I0740111

Publisher's Note:

Thank you for purchasing this book. It began as an idea, was shaped by the creativity of its talented author, and was subsequently molded into the book you have before you by a team of editors and designers.

Like all EDGE books, this book is the result of the creative talents of a dedicated team of individuals who all believe that books (whether in print or pixels) have the magical ability to take you on an adventure to new and wondrous places powered by the author's imagination.

As EDGE's publisher, I hope that you enjoy this book. It is a part of our ongoing quest to discover talented authors and to make their creative writing available to you.

We also hope that you will share your discovery and enjoyment of this novel on social media through Facebook, Twitter, Goodreads, Pinterest, etc., and by posting your opinions and/or reviews on Amazon and other review sites and blogs. By doing so, others will be able to share your discovery and passion for this book.

Brian Hades, publisher

DARK SEA RISING

Barry Broad
Drew Mendelson

EDGE SCIENCE FICTION AND FANTASY PUBLISHING
An Imprint of HADES PUBLICATIONS, INC.
CALGARY

Dark Sea Rising

Copyright © 2018 by Barry Broad and Drew Mendelson

This is a work of fiction. Names, characters, places, and incidents are the products of the author's imagination or are used fictitiously and are not to be construed as real. Any resemblance to actual events, locales, organizations, or persons, living or dead, is entirely coincidental.

EDGE SCIENCE FICTION AND FANTASY PUBLISHING
An Imprint of HADES PUBLICATIONS, INC.
P.O. Box 1714, Calgary, Alberta, T2P 2L7, Canada

The EDGE Team:
Producer: Brian Hades
Acquisitions Michelle Heumann
Edited by: Maylon Gardner
Cover Design: Darrin Geisinger
Book Design: Mark Steele
Publicist: Janice Shoults

ISBN: 987-1-77053-176-5

EDGE Science Fiction and Fantasy Publishing and Hades Publications, Inc. acknowledges the ongoing support of the Alberta Foundation for the Arts and the Canada Council for the Arts for our publishing programme.

Library and Archives Canada Cataloguing in Publication
CIP Data on file with the National Library of Canada
ISBN: 987-1-77053-176-5
(e-Book ISBN: 987-1-77053-175-8)

FIRST EDITION
(20180501)
Printed in USA
www.edgewebsite.com

"How inappropriate to call this planet Earth,
when it clearly is Ocean."

—Arthur C. Clarke

Chapter 1

The Above: Honolulu International Airport, Hawaii

Gusman felt like hell. No, it was worse than that: he felt like death. It had started out as a cold but had gotten nastier the farther west he flew. By the time he completed the first leg of his flight from O'Hare to LAX, his head felt stuffed enough to explode. Just before he took off from LAX, he dry-swallowed four ibuprofen and a couple of Sudafeds. He didn't think he had ever experienced such sinus pressure. The pain spread from his temples and across his forehead, settling like a dead weight behind his eyes. He kept massaging his temples and pressing gently on his eyes to ease the pain. It barely helped. He downed more ibuprofen.

He made his way over to the private terminal to wait for the arrival of the company plane that would take him to Midway.

The next thing he knew, he was being shaken.

"Wake up, sunshine," said a disembodied voice.

He groaned and put a hand to his neck, which had a huge kink in it.

"You look like shit, Gusman."

Gusman looked up at the co-pilot and attempted a half-assed smile. "Hey, Butch. As a matter of fact, I feel like shit."

"Too bad. You ready?" Butch looked at his watch. Not much sympathy.

"Time to go," he said.

Gusman didn't argue. He got up, shouldered his duffel, stumbled out of the shabby waiting room, and followed Butch onto the tarmac.

The company plane was an old surplus C-130 Hercules. It was great for carrying cargo and could land just about anywhere, but it was slow. Although Midway was technically at the beginning — or end, depending on your point of view — of the Hawaiian Islands chain, it was still 3,000 miles and a nine-hour flight from Honolulu on the C-130. His final destination — Platform Faith — was another 500 miles west of Midway.

When Gusman got on board, there were two other passengers already waiting: a pair of roughnecks on their way back to Faith to relieve some guys who had finished their six-month tour. They nodded at him, but didn't try to make conversation, which was fine. Gusman just wanted to sleep.

Butch handed Gusman a couple of little white pills. "Take these. They'll knock you on your ass. You'll sleep the whole way, I guarantee it."

"What are they?"

"Dunno, exactly. Gorazapam… Dorazaman… something like that."

"I'll take it on faith," Gusman replied, swallowing the pills.

The co-pilot snorted.

Gusman didn't even remember the plane taking off. He woke up briefly a couple of times during the night, both times grasping fleetingly at the fragment of a watery dream that promptly dissolved as he lost consciousness again.

He woke once more when the plane bounced hard on the runway at Midway before braking to a stop.

No dreams this time as Gusman groaned and tried to clear the cobwebs from his brain.

One of the roughnecks was looking at him.

"Hey, dude, you snore."

"Sorry," Gusman replied. "I have a cold."

"No biggie," the roughneck said with a toothy smile.

As usual, the mid-Pacific sun was blazing. The Midway atoll, famous for the naval battle that took place in 1942, was no longer the home of the US Navy. It had been turned over to the National Park Service to manage as a wildlife reserve because about a million seabirds nested there. It was also the staging area for the company's drilling operation on Platform Faith. The company had expended considerable political influence to obtain permission to use the airport.

The three men headed over to the helipad on the far end of the island, where the company's Sikorsky Jolly Green Giant, a reconditioned but still creaky Vietnam-era war bird they all called "The Beast," was waiting for them. The Beast was painted orange. The words "Clearsea Energy" were emblazoned across the length of its long, sausage-like fuselage in huge white letters, except for the first letter in Clearsea, which was bright green and spiral-shaped. The company's original name, West Texas Offshore Drilling Corporation, had been unceremoniously dumped some years earlier in the wake of a huge disaster at one of the company's platforms in the Gulf of Mexico. The spiral-shaped logo was green for a reason and — along with the company's new slogan, "For Our Planet" — was intended to convey Clearsea's commitment to environmentally sustainable oil production.

This corporate "rebranding" — in the terminology of the Madison Avenue experts who dreamed it up — was total. It got a jump start when the old CEO, a craggy, plain-talking Oklahoma oil man right out of central casting, was fired after he infamously joked that the fish die-off resulting from the oil disaster was "a shame... hell, some of those fish would have made damned good eating." In a move that surprised Wall Street and delighted the press and public, he was replaced by the company's charismatic young General Counsel, Enrique Gonzales. Gonzales was a Harvard-educated former-Republican Attorney General of Texas, whose calm competence was matched by his amazing rags-to-riches story. Gonzales had risen from being the impoverished son of Mexican farm workers to a leading light of the American legal profession and a potent symbol of the increasing power and influence of Latinos.

"From this day forward," Gonzales said at his first press conference, "Clearsea will be a new company, dedicated to the stewardship of our planet's resources and measuring success not simply by profit, but by our contribution to repairing our world. I apologize for the disaster that has occurred and pledge that we will spare no expense to restore the Gulf. As a company, from now on, Clearsea will — and must — be forthright, transparent, and humble. We will do everything in our power to regain the confidence of our shareholders, our government, and, most importantly, the American people. Ultimately, we recognize that our world must end its dependence on fossil fuels and, while that may be an unpopular thing to say in our industry, it is the truth. Until that day comes, Clearsea is committed to producing energy safely and sustainably."

The remake worked, leavened by Clearsea's massive financial commitment to environmental restoration and alternative energy projects around the globe. Clearsea returned quickly to profitability. Its stock, which had lost a third of its value in the wake of the Gulf oil crisis, rebounded — and then some. Gonzales was awarded the Malcolm Baldridge Award for corporate excellence and named Time's "Man of the Year." The disaster soon faded from public attention, except for some hard-core environmentalists, like Gusman's marine biologist sister, who could never bring themselves to trust an oil company, regardless of its sincerity.

As Gusman plopped himself down on one of the webbed seats of The Beast, he felt the full impact of his depleted physical condition. His throat was raw, his sinuses throbbed, and his back was stiff. Even his teeth hurt. He still felt woozy from the pills Butch had given him, although at this point he wouldn't have minded swallowing a few more. It was 500 miles to Platform Faith... a long way in the slow-moving, fearsomely noisy, vibrating Sikorsky. At least the weather was calm and they'd be flying at low altitude, sparing his wounded skull further punishment.

Chapter 2

The Below

There is turmoil *in the Dream.*

For many hungers now, the body of a monstrous worm has been descending from the waters Above, many arm spans away from the vents and the gathering of dwellings that is the urb. The He'e have felt its movements, but a few He'e exploring far from the urb have caught glimmers of it in the murky darkness Above, too far away to be lit by any smoker spewing its heat and light from beneath the ocean floor. Is this worm different from the four dead giant worms that have fallen in the recent Dreamtime, whose heavy heads lie inert on the ocean floor, but whose twisted, fibrous worm bodies stretched endlessly into the Above?

One of the He'e, the hunter called P'mul, who is so skilled that he has even killed the fearsome great tentacled muhe'e, has been sent to take the measure of this massive worm. He clicks it and the returning echoes tell him this thing also stretches seemingly endlessly into the Above. He feels its pulsing movement—but not the beat of a heart, even a faint one. In the Dream of the He'e, the collective vision that stretches all the way back to the Great Father and Mother who were the first He'e, there is a memory of such a thing coming down from the endless Above to lay waste to one of the conurbations of the faraway He'e. It drove its evil head into the sacred pool of hinu and killed many He'e. Some believe the tale and some do not, but every young fry knows the story of the great devouring worm.

In the Dream, there is a ravenous mouth like a snail's radula inside the worm's massive head. The mouth is an eighth of an arm span across with a triad of biting ribbons that mesh together and rotate like nothing should that is alive. The tail is thick and segmented, and vibrations can be heard inside it. The creature that P'mul encounters is enough like that image to send him jetting back toward the urb with the frightening news that the devouring thing will soon be upon them.

Pulsing white with bursts of red fear, P'mul interrupts a meeting of the urb's Chamber of Decision. "The great worm monster will soon reach the ocean floor. It has a radula mouth like the great worm of the Dreamtale."

A shiver of fear pulses through the Dream of the gathered He'e. What this thing is may not be clear, but it is a threat. P'M'heen, the mates P'heen and M'heen who together lead the council, are disturbed by the dangerous image from the Dream and send a trio of young watchers off to observe and report on the worm.

"Is this worm like the others?" asks the venerable P'dal'o.

The Chamber of Decision has been meeting almost constantly since the four giant worms recently descended to the ocean floor, bracketing the urb and causing the whole conurbation of He'e to feel agitation and dread.

"Perhaps," says P'heen, "but those are dead worms, whose inanimate heads are made of fused sediment and whose worm bodies are made of hard and intertwined fibers like the stalk of the d'al'ma seaweed. It is more like a plant than a creature. We have already set the benthic worms upon them to dissolve those worm heads. But this beast has a devouring mouth and is much larger and has a moving, segmented worm body. A benthic worm would likely be useless against it."

The watchers soon rush back, almost incoherent, able only to warn. "The worm's tail rises high into the Above, far past where we can click it. It's not made of flesh or bone or shell."

The watchers are sent back once more and return after two hungers of silence to report that the worm is now less than ten eight-eights away from the seafloor, directly above the great pool of sacred hino that is trapped beneath the rock and sediment. It is moving slowly, but relentlessly, downward.

Aroused, four members of the chamber call out another eight of the He'e and together they rush from their dwellings in the Urb and jet across the seabed toward where the worm is descending. At the front is P'aldil, the Chief Examiner of the Strange. He, too, observes the worm and his arms glimmer with apprehension. As it did for P'mul, the presence of the worm calls up for him a nightmare vision of the devouring worm from the collective Dream of the He'e.

P'aldil believes the tale of the giant devouring worm is real. Once, on an expedition to investigate a strange object that had fallen from the Above, he encountered an ancient He'e from the nearest conurbation, who also was searching for this fallen object. They spent nearly a whole hunger pleasantly exchanging stories from the Dream, some serious and some mirthful. This He'e, whose name was P'a'l, said that the story of the worm was no falsehood concocted to frighten fry and teach them to fear the strange, but a catastrophe in a conurbation far upstream along the clockwise gyre of the great waters many eight-eights of arms away. In truth, according to P'a'l, the worm descended into the faraway He'e habitation just a few dozen generations of fry ago — at a time no more distant than the early life of his own parents — killing many He'e when it released the pressured pool of hinu under their Urb. P'a'l then told P'aldil a part of the tale of the devouring worm that he had never heard before: that the worm was not alive, but dead, and that it was fashioned like an enormous tool.

"And what about the part of the tale where the faraway He'e kill the creature?" asked P'aldil.

"You cannot kill a thing that is already dead, but you can kill the creature that uses the tool," replied P'a'l.

"And those He'e did that — killed the maker of the worm?"

"So it is told," said the ancient one, turning his arms the darkest gray to convey his earnestness.

"But this would mean that a creature other than the He'e has been given dominance over the lesser living things and the full power of the Dream."

"Yes, it would."

P'aldil pulsed a blue-red flash of confusion, but, as the Chief Examiner of the Strange, he had always suspected as much from the odd objects that had floated to the ocean floor. But such a thought was contrary to the gift of the Great Father

*and Mother, P'lo and M'lo, who gave the He'e the Dream —
and, with it, singular dominance over all other creatures
through insight and the pulse of control. Such a thought
would disturb the tranquility of the Dream, so P'aldil kept
such thoughts to himself.*

*Could the giant worm he could now plainly see with his
own eyes be another of the same evil creatures?*

*Just then, the worm's head awoke with a tremendous
gnawing groan, its radula turning slowly. After perhaps a
quarter hunger, the radula stopped turning, but the worm's
head still descended relentlessly, if slowly. They jet away again,
across the dark seafloor, back to the Chamber of Decision
where P'M'heen and the other elders await their report.*

*P'aldil says, "It is like the story in the Dream where the
head of such a worm came down to bite into the Urb of the
faraway He'e. You must know that Dreamtale. How it bites
down into the seafloor until it finds the hinu and awakens
it. How the spout of hinu makes the seafloor throb with the
thunder of its escape. How many He'e lived there and all their
dwellings were swept away in that gush."*

*P'heen shivers at that. His arms curl and twine restlessly.
"We all see it in the Dream," he says. "We all hear the faraway
He'e click in fear as they try to flee, only to die so that they are
not anymore."*

*The voices of the Dream declare that the worm diving from
above must be insensible or it would never dive so recklessly
into a chamber of the hinu essence, which is ready to burst.
P'heen and P'aldil's arms lash the seafloor in mourning.*

*M'heen, intertwining one of her arms in P'heen's to
comfort him, says, "And this worm is now the fifth such
creature descended from Above with tails that also climb
endlessly upward."*

*"But this one seems very much alive, whereas the others
are dead things, whose heads are made of sand fused with
small stones and whose hardened tails are intertwined and
not segmented," says P'aldil. "Elders, there is something I
must show you. Follow me to the Chamber of the Strange."*

*The Chamber of the Strange is a cavernous place that is
the domain of P'aldil. It is filled with the carcasses of creatures*

preserved in hinu so they do not decompose, objects of metal and glass that have fallen from the Above or have been found in the stomachs of fish or squids, and all manner of colored stones and unusual formations of minerals found near the smokers. Stretching above the space is a huge object, several arms lengths across, which is suspended from the roof of the chamber.

P'aldil's grandparents — their voices still alive in the Dream — recounted it from their youth when the object came drifting down from the Above. Though crushed and now eroded by the sea water, it is finned and has a partial tail, and once must once have been as sleek as the hahalua rays whose bodies sometimes drift down from far up in the Above. Both of the object's fins, though, are broken off short. A hole a full one eighth of an arm span across pierces the carapace of the object and through that hole its inward parts dangle like dead arms. And there are other little holes, as if it was pierced by an eruption of small round stones, all of the same size. It has a thin skin of metal, which is attached to a skeleton of thicker metal.

When he goes into the Dream, P'aldil relives the tale of how the object floated down from the Above and settled near the black smoker. Inside were two strange things made of something like chitin and also flesh and muscle, but with the hollows in them crushed and their substance smeared inside the object. Yet their outside is covered by a thin, fibrous, dead skin, torn in many places. In the Dream, he sees the shrimp and the crabs gathering to make a meal of it. It is this way in the Dream, but out of the Dream, the finned object is just ruined metal that the soul of the waters is eating away; the remnants of meat and muscle long gone, the hard cores of the bodies eroded, a curiosity now. The Dream holds tales of other objects, some so enormous they cannot be moved, scattered among the other vents that are the habitats of the He'e, both faraway and closer by.

P'aldil describes the new worm, saying, "This thing, with a mouth and teeth much like a snail's radula that could bite into the seafloor, thrusting its toothed tongue deep to cause destruction, also has come from the Above and may be made of metal and not flesh."

A deep green gleam of worry wraps the arms of the elders.

"Is it possible that these inanimate things that fall from the Above are made by creatures and do not spring out of eggs or the bellies of fish? Since we do not know these mysterious objects, could it be that they come from out of the Above?"

There's a murmur among elders, both in voice and glimmers. Out of the Above? Made by creatures? But this cannot be. There is nothing above but the waters and the dwellers that swim there. Above that is just more of the same. Eternally. Is that not the eternal truth of P'lo and M'lo, the first father and first mother of the He'e who made the Dream and gave the He'e dominance over all other creatures great and small?

P'heen pulses with anger at P'aldil. "It is not the time for reaping confusion with your wild dreams, P'aldil. It is time to determine whether this thing is a threat and what we should do about it. Now, go out and examine the new object and bring back the knowledge we need to make a decision."

P'aldil takes his mate M'aldil — together they are P'M'aldil — and they go back to observe the worm yet again. They watch and Dream. In their Dream of the other worm, an ancestor says there should be a way to stop it. Her voice, as strong as if she were still alive, whispers that the benthic clams should awake. She says to whisper to the clams about the peril to the essence of sea below. She sings to them softly of the clams' good nature and of their talent of coalescing hard objects from the substances dissolved in the waters. In the Dream of P'M'aldil, the benthic clams burrow deep, sending up their long siphons to sup at the substances from the waters and make a large shell formed from kaimana — harder than diamonds — to stop the descent of this thing and protect the Urb.

In their Dream, the kaimana shell stops the worm and shatters its radula. The evil worm is no more.

P'M'aldil bring back the advice they have received from the Dream to the Chamber of Decision and the elders quickly order that a kaimana shell be placed in the sediment directly beneath the place where the worm's radula will bite into the seafloor.

This requires fast work, but they have planned in the Dream for such a defense and every He'e knows what task must be performed. The kaimana is brought from its hidden places, the clams gathered, and they make quick work with their secretions. The shield — no thicker than the arm of a juvenile He'e — is carefully transported to the nearest hot smoker and cured in the intense heat. Though thin, it is harder than the thickest, densest stone — one of the great gifts given to the He'e by the Great Father and Great Mother at the beginning of the Dream.

Meanwhile, the sediment where the worm will bite has been moved aside to create a place for the kaimana shield. It is transported by a dozen He'e, their arms bracing it, who then lower it into its place and secure it by layers of rocks and seafloor mud. The radula-headed worm is a mere eight-eights away from the seafloor when they are finished. They scurry away for cover.

The young fry are moved to the furthest reaches of the Urb. P'aldil and a few others take refuge among the large chimneys of a nearby dead smoker to wait and observe.

As the thing nears the seafloor, its radula begins to turn again, the grinding noise it makes unlike that of any other creature known to the He'e. It causes them to pulse in fear.

Finally, the worm hits the seafloor above the buried kaimana. There is a brief pause and then its radula begins to whirl, and it bites into the sediment, spewing mud and crushed rock violently around it. As it goes deeper, a vast billowing cloud of the floor's substance rises from the now half-buried head of the worm and sweeps slowly off into the current.

M'aldil, who clings to P'aldil behind a rock that rises from the seafloor, asks, "Will it do as in the Dream and bite until it reaches the hinu?"

"I think it will try," P'aldil answers, "though in the Dream we see that the worm has not the power to break the kaimana shield."

"From your radula to the sound holes of the Great Father and Great Mother, may they hear your plea," says M'aldil to her life mate, with grim mirth.

The grinding teeth of the worm bite deeper into the seafloor, the plume of disturbed mud billowing thicker, the scream of the worm's churning teeth rising as it tries to eat into the kaimana's hardness. The mud plume has stretched far until its top towers far above the nearby chimneys. The scream of the worm's teeth against the kaimana rises to a screech that sends shivers up P'M'aldil's arms and sends them both burrowing into the seafloor mud to escape it. Now there is a sharp sound, a screech, and a rattle. The seafloor heaves as if alive. Their clicks show the body of the worm writhe, snapping back and forth all along its length, as it snakes upward into the Above. The biting head throws itself upward, teeth and tongue flying apart, pieces soaring into the waters above the seafloor. The clash of its shattering shakes the floor and rattles through P'M'aldil who cower together, shoving themselves farther down into the mud.

Silence.

The last bit of crystal tooth and metal tongue settle to the seafloor. The worm stops its writhing and hangs still, its mangled head and what is left of its mouth slack and dead. Mud settles onto the torn seafloor, into the hole the worm's mouth had bitten over the kaimana shell. Echoes from many of the He'e show the uncovered part of the kaimana shield, where it was struck by the worm's radula, is unscathed. Not a scratch or rent marring it.

After a small hunger passes, the watching He'e venture over to inspect the dead worm.

They approach it cautiously, in case it is just wounded. But it does not stir; it is truly dead. One of P'aldil's arms reaches out half an arm's length and takes up one of the crystalline teeth, another arm finds a bit of the metal torn from the worm's mouth. He holds the broken mouth parts up for M'aldil to sense.

Together, P'M'aldil squirm along the surface of the seafloor an arm's length or so away, then propel themselves up into the waters and jet away.

They must report their great victory to all in the Dream.

Chapter 3

The Above: Platform Faith

It was late in the afternoon when The Beast approached the helipad on Platform Faith. It never ceased to amaze Gusman how, from a distance, the oil platform looked like such a tiny dot in the ocean, but, as they neared, it transformed into something truly massive — a feat of modern engineering and a towering example of the human capacity to conquer nature. Faith was the largest offshore oil platform ever constructed. It contained more steel than the largest aircraft carrier. Unlike the earlier generation of platforms attached by huge legs to the ocean floor, Faith was a semi-submersible platform. It was kept in place by powerful GPS-linked engines that constantly reacted to the ocean currents, moving the platform to keep it centered over the borehole.

The platform sat atop four giant pontoons, each over two football fields in length and as tall as a five-story building. Platform Faith operated on the principle of a submarine. A heavy cable stretched to the seafloor far below from each pontoon, anchors that added even more stability. By keeping its pontoons filled with the proper ratio of ballast water to air, it could be submerged to a depth that, along with the mooring cables, stabilized it even in the strongest ocean currents. If the platform needed to be moved, the mooring cables would be raised and the ballast water ejected allowing the pontoons to rise to the surface, where it could be towed to a different location.

Gusman walked down the rear gate of The Beast onto the deck of the Platform Faith. He still felt sick — drug-woozy and congested — but he was relieved to be at the end of his voyage. Beyond the edge of the platform was the ocean, an endless soft blue reaching to the horizon in every direction. At its center, the huge drilling structure rose high into the sky, a jagged and jarring pile of sharpened steel. Various species of sea birds flew above, diving into the ocean to feed on the fish that congregated underneath its massive bulk. *Instant habitat*, thought Gusman.

Gusman and the two roughnecks lowered their heads against the wind and headed for the entrance that led to the guts of the behemoth called Faith.

Chapter 4

The Below

For several hungers *now, since shortly before the worm descended into the Urb, the Dream has been invaded by a weak presence from the distant Above. Some — but not all — of the He'e felt it: a stray thought from creatures they do not know, odd clicks and whirs from voices that do not sound like fish or blow-holers, snippets of fear or mirth, They click back, but there is no answer. Such odd voices invade the Dream from time to time and they are not disturbed.*

Then the giant mouthworm struck. When P'aldil thinks of the giant worm's destruction, he stretches an arm and says, "It is good."

But just before the giant worm descended and struck the kaimana shield, P'aldil sensed the strong presence of another in the Dream, though in a brightness unlike anything on the seafloor. P'aldil's eyes sink back for shelter from this blaze and his arms curl by themselves in front to shield his vision. There is no water, none; the sea has vanished. If this were not in the Dream, where all things that have ever been and are now exist together, P'aldil would flounder, unable to breathe without life-sustaining water bathing his gill slits. In the Dream he burns, the fierce light wraps him in stinging heat and he shrivels and would die. But it is the Dream. Eyes look at him from a being as strange as ever he has seen — a being awkward and constrained. P'aldil has the impression of simplistic extremities, rigid as those of a crab, but softer outside than in, with the hardness of its shell on the interior, like the bones of the bony fish. Still, it moves and its eyes are like P'aldil's: bespeaking an intelligence that seems to wonder, watching him as he burns in this void without water. Could it be the same as the creatures from the Dream of the He'e no longer here, of the generation of He'e that gave birth to his mother and father? The creatures with soft skin covered in a fibrous layer that cannot be eaten, but whose inside has meat that is soft and also has bone? The same as the creatures that floated down, encased in the metal carapace which is suspended from the ceiling of the Chamber of the Strange?

Yes.

In the Dream, P'aldil realizes that the strange creature that has caused the terrible worm with its radula to attack is the same as the dead ones from the ancient Dream.

He says to the creature, "Go away."

P'aldil has not told another soul, not even M'aldil. But when he wakes from the Dream where he has sensed this strong presence again, he shares it with M'aldil, who tangles arms with him in sudden fear.

"Where is this strange creature?" she asks.

"The Above," he says. "Many, many eights of arms above."

"And it looks at you and knows?"

"It knows," says P'aldil, his arms twisted and tangled in hers. "In the Dream, I could see what it saw. It knew of the worm that had come from above, and how its mouth had bitten into the seafloor and had been stopped. But it knew not why; it knew nothing of the kaimana shield. And so, what was a triumph for the He'e — the death of the worm's biting head — was a disaster for his kind."

The Above had always been remote, ascending forever into the waters. But now there comes a giant worm that bores into the seafloor with long tethers and feet like limpets, clutching... and, with it, this inexplicable intrusion in the Dream of a being from a waterless place of light.

M'aldil tells P'aldil that he must tell P'M'heen and the other elders of this invasion of the Dream.

Change does not come easily to the He'e living in the timeless seas, nor is change easily accepted. P'aldil clicks to P'M'heen of his Dream and of the creature who has sent the giant worm. P'M'heen know that P'aldil has powerful Dreams. So P'M'heen call a gathering of the Chamber of Decision to worry at this because it is change nonetheless. They will do what they must do.

M'heen recalls for them the recent Dream of the flock of muhe'e each half an eight of arms long that came to raid the He'es' dwellings. Many of the He'e are dead because of this raid and the muhe'es' tentacles reaching and massive beaks biting and eating the He'e. Like the He'e, the giant muhe'e has eight arms and also two long tentacles. It has a spear-like fin at the end of its mantle, eyes as big as giant clams, and a tearing beak. But the He'e are beings of thought as well as muscle — strong armed, but also with brains and minds, who build their conurbations and live in communities ruled by thought. The muhe'e are creatures of the wild and the cold dark of the seafloor away from the warmth of the vents. They are ones who hunt and eat and have no care for what they eat, whether fish and shelled creatures of the deep seafloor or thinking ones like the He'e. Sometimes they kill He'e and do not eat, doing so as if for the pure pleasure of killing, which marks the muhe'e as evil, unlike any other creature.

In the Dream, they all understand why M'heen recalls the attack of the muhe'e.

When P'aldil was little more than a fry, the muhe'e raiders came jetting across the seafloor out of the darkness, down from the Above. Their voices were simple rumblings in the water and no lights ran on their arms and no intelligence glowed in their giant eyes. One would jet close and shoot out an arm to grab one of the He'e, an eighth its size, and pull him or her to its beak to be torn apart and eaten or perhaps just discarded. But P'na'au — He of the Strong Hearts — had a Dream that the He'e should gather as one, swarm around the giant muhe'e, and cast the tubeworms' anchoring feet first at the muhe'e.

They did, and the anchoring feet bored deep into the giant predators, thrusting into the flesh of the muhe'e and tormenting them with their juices of digestion until the muhe'e bolted away.

"Together," P'M'heen says to the gathering of He'e in the Chamber of Decision, "we are powerful; overwhelming. No enemy can resist us."

"But in the Dream, the creature was of thought and did not seem to know of the He'e or our conurbation. Perhaps they are not like the muhe'e and mean no harm?"

"Or perhaps they are more evil than even the muhe'e?" says P'heen.

They Dream together again of the strong, reaching arms and the beaks of the raiders suddenly jetting away across the sea bottom, their voices full of fear and surprise, the He'es' voices full of anger and triumph.

In the Dream you learn.

Chapter 5

The Above: New York, New York

Enrique Gonzales looked out the enormous plate glass window of his office at the panorama of New York City below. He never tired of the view: the harsh sunlight set against the dark shadows cast by the buildings of upper Manhattan, the birds that soared between the buildings, the green of Central Park, and the blue of the Hudson River beyond. He was wealthy and respected — a much sought-after and brilliant voice of compassion and reason; a corporate leader Americans could trust. Gonzales was being openly talked about as a possible presidential candidate.

Of course, it was all a lie; a facade created by image-makers and spoon-fed to the American psyche by an army of consultants with big retainers and sophisticated computer algorithms. When Gonzales persuaded his board of directors to approve investing an enormous chunk of the company's capital reserve into oil exploration and production in the central Pacific, in water much deeper and more inhospitable than conventional wisdom thought possible, the markets had, at first, been skeptical. But the oil turned out to be there: a huge reserve of light, sweet crude they named "Leviathan." The Leviathan field was so rich that it was estimated to be equal to the known reserves of Saudi Arabia, Iraq, and Iran combined. The all-powerful stock analysts, who had at first been skeptical when Gonzales announced that Clearsea would "bet everything" on the Leviathan field, now rated the company a "buy." Three state-of-the-art platforms — Faith, Hope, and Charity — would be built at a cost of nearly three billion apiece. Faith was the first to be completed. Hope and

Charity — now under construction — would be towed into position across the Pacific in the next two years.

What the Wall Street stock analysts did not know was that Clearsea had spent so much money on Leviathan that the company would be functionally insolvent if the crude did not start flowing from Platform Faith within six months of it being towed into place. Once Faith started producing, Gonzales could go to the capital markets.

However, his six months had turned into a year and he needed to buy time. There were cost overruns and then there were geological complexities. The seabed near Midway was riddled with deep sea vents and underlain with live veins of magma. In their first attempt to drill, they hit magma and had to move the platform. Gonzales had brought in his Chief Financial Officer and ordered him to do whatever it took to hide the company's true financial condition. They were on the knife's edge: fabulous wealth on one side of the blade, and failure, humiliation, and disaster on the other.

Gonzales turned away from the window and looked at the brightly lit green digital numbers that, as if by magic, appeared on the thick frameless glass clock on this desk. 7:59 a.m.

One more minute.

He sat down in his leather desk chair and opened his laptop that, along with the clock, were the only objects on his desk.

When the excited atoms in the liquid crystal display realigned themselves into symbols that read 8:00, Gonzales pressed the key on his laptop that activated the encrypted video conferencing line.

On the other side of the world, Drake saw Gonzales' image appear on his computer screen, crystal clear.

"Hello, Drake," said Gonzales, his tone even and unenthusiastic.

"Good morning, Mr. Gonzales," responded Drake. "How are things stateside?"

Gonzales ignored the question. "More to the point, how are things there?"

"Fine," said Drake, a little too brightly.

"I'm in no mood for pleasantries. We're behind schedule. Why?"

Drake cleared his throat. "We've had a setback."

"What does that mean, 'a setback?'"

"We were drilling the new borehole and we hit something hard."

"Hard?"

"It caused the drill bit to shatter."

"What could do that, Drake?"

"I don't know. In my thirty years in this business, I've never seen anything like it. Drill bits crack; they sometimes break. But they don't shatter. I've searched the literature and nothing like this has ever been reported."

"So what are you going to do about it?

"Well, we're going to switch to a larger roller bit and increase the force."

"Who knows about this?"

"Besides me, the video guy; that's it. Everyone else just thinks we had a standard sheared bit."

"Well, keep a total embargo on the information. Send me the video and then destroy your copy of it. We don't want anything getting out that suggests that we're encountering more problems."

"Yes, sir."

"And get that drill going again."

—— «》 ——

"Well, Frank, what do you make of this?" Gonzales asked, pausing the video playback and staring up at the older man standing over his shoulder.

Frank Stanton was the company's Chief Engineer, a solid hand who had been with Clearsea for nearly forty years and knew the oil business from top to bottom. He rubbed his chin and hesitated, carefully forming his words.

"I've heard of something like this happening once before. In Angola. Back in '77."

"Angola? What happened in Angola?"

"Back then, I was a young safety engineer for the company and there was an incident at one of our platforms in Cabinda province. The platform was in relatively deep water for the time, maybe three hundred and fifty feet. It was the farthest one out and isolated from the rest, which were much closer to shore. There was an explosion and a fire. I was sent in to investigate. Only one man survived — a diver. He was picked up in the water, badly burned. He died a few days after we rescued him. He told me their drill bits kept shattering like 'glass hitting a hammer,' he said. They couldn't figure out what the problem was since the platform was not drilling into particularly challenging substrate. He said that in the days and weeks before the accident, the men started getting sick — they had these awful headaches and started behaving strangely. There were fights. Discipline broke down. Some of the men wanted to quit."

"What caused the explosion?"

"What actually caused it or what we reported as the cause?"

"The truth."

"Sabotage."

Chapter 6

The Above: Platform Faith

Gusman walked along the row of steam tables, trying to figure out what to eat. He was always mildly amazed at the sheer excess of food served on offshore oil platforms. As a young man just starting out, he couldn't believe his luck: endless mounds of bacon, sausage (three kinds), ham, steak (chicken fried or blood red fillets), pancakes, waffles — you name it. He was skinny as a rail then and could eat whatever he wanted and never gain a pound. And, at first, he indulged. But eventually, the novelty wore off and his metabolism began to change. With every passing year, he ate less and less of the heavy food, to the point where he now found the whole thing mildly depressing. He spooned a lump of oatmeal into a bowl and filled a mug with black coffee. Prison food. Excellent prison food, but prison food nonetheless.

There were two big tables and a few small ones scattered around the dining room. When it came to a choice of dining companions, the workers on the platform segregated themselves according to status: management and professionals at one table, production workers at another. Gusman had learned long ago that social class was a line that was not crossed on an oil platform.

"You're back, Gusman." Drake's tone was flat and his expression neutral. Their relationship was built on biting sarcasm, but, for some reason, the sarcastic tone was gone today. It took Gusman by surprise.

The others — Morrissey, the head of security, and Samson, the chief production supervisor — looked at

Gusman with half-smiles and partial nods and a touch of something else. Embarrassment?

Gusman put his tray down and took a seat across from Drake.

"I love you, too, Drake." Gusman wasn't ready to give up his own deeply embedded sarcasm.

"What did you say, Mr. Gusman?"

'Mister Gusman?' Drake had never called him anything but Gusman — typically with a tone that alternated between mild disapproval and utter contempt. Gusman scanned Drake's face. The usual sneering downturn of his lips was absent. Gusman did not know how to react.

Morrissey broke the ice. "That would be 'I love you, too, Mr. Drake, sir.' Never forget the chain of command, son."

They all laughed, but it was more of a nervous titter than a genuine guffaw. Drake was a petty tyrant and they all knew it. Drake laughed, too, but his steel blue eyes were not smiling. Still, they lacked their usual malevolence.

"Never, sir," replied Gusman, and gave his boss a crisp salute.

An awkward silence followed. Something had changed. Then a few minutes later, Drake said to Gusman, his tone still even, "When you get settled, come see me. There are a few things we need to go over."

Gusman looked around at the others. No one met his gaze.

— «» —

His meal finished, Gusman wandered outside onto the platform deck. The air was clear and clean, lacking the vaguely metallic smell that filled the relentlessly air-conditioned interior of the platform. He watched one of the kitchen crew, an old Filipino man he knew only as Rizal, dump buckets of uneaten food off the side of the platform. It was, of course, a total violation of company policy — not only because the local life forms would consume food completely unhealthy for them, but for a more pragmatic reason: it encouraged sharks to hang around Faith. Years ago, Gusman would have said something, but he had long since given up caring about the environment or much of anything else. All he wanted was to cash in big on his stock options and get out while the getting was good. Hopefully, this was 'the one' — an oil field beneath the ocean so immense that it would rival, and maybe even exceed, the proven reserves of the Persian Gulf. The test drilling in the general area seemed to confirm the possibility. The crude that came up was light and sweet, something unheard of in deep-sea fields. His sister, Ms. Environmentalist, would have a field day at the family Christmas beating the crap out of him. Luckily, there hadn't been a family Christmas in quite some time.

The water roiled with fish where the chum floated temporarily on the surface several hundred feet below. Birds dive-bombed the floating garbage pile, grabbing the fish that rose to the surface to feed.

It was at moments like these that Gusman thought about taking up smoking again. The old addiction gnawed at the receptors in his brain like a faint, unscratchable itch. He swallowed, gathering up thick phlegm in his throat and spit the yellow-green ball off the side. He watched the remnants of his cold ascend in an impressive arch and then fall toward the sea before he lost sight of it somewhere about halfway to the surface.

"Charming," said a woman's voice behind him.

Gusman turned.

"Woulda, coulda, shoulda Gusman," she said.

"Hey, Nancy," he replied. She stood next to him at the railing. "How's it going?" he asked, more out of social habit than real concern.

She did not answer immediately, hesitating. "Truthfully? There's some weird shit going on."

He miscued. "There's always weird shit going on here. Just as long as it doesn't interfere with my plan to turn this into the most productive oil field on the planet, so I can get rich and get out."

"I'm serious, Gusman."

"I'm serious, too," he said, smiling.

When she didn't smile back, he knew she really was serious.

"You're not kidding, are you?"

"No, I certainly am not. There's weird shit going on with the drilling equipment. Drake has it all locked down. Even though I'm supposed to be told if something's happening like that, they've kept me in the dark."

Her playful expression was gone, replaced by a furrowed brow and worry lines at the corner of her eyes.

"What do you mean 'weird shit' with the drilling equipment?"

She lowered her voice and moved closer to him, their bodies touching. Just like old times, but without the sexual energy. She was married now; beyond reach. "One of the drill bits shattered."

"Shattered? Like glass shatters?"

"Yes."

"Come on, Nancy, that's impossible. Those things are made of super-hardened steel and the cutting edges are coated with carbide and industrial diamonds. They can shear off, but they don't shatter."

"Well, it shattered. I don't know how — it hit something and the bit disintegrated into fragments. When they pulled it up to the ocean floor, the camera could see chunks of metal flying all over the place."

"You've seen the video?"

"Yeah, Noguchi…"

Gusman interrupted. "…Andy?"

"Yeah. He had it on his phone. Wanted to know what I thought of it."

"What would cause that kind of metal failure?"

"You got me. You know what else?"

"What?"

"He told me that Drake ordered him to lose the footage and sanitize the computer record."

Gusman looked at Nancy. There was a silence. Gusman didn't quite know what to say next.

"There's more," she said.

"More what?"

"More weirdness."

"How could it get any weirder?"

"It's the guys. Everyone's on edge. They're fighting with each other for no reason. The calmest ones are totally stressed out. Some of them are getting drunk or stoned. And Drake is being an even bigger asshole than usual. It's not normal. It's like an Angola waiting to happen."

"Oh, come on Nancy. Angola? That's a fucking myth."

"It happened, didn't it?"

"Well, a platform blew up on Angola in 1977. Yeah, that happened," he said, rolling his eyes. "But the part about the guy who got demonically possessed or some such bullshit and blew it up? No, I don't believe that for a second."

"The way people are acting around here, I'm starting to wonder," she replied.

Chapter 7

The Above: Platform Faith

Gusman lay in his bed, staring up at the ceiling and listening. It was silent, except for the constant hum of the ventilation system and the faint buzz of electricity. Occasionally, he would hear footfalls in the hallway or a cough from one of the other cabins.

Whenever Gusman returned to Faith, he had to get used to the feeling of being entombed — buried alive — in a giant windowless metal box.

Gusman was thinking about the story Nancy Jones had told him: the broken drill bit and Drake covering it up. She also told him she wasn't coming back. She was sick of Drake, who never ceased his constant barrage of sexual innuendo. And sick of the isolation she experienced when she was on Faith. Yeah, the pay was great. But it was affecting her. She was depressed and it was putting pressure on her marriage. Nancy hinted that her marriage was in trouble, failing. She used to say to him, joking, "The third time's the charm."

She wasn't saying that any more.

He listened to his breathing, then to the beat of his heart, then he closed his eyes and stared at the darting white flashes that danced on the back of his eyelids.

Then nothing.

Chapter 8

The Above: Platform Faith

Gusman woke. He reached over to the desk and looked at his watch. Two hours had elapsed since he had lain down after lunch to take a nap. He was thirsty and momentarily thought about drinking the rest of the water from the cup he had half consumed before he fell asleep, but he felt a wave of claustrophobia and decided to get up and get some air on deck.

As he rose, his hand grazed the book he had been reading. He thought about picking it up, but rejected that idea, too. He put on his shoes, tying the shoestrings in perfect double knots. Gusman reached the door in two even strides and opened it, the lock making a satisfying click as the tumbler disengaged. He walked down the fluorescent-lit corridor toward the elevator. He stepped in, turned around, and pressed the button that would take him down to the platform level and to the outside. It was then that he first heard a rhythmic sound — *bang, bang, bang* — quiet at first, then louder, the sound somehow coming from no specific direction, but all around. When the door opened, he was struck by the searing light of the sun, which temporarily blinded him. The banging was now so loud it became a single, incessant sound that blended into the whiteness of the world, reaching into the center of his brain and becoming the totality of the world itself.

He stepped out of the elevator and fell weightless into the blinding whiteness.

And then he heard a disembodied voice whisper, "Go away."

— ⟨⟩ —

The Below

Again there is nothing in the Dream, no memories either new or ancient and faint that can explain the searing brightness that has returned. Even pulled back behind the folds of his mantle, P'aldil's eyes seem scorched. This is not the dream from sleep, but the real Dream that touches all the He'e and threads their memories together. He is in a not-land that has flickered into his dream before, a not-land, as hot as if it is formed from the plume of a smoker, but wondrously without water. There are colors that gleam in it, but so bright that they are almost burned away by the overwhelming presence of the light. In it, through eyes he has narrowed to the slightest slits, he sees something alive moving toward him. It is ungainly, moving on stiff legs like an 'opae shrimp skittering across the seafloor. It moves into the full brightness and P'aldil lurches away from it, back out of the Dream, back into the cool gloom of the seafloor. His eyes ache and M'aldil exudes an anodyne to soothe them.

— «» —

The Above: Platform Faith

Gusman sat up, his body bathed in sweat. *What was that?* And then the banging again — quieter, but no less insistent. *The door. Someone was knocking at the door.*

"Just a second," he said, his voice gravelly, irritated.

He stumbled to the door and opened the lock. The same smooth click of the mechanism again. He opened it.

It was Nancy.

"I was asleep," he said, groggily. "What time is it?"

He turned and sat down heavily on the desk chair.

"Does it matter, Gusman?" she said, sitting down on the bed. She put her hands on her lap, and stared at him, her head slightly cocked.

"What's wrong?" he asked, rubbing his fingers to massage his sore temples.

"I've missed you." Her voice was softer, the tone she used for their rough banter gone. She patted the bed to motion him to sit down.

"Do you think that's really a good idea?"

"Of course not. It's a terrible idea. But my marriage is going to shit, I'm lonely from being stuck on this tin can for six months..." she paused and smiled absently. "We always did have a good time together."

Gusman sat on the bed next to her. He stroked her cheek with the back of his hand. "We certainly did."

He wasn't sure if he was up to it.

Nancy pushed past his hand and they embraced, kissing hard, as always, her raw physicality blowing past any hesitation he felt. It had been a few years and he had forgotten what a powerful lover she was. She uncoiled like a snake, pushing him down and climbing on top, grinding her pelvis into his.

He was up to it.

They began a lover's wrestling match, he pushing to get at her breasts, she resisting, then tearing her shirt off and pushing her breasts into him. Her runner's body was strong and lithe.

She laughed wildly, then said, almost yelling, breathless, "This is good," and resumed her grinding and pulsing.

It was taking all Gusman had just to keep up. *Had she been like this before?*

Chapter 9

The Above: Platform Faith

Nancy looked back and waved at Gusman, a crooked smile on her face, then climbed the aluminum ramp and entered the belly of The Beast. He watched the rotors begin to turn, slowly at first, then more quickly until the pilot pulled pitch and The Beast lifted off, heading east toward Midway. Gusman waited at the railing until the helicopter disappeared from view. As he turned to go inside, he saw a man in the shadow of the open bulkhead door as it shut quickly.

Was someone watching him?

He tried to shake off the feeling of foreboding that had plagued him since before dawn, when he awoke from another strange dream full of light and heat and that strange disembodied voice telling him to go away, and saw Nancy staring at him in the half-dim yellow glow of the night-light.

She whispered, "I'm scared for you," and closed her eyes. Had that really happened or was it part of the dream — a dream inside a dream? He had meant to ask her about it, but later, in the tumult of their hurried kiss goodbye, he had forgotten.

It was time to get to work, to test and record, to take the measure of the monster that was Platform Faith. Time to get to the bottom of things.

— «» —

Gusman spent the morning in his tiny office going over Nancy's maintenance entries. There was an inspection routine they followed, and it was all meticulously documented and entered into a computer program. Ultimately, the computer records would be forwarded to BOEMRE (the Bureau of

Ocean Energy Management, Regulation, and Enforcement), the old Minerals Management Service — renamed after BP's 2010 oil spill in the Gulf to make it sound like it wasn't owned lock, stock, and barrel by the oil industry. Some government bureaucrat was supposed to review them, at least in theory, but Gusman thought that the records were probably simply filed away, only to be retrieved if there was an accident — in which case BOEMRE would, as usual, cover its ass by simply stating that the records were incomplete. Blame would be conveniently fixed on the company and BOEMRE could pretend it had clamped down on the oil industry. It would all work out very nicely for everyone — except the fish.

They had started drilling several kilometers away from their present site, but the hole was not sufficiently productive, and Faith had been moved to its present position six months later. They were now very close to one of the vents and there was a significantly increased risk of pressure surges that could lead to a blowout, but corporate had deemed it was worth the risk. Two weeks earlier, the 'spudding' process — assembling the articulated thirty-foot lengths of drilling pipe all the way down to the seabed — was completed.

When it came time to commence drilling at the new location, Nancy received orders right from the top to use a roller cone, or 'rock bit' as it was known in the trade, rather than use a conventional drill bit. While conventional bits had a lower risk of a blowout if they hit a gas-pressurized void, they were slower and obviously corporate was in a hurry. Rock bits, constructed of three rotating, interlocking tungsten-carbide, diamond toothed cylinders, reminded Gusman of the mouth of some primordial sea monster, devouring everything in their way.

Actually, Gusman's more immediate concern was the structural integrity of the platform itself. Ultra-deep drill platforms were under immense stress and were engineered to withstand tremendous forces: corrosion, waves, wind, earthquakes, potential collision with vessels, and — God forbid — fires and explosions. The pontoons, structural members, pressure vessels, and the hundreds of miles of cables, pipes, and exhausts had to be constantly inspected for metal fatigue and hairline cracks. Anything more than fifty feet below the surface, including the array of stainless steel cables that loosely moored Platform Faith — like Gulliver tied down by the threads of the Lilliputians — to the seabed more than five miles below, was inspected by a small army of remotely controlled cameras. All of the data was fed into the central computer system that analyzed it, searching for anomalies which would show up on Gusman's oversized flat-screen computer monitor.

For repairs, Faith was equipped with an ROV, a remotely operated vehicle that could function in the deepest water. The operator was an ex-Navy guy named Kent Telfer who had learned to operate an ROV while stationed aboard a minesweeper in the Persian Gulf. Telfer loved to regale anyone who would listen with stories of his exploits piloting an ROV in the cat and mouse game the US Navy played with the Iranians — pronounced '*Eye*-ranians' — who would plant mines in the sea lanes of the Persian Gulf which he'd blow up by the next morning. In his last tour, Gusman had gotten Telfer to give him lessons on how to work the ROV. Operating it was slow going and took the patience of a saint.

Gusman spent the morning half-heartedly reviewing various maintenance logs, but he couldn't concentrate. His thoughts kept returning to Nancy's story of the shattered drill bit and the evident cover-up that followed.

Should he confront Drake directly? Probably not a good idea. As his Uncle Mike, a wiseass career prosecutor in Chicago, once said to him, "Kid, the second commandment of being a lawyer is to never ask a witness a question unless you already know how he's gonna answer." Uncle Mike went to his grave without revealing the first commandment of lawyering — or any of the other commandments, for that matter.

No, he would poke around and see what he could come up with on his own. The logs showed that drilling had been suspended three days earlier but didn't say why. Obviously, he needed to start with Andy Noguchi.

He made his way around the corridor to Noguchi's little office. The door was closed. Gusman knocked.

There was no answer.

He knocked again.

Nothing.

This time he banged hard on the door.

"What?" barked an angry voice.

"It's Gusman. I need to talk to you."

"Fuck off, Gusman."

Gusman, taken aback at Noguchi's angry response, tried the latch. It was locked.

"Come on, Andy. I need to talk to you about something important."

"Get the fuck away from me."

"What did I ever do to you? I just got back here yesterday."

There was no response. Andy Noguchi was one of the mildest men Gusman had ever known; level, friendly, helpful to a fault. He had never heard him using profanity. This was weird. Gusman lowered his voice and made his best effort to speak in a soothing tone.

"Hey Andy, Nancy told me that we ought to talk about something that happened. I need to know what's going on. It's my job."

Silence. Then, "Okay, not now. Meet me at the injection control room at 2:15. Now go away."

— «» —

Gusman showed up at the injection control room on the third level a few minutes early. Since drilling was suspended, no one was on duty. Of course, Noguchi would have known that. He decided to wait inside. He waved his security card in front of the scanner and entered the small office. The company's green spiral "C" logo swirled across the screens of the control room computers.

Gusman waited in the semi-darkness.

His headache had returned, but the pain was less ferocious this time — more constant throb than stabbing pain. He closed his eyes and rubbed his neck, which seemed to relieve the pain until he released the pressure. Then it came back, dull and constant. He just couldn't shake his sense of malaise, as if his raging cold had retreated but not surrendered and was settling into a low-intensity guerrilla war against his body. This feeling of illness was heightened by the strange, inexplicable sense of anxiety he had felt from the moment he stepped off the helicopter onto the deck of Faith.

There was a click of the control room door and Noguchi slipped in.

"Gusman," he said in a loud whisper. He turned his head jerkily to survey the small room.

"We're alone, Andy."

"Yeah, okay. Good."

His eyes still darted back and forth as if he didn't trust Gusman's assurances. Noguchi's hair was longer than usual, and unkempt.

"Sit down," Gusman said, gesturing to one of the other chairs.

Noguchi plopped himself down heavily in the chair, which emitted a loud hiss from its cushion.

"So, what's happening, Andy?" asked Gusman, a little too matter-of-factly.

"Some bad shit, man."

"What kind of bad shit?"

"You said Nancy told you."

"She did, but I want to hear your version."

"Yeah, okay. But you can't tell anyone."

Noguchi's dark eyes widened and Gusman saw real fear in them.

"Not a soul," responded Gusman.

"Nancy said I could trust you."

"You can."

Gusman reached out and patted the younger man on the shoulder to reassure him. Noguchi stiffened at his touch and Gusman pulled back quickly.

"So last week, when the drill bit failed, I reviewed the video and I saw something that I've never seen before. The bit did not sheer off, as is generally the case when it hits a hard substrate — it shattered into tiny pieces. You could see thousands of shards of metal exploding up from the hole when the bit — or what was left of it — was extracted."

"Yeah, Nancy showed me the video clip you gave her."

"So then that asshole Drake comes to see me. He just walks into my office without knocking and locks the door behind him. Without so much as a 'hello,' he sits down and gives me this strange, far-away look. Not his usual nasty-ass smile, like he wants to slit your throat. But somehow his weird calmness scared me even more. He orders me to edit out the part with the drill bit exploding and substitute footage from a previous normal break before I send it back to the company and the Feds. When I tell him I'll get fired for doing that, he says that it's a direct order from the top and that I'll get my ass fired if I *don't*. That I should just 'do it' and not ask any questions. Also, he tells me not to tell anyone."

"Then why did you tell Nancy?" Gusman asked.

"I don't know. Nancy's always been a friend of mine and I was scared, and I needed to talk to someone."

"Did you edit the film?"

"Yes, but I kept a copy of the real video on a thumb drive that I hid."

"And now Nancy has seen it. That's dangerous. Drake's a ruthless bastard. You need to be careful. Watch your back."

Andy looked down and wiped his nose quickly with his finger. When he looked up, his face was strained and gray.

He stared straight into Gusman's eyes. "Do you think Drake would do something to me?"

Gusman decided to lie. "No, no. Drake's not the violent type. I just meant you should watch out for your career. He wouldn't hesitate to fire you if he found out you gave Nancy that footage or were talking to me about it."

"Yeah, okay." Noguchi sighed, relieved. "Hey, Gusman — what could cause a drill bit to shatter like that?"

"I don't know. I've done a literature search and I came up with nothing."

"Well, we know it happened here. What could cause that?"

"I really couldn't say. If it had hit magma, like at the first drilling site, it would have just melted. To shatter like that, it would have had to hit something harder than hardened steel. I suppose it could also be caused by a very large explosion in a confined space, but that is not very likely, or you would have seen evidence of it. The drill bit had barely penetrated the seafloor."

"Well, if it wasn't an explosion, then what could be hard enough to shatter hardened tungsten-carbide steel?"

"Fuck if I know," said Gusman. "How about the largest diamond ever discovered thrust up at the bit with great force as it was bearing down with equal force?"

"Really?"

"No, but it's the only thing that I can think of that fits the situation. The core sample, which was taken from a test hole in the same spot before we started drilling, showed no diamond studded substrate and extended farther than the drill bit did before it shattered."

"That doesn't make sense."

"No, it doesn't."

Noguchi was silent for a few seconds. "Hey, maybe you should talk to Kent. Drake had him send his ROV down there to collect soil samples from where the bit exploded."

Noguchi stood and began to pace around the office. "I guess I better go."

"Take care of yourself, Andy."

Gusman went directly to Kent Telfer's office, a little hole-in-the-wall a few doors down from the main control room.

Telfer was one of those guys who never stopped talking and never seemed to realize that others had tired of the conversation. Still, his eternally sunny disposition made him impossible to dislike. He also seemed to have the largest vocabulary of American idiomatic expressions of anyone Gusman had ever met and knew the right one for every occasion.

"Well, hello, Gusman," said Telfer when Gusman strode into his office. "Welcome back. What can I do you for?"

"I hear you collected samples from the site where the drill bit exploded."

A surprised and frightened look came across Telfer's face.

"Who told you that?"

"Andy."

"I can't talk about that. Andy shouldn't have said nothin'." Telfer averted his gaze.

"I need to know. I'm responsible for all this."

"I'm sorry, Gusman. Drake said not to talk about it with anyone."

"Just give me the basics."

"Hell's bells, if I say anything, I might as well kiss my sweet ass goodbye."

"Come on, Kent. We've been friends for about a thousand years. Just give me the basics."

Telfer dithered, playing with a pen on his desk and looking uncertainly at Gusman, finally nodded and said, "What the hell. You out of anyone here ought to know. But there isn't much to tell. I sent the ROV down there to the drill hole. I scooped up samples. As soon as I got them to the surface, Drake confiscated them and told me not to discuss it with anyone."

"Did he say anything else?"

"Only that he was sending the samples to the mainland for analysis."

Chapter 10

The Below

The He'e have abided in the Urb as long as they remember in the Dream of it. Far away, many eights of eights of arm spans away are other Urbs, spotted along the seafloor where other smokers bring heat and the stuff of life. Heles, the travelers among the He'e, journey among the Urbs along the vast route over the sea's benthic floor.

All are connected in the Dream. But the heles bring the variety of their own bloodlines to the far-flung Urbs, bringing their eggs or fertilizing others. In this way the He'e, though dwelling apart on the vast seafloor, nonetheless remain close cousins. They remain ho'omaka, evolving together, and so have become the ka mo'I kings and queens of the deepest of the deep.

The great muhe squid are a danger. But they are no longer the terrifying predator of the past. The He'e can handle them now as they handle most dangers of the Below. And so the benthic world of the He'e has become tame for them, its dangers few. So, they have lived for many eight eights of hungers, placid as the placid flow of the waters that move across them in its gyre.

Now, at the dark borders of the Dream, something new has entered that defies classification. P'ke'imi, who has taken the name 'curiosity,' moves in the Dream to touch the most distant He'e. More than just P'aldil have experienced the apparition. The danger is something that also seems to dream, though in its own Dream, separate from the He'es'. But in places where the Dreams intersect, the mixed vision is alarming.

P'ke'imi's touch with other Urbs brings no clarity, only a sense of foreboding, of wickedness. His arms seethe with the varied colors displaying a welter of emotions. He doesn't know why yet, but he tells M'ke'imi, "We have to prepare."

She knows no more than her mate, but flickers with the white of agreement. Together they go to P'M'heen to say that the great neck and radula that descended on their Urb from the Above hold a hideous new danger for them and all the He'e.

Chapter 11

The Above: Platform Faith

Gusman dreaded dealing with Drake. They had never liked each other, and over the years their mutual loathing became more intense, marked by stiffness and sarcasm. Drake had started working as an engineer for the company a few years before Gusman but had risen quickly. Gusman had not been interested in becoming a manager and Drake held it against him, as if his failure to seek promotion was an incurable personality defect deserving of abject contempt. Some days Gusman beat Drake to the punch, wallowing in sufficient self-loathing to occupy the field.

Befitting his standing, Drake's office was large and well decorated — even on this metal hulk in the middle of the Pacific — lined in dark woods and tasteful corporate art. Characteristically, when he entered, Drake gestured for him to sit, but then left him cooling his jets as he self-importantly finished reading some papers. Gusman busied himself in his moment of petty humiliation by studying the photographs on the credenza behind the desk: Drake with his perfect Texas trophy wife, blond and leggy and twenty years his junior — the one he had predictably acquired after dumping the woman who bore his three children; Drake with Enrique Gonzales on the occasion of his last promotion; Drake with George Bush — the second one — at some confab or other. A grinning Drake at a Trump rally. Power. It was always about power with Drake. And control. No nuance, no subtlety; just fuck you and the horse you rode in on.

Gusman had enough. He stood. "I'll come back later when you're less busy."

Drake looked up over his reading glasses. "Are you in a hurry, Gusman?"

"As a matter of fact, I am."

"With what?"

Gusman lost it. Spontaneously and completely. Afterward, he could not explain it. Perhaps it was that smirk on Drake's face or the untrimmed hair in his nose.

"I'm trying to get to the bottom of why a perfectly good carbide-tipped tungsten steel drill bit shattered into pieces. And why you're trying to cover it up. And what the fuck I'm supposed to do about it."

Gusman turned his back on Drake and walked to the door.

Drake stood, red-faced, the veins in his neck bulging.

"You walk out that fucking door, Gusman, and you're history."

Gusman turned and attempted to assume a calm and confident expression. God knows what expression he actually had. His stomach was doing somersaults. The honest truth was that he found Drake as intimidating as he did loathsome.

"Look, Drake. We've known each other for a long time. You don't like me, and I don't like you. I get that. And I also get that you're the boss. I'm not trying to take you on or make you look bad. I just want to do my time and get off this hulk."

Drake sneered. He wasn't buying.

"When I want your opinion on something, I'll ask for it. In the meantime, you don't walk out on me. Is that clear?"

"Perfectly."

Gusman turned from the door. The adrenaline rush and, with it, his sense of bravado had passed and he sat back down, trying his best to make it look as dignified as possible. He knew Drake was capable not only of firing him, but of blacklisting him so that he'd never work for a big-league oil company again. He needed his job; he had alimony to pay.

Drake's smile returned; the triumphant smile of a petty tyrant. The man granted no quarter. He sat down slowly, never taking his eyes off Gusman, obviously savoring the moment. Gusman stared right back. It was the least he could do to retain a semblance of pride.

Drake started to shuffle the papers on his desk and Gusman thought he was going to resume reading and extend the humiliation.

But something else happened, something entirely unexpected.

Drake put the papers down and exhaled hard. Then he looked up at Gusman and said quietly, hardly above a whisper, "I need your help."

"What?" asked Gusman, leaning forward. Drake's sardonic smile had vanished. His expression was deadpan.

"Look, Gusman, I need your help."

"Help? With what?"

"That's just it. I don't know. I can't explain it."

"The drill bit exploding?"

"That's just part of it. There's more."

"Like what?" Gusman asked.

"Take a look at this…"

Drake pulled a photograph out of the stack of papers and put it on the end of the desk, gesturing to Gusman to pick it up.

Gusman studied the photograph. It was a single frame from video footage showing one of the mooring cables attached to what remained of its concrete anchor block. The anchor block was riddled with holes like a Swiss cheese. Gusman did a double take, shaking his head and looking up at Drake.

"These are clean holes, right?"

"Yes, whatever did that bored a hole smooth as glass right through both the concrete and the rebar. Can you think of anything that would cause that?" Drake asked.

"Not in nature, but I suppose anything is possible."

"How about this?"

Drake reached into one of his desk drawers and brought out a foot-long piece of the four-inch thick twisted stainless-steel cable that was used to moor Faith to the ocean floor. He handed it to Gusman.

Gusman lifted the piece of stainless steel. It must have weighed at least forty pounds. One end had obviously been cut by a saw. The other end was black and melted-looking, like a piece of plastic exposed to a flame.

"Where did this come from?" Gusman asked.

"From one of the other mooring cables that broke off. It was detached about twenty feet above the seabed. We found it dangling about four hundred meters from where it was attached to the pier."

"It must have been severed by some kind of chemical or intense heat."

"Yes. Something like that."

"And what happened to the pier block?"

"We couldn't find it. The rest of the cable below the break vanished."

Gusman said nothing. He was trying to make sense of it all.

"So, let me get this straight. Something severed the line, but you couldn't find the other end? I mean, there should've been cable sticking up from the bottom where it was anchored. You're telling me there was nothing there?"

"When we sent the submersible down to take a look, the anchor was gone. Two of the other three cables were intact but just barely."

"It sounds like sabotage."

Drake nodded and said, "Yes."

"But who or what could do that?"

"I don't know."

"Is there more?" asked Gusman.

"God, I hope not."

Chapter 12

The Above: Platform Faith

Gusman woke up. He looked at his watch. It was 5:32 a.m. Just before dawn. Should he go back to sleep? He lay in bed, staring at the ceiling thinking about it, but decided to get up and watch the sun rise. He dressed quickly and stepped into the corridor, heading for the elevator that would take him down to the deck.

Gusman reached the railing at the edge of the platform just as the edge of the sun's red ball was beginning to illuminate the eastern sky. It was dark enough that the sky behind him was still ablaze with stars. Even the moon, a hand's breadth from the rising sun, was visible just above the horizon. Gusman stood on the edge of the platform, looking at the quickly brightening surface of the water. The ocean was calm and flat, streaked by light and shadow. And then he saw it, a growing stream of yellow-green bioluminescence snaking along just beneath the surface. It was perhaps a few feet in length, but it had no obvious beginning or end. He could see it turning, undulating, stretching, growing fatter and then thinner like the night crawlers he used to dig up as a kid to use for bait. Suddenly, it breached the surface and drove straight up in the air.

It had a face with eyes that were locked onto his. He realized the mouth was open and screaming. He wanted to look away, to run, but he could not move or even avert his gaze. His feet felt like they were locked to the deck and his body was impossibly heavy. The apparition continued to rise, gaining speed as it flew directly toward him. How could this be? He felt overwhelming fear, but also fascination. When it reached the height of the platform, it stopped suddenly, inches from his face. The thing he saw was vibrating, inchoate, and ghostly. The mouth was open and inside there was blackness. The scream grew louder and louder, expanding in pitch and timbre. Then, abruptly, the noise ceased and there was total silence. From the silence he could hear words, but the words were somehow coming from inside his own head.

"Creature, leave this place or you will all die. We do not harm your fry. Why do you endanger ours?"

Gusman blinked.

He sat up and looked around. His cabin. A dream. It was a dream. He wiped the sweat from his face and felt his rapid heartbeat. He vividly remembered what the being had looked like and the warning it had screamed. He looked at his watch. It was 5:32 a.m. Just before dawn. He got out of bed, stumbled over to the sink, and looked at himself in the mirror. The man who stared back looked gaunt and old. He splashed himself with cold water and ran it through his hair, which made him feel a little better.

He was having nightmares about monsters. Sea monsters. "Jesus fucking Christ," he muttered, shaking his head.

He was wide-awake and, if the truth be told, he was scared to go back to sleep.

So he decided to go outside and watch the sun come up.

For real this time.

— «» —

The Below

M'ke'imi lets out a bleat. "I touched our Dreams together. I told it to go." She grasps P'ke'imi's arms and shudders with a well-worn fear. "What is this creature? What does it want?"

Chapter 13

The Above: Platform Faith

Drake was standing, arms crossed, staring over Andy Noguchi's shoulder at the control room video monitor. Noguchi kept stealing anxious glances at his boss. Gusman, who stood over Noguchi's other shoulder, saw raw fear in his drawn face and watery, dull eyes. Fear of what? Failure? No, that wasn't it. It was a fear more intense, more basic, like the fear of death.

On the monitor was a static, oblique-angled camera shot of the borehole as the big roller bit was lowered inch by inch into it. Other than the occasional sea creature that swam by, the only movement that could be detected was a fine cloud of pressurized drill mud that blew steadily out of the borehole.

"How far in are we?" asked Drake.

"Twenty meters," replied Noguchi, looking at the computer screen with its flashing green numbers, reporting the statistics: drilling depth, mud pressure, water temperature, and revolutions per minute.

"It blew last time at thirty-six, right?

"Thirty-six point five," interjected Gusman, if for no other reason than to take the pressure off Noguchi.

"So, ten minutes," said Drake.

"Yeah, that's about right," Gusman replied.

They waited in silence, the seconds ticking away. It was so quiet that Gusman could hear their breathing.

"How's the video feed to New York, Andy?" asked Drake.

Drake's voice startled Gusman.

"It's perfect," said Noguchi.

"At least something's working right," replied Drake.

They lapsed into silence as they watched and waited. Time seemed to slow and Gusman kept looking at the clock for no reason.

Finally, Noguchi spoke. "We're at thirty-four meters."

"Almost there," said Drake.

"Thirty-four point five."

"Thirty-five."

"Come on, you can do it," said Drake, exhorting the roller bit like he was a high school football coach giving a locker room speech.

"Thirty-five point five," said Andy.

"Come on..."

"Thirty-six."

"Thirty-six point five."

"Good," said Drake, smiling for the first time.

"Thirty-seven."

Across the room, Jones, the bore operator, said, "We're now beyond where we were before."

"Jones, how does everything look?"

"The drill is slowing, but that's normal," said Jones.

"Thirty-seven point five."

When Noguchi called out forty meters, Drake said, "I think things look good now. I'm going back to my office to call New York."

"Yeah, okay," responded Gusman, who felt relieved both that things were back on track and that Drake was leaving the immediate vicinity.

Drake was almost to the door when Jones said, "Wait," and, almost simultaneously, Noguchi said, "Something's happening."

Drake turned around.

On the screen, in soundless black and white, nearly six miles down, the camera recorded a sudden plume of rock and metal and mud explode out of the hole, like a small mushroom cloud, expanding rapidly and then obscuring the view as it engulfed the lens.

"Fuck," said Jones.

"What's happening?" asked Drake, his voice quivering, panicky.

"I dunno. We're dead."

"Jesus Christ," said Gusman. "It happened again."

— «‹›» —

The Below

The He'e get no pleasure from the destruction of the thing of metal. While it is not alive, it is a thing of life, articulated and purposeful. With its destruction, something has died. In its death, P'heen perceives not the end of any struggle, but the beginning of something far worse. "It doesn't seem like a victory," he tells M'heen.

"No, my love," she says, "it does not."

— «‹›» —

The Above: Platform Faith

Gusman knew something was wrong the moment he saw that Nancy had sent the email to his personal account. He read it with rising anger. She had returned to Houston and had promptly been fired. She was certain it had something to do with the problems on Faith, but she said no one was willing to talk to her, let alone provide an explanation. They simply told her to pack her things and go. On top of that, her marriage was ending. Gusman felt a twinge of guilt, but it was passing; he wasn't that prone to guilt.

Gusman took his time composing a response to Nancy's email. He wanted to sound supportive and sympathetic without sounding fake. It was difficult because he wasn't exactly a touchy-feely kind of guy, and Nancy knew it. Eventually, he managed to bang out something that seemed appropriate.

He pressed the send button.

Nothing happened. He tried to refresh his browser. Again, nothing.

The Internet connection was dead.

Chapter 14

The Above: Austin, Texas

Nancy was having difficulty collecting her thoughts. Half the problem was the booze — she was on her third Cosmo. The other half was her emotional state, which was bad and descending rapidly into the deep self-pity zone. She took a deep breath, crossed her legs and straightened out her skirt before she spoke to the woman sitting across from her.

"How do I feel? Well, Annie… I'm angry. At Bob, at the fucking company, at your brother."

"My brother? I thought that was over years ago."

Annie Gusman detested what her brother did for a living. Somewhere around 1995, they reached a *modus vivendi*: Gusman never mentioned his job and Annie stopped denouncing him as a rapacious pig at every opportunity. Of course, Gusman, ever the cynic, more or less agreed with Annie's views about the oil industry — not that he would ever admit it in front of her. Her earnestness annoyed him to no end. So, at their family gatherings, whenever Annie mounted her high horse, Gusman quietly wandered into another room to wait out the storm.

Then Gusman avoided the problem entirely by no longer attending family gatherings.

"He's letting those bastards at the company get away with murder."

Annie perked up. "What do you mean, 'murder?'"

Nancy moved her head slowly from side to side and said, "No, I can't talk about it." Then she took a big gulp from her drink, which seemed to have an immediate impact on her resolve. "Okay, I shouldn't tell you this," she said, leaning in close to Annie with a conspiratorial grin, "but, shit, I don't owe those bastards anything, now."

"I should say not," Annie said indignantly. "They fired you."

"You got that right. After fifteen years of loyal service, they called me in and fired me. No explanation. Nothing. Just, 'clean out your desk and go.' That was it. Then I get home and Bob tells me he's leaving me."

"For another woman?"

"He didn't say. But I suspect."

Annie reached over and patted Nancy on the arm. "I'm so sorry."

"Me, too," she said, almost in a whisper. She stared into her drink.

There was an awkward silence.

Then Nancy picked up her glass and, smiling a little too brightly, said, "To better times."

"To better times," responded Annie, clinking glasses.

"So, where was I?" asked Nancy, her eyes looking slightly unfocused.

"You were telling me why you're pissed off at my brother." Annie's tone was tentative. Nancy was about to tell her what she *really* wanted to know, but she didn't want to sound *too* interested less Nancy, inebriated as she was, think she was insensitive to all her other problems.

"Oh, yeah, your brother."

"What did he do now?"

"It's not what he did. It's what he won't do."

"I don't understand."

Nancy leaned in close to Annie and looked around conspiratorially. "Do you promise you won't tell anybody about this?"

"Of course," responded Annie, not quite sure if she was lying or not.

"Some really strange stuff is happening on that oil platform."

"Like what?"

"Well, the drill bit shattered just a few meters beneath the ocean floor."

"Shattered? Does that happen often?"

"Never. They break, but they don't just shatter. There is nothing that I know of that could do that. Even a high-yield explosive would probably just twist the metal or cause it to crack or shear off — but not shatter."

"Wow. When you say 'shattered,' do you mean shattered like glass shatters?"

"Yeah. Exactly. And that asshole, Drake, was trying to cover it up."

"Who's Drake?" asked Annie.

"He's the Project Director — the head guy — aboard Faith. I think he got me fired."

"Why?"

"Because I knew what was going on."

"Which is what, Nancy?"

Nancy leaned in close and looked around. In a whisper so low, she was practically mouthing the word, she said, "Sabotage."

"Oh, my God," said Annie. Then, shaking her head, she asked, "What does my brother have to do with it? Is he part of the cover up?"

"I don't know. It doesn't seem like him, but I keep emailing him and he's just ignoring me."

"I don't understand something. How can someone on board cause a drill bit to explode miles below the surface?" asked Annie.

"What if it's not somebody on Faith?"

"What could it be? Maybe seismic activity, or hot gas or steam. But caused by what?"

"I have no idea. The bit would have had to have been subjected to enormous pressure to shatter like that." Nancy seemed suddenly more sober now. "Whatever's down there, it's dangerous and they have no idea what to do about it."

Chapter 15

The Above: Sacramento, California

The blogger who called himself "Oil Foil" did his best work at a coffee shop located off the lobby of a residential hotel in downtown Sacramento. The place was incongruously named the Pine Top Grill and attracted a clientele roughly split between elderly alcoholics and kids, primarily of the inked-up and strung-out variety. Oil Foil, whose real name was Noah Reiner, hated corporate America with a passion and the Pine Top was, if nothing else, the complete antithesis of everything corporate, down to its last cup of bad coffee.

Noah, who had spent the last two hours busily writing at his favorite corner table, let out a self-satisfied chortle — loud enough to draw momentary dull stares from a number of the other patrons. The Pine Top was a tolerant place, and people emitting strange noises, erupting into arguments — frequently with themselves — or laughing too loudly were commonplace. The waitresses were tough, hard women whose lives were a string of bad choices and even worse men who absolutely loved Noah. They called him "hun" and "sweetie" and "darlin'" and brought him extra food because they thought he was too skinny. He was an emissary from the outside world, that strange place where people voted, owned homes, and believed they had a stake in the outcome of society.

For Noah, the Pine Top was authentic and nurturing and it evoked the romantic image of beat poets suffering for their art. He used to tell people that he loved the Pine Top precisely because he was certain that he was the only person who had ever set foot in the place who had had a bar mitzvah.

Noah had just finished his latest blog entry, which he entitled *Sludge-gate?* He was excited. This time he was not just blasting the oil industry but was actually breaking a big news story. Images of interview requests and invitations to write for the *Huffington Post* danced around in his head.

In a strange way, he had a grudging respect for the rough candor of the old-school Texas oilmen he constantly attacked. They didn't mince words and thought that all the talk of protecting the environment was just so much stupid prattle from liberal do-gooders — hypocrites who were utterly dependent on oil to fuel their pampered middle-class lives but lacked the honesty or good grace to admit it. And embedded in that paradoxical admiration was the essence of why Noah Reiner particularly detested Enrique Gonzales, Clearsea Energy's charisma-spewing CEO. Gonzales was a panderer and a fraud, an ambitious social climber who ruthlessly exploited his own ethnicity to rise up in the world. What enraged Noah more than anything was that people fell for it, treating Gonzales and Clearsea with kid gloves. To Noah, Clearsea was the epitome of corporate evil. He had even taken to calling the corporation Dark Sea Energy in his blog posts. Dark Sea, like something hidden and corrupt.

With any luck, that is about to end, Noah thought and pressed the send button which launched his latest blog into cyberspace.

Noah sat back against the worn brown fake leather of the booth and closed his eyes, conjuring up the image of Annie Gusman sitting across from him, talking about Clearsea Energy's off-shore oil crisis. She had emailed him out of the blue to ask if he could meet with her in San Francisco to discuss a matter in strict confidence. Noah was flattered and, quite frankly, amazed that a veteran activist like Annie Gusman, who had been battling corporate America for years, wanted to meet with him. They sat in a dark booth at a hip coffee house in the Mission District called the Ritual Café, a place way out of Noah's usual ambit— not to mention price range. Noah listened with rapt attention while Annie revealed the unfolding disaster at Clearsea's offshore platform in the central Pacific. Annie Gusman was intense, articulate, and beautiful. Her thick curly hair, high cheekbones, and dark, sensual eyes made her look like one of those women who perpetually seem to have just rolled out of bed. For Noah, there was only one word to describe Annie Gusman: hot. Actually, two words: smoking hot. He developed an instant — and intense — older-woman crush.

Annie gave no indication that she noticed.

The oil operation on Platform Faith was apparently in serious trouble: drill bits mysteriously exploding, steel mooring cables shearing off, concrete footings full of holes, and not a drop of oil to show for it. Clearsea was shutting down internal communications and firing employees who had knowledge of the disaster.

"Why me?" asked Noah.

"Because I read your stuff and it's good. Very good."

Noah could feel his face reddening. "Yes, but there are environmental bloggers who have a lot larger readership than I do."

Annie smiled and put her hand on Noah's.

"That's true. But, frankly, you're the real thing — and many of them are just opportunistic egomaniacs. You're talented and we need to bring our younger people along in the environmental movement."

"Thanks," Noah stammered, looking down.

"Now, you've got the information. Go with it."

Chapter 16

The Above: Cyberspace

Sludgegate?

Oil Foil has this burning question: what in the hell is going on in the deepest Pacific at Clearsea Energy's Platform Faith? Oil Foil has received secret information that mysterious happenings are occurring on — and beneath — the world's deepest offshore oil platform.

Unprecedented things that cannot be explained by science.

I will reveal all, but first a little background.

Two years ago, Enrique Gonzales, the smooth-talking CEO of Clearsea, announced the company had located a huge oil field in the vast Pacific between Midway Island and the Marianas Trench. Its estimated contents are at least forty billion barrels of light, sweet crude — an immense discovery that would be among the top ten largest known oil fields in the world. The problem is that the bottom is almost seven miles down and located not far east of the Pacific 'Ring of Fire' — the undersea vents where hot gases and molten lava erupt from fissures in the Earth's crust. "No biggie," exclaimed the ever-confident Enrique, a salesman so extraordinary that he has managed to fool a good part of the public into thinking Clearsea actually cares about the environment. It's enough to make you want to vomit. Gonzales declares that he is so confident of the find, that despite the enormous cost and technical challenges of drilling in such a remote location, Clearsea is going to bet the financial farm on the project.

Untold (and I believe underreported) billions of dollars later, and amid much ballyhoo and bullshit, Faith was towed in place. It is the largest and most expensive offshore platform ever built. Yours truly predicted that it would fail.

Nobody believed me.

Jump ahead to last month. Time to drill. They start to bore the first hole. (Well, their second. The first bore a few miles east was an expensive bust.) Everything is good… at first. Then they get to just shy of forty meters beneath the bottom and something happens.

The drill bit breaks. Which might be routine, but this is no ordinary break. The drill bit explodes into thousands of tiny pieces. Now, these drill bits are made from hardened steel and the teeth are coated with carbide and industrial diamonds.

Oil Foil is no slouch. I did an exhaustive literature search. These things don't shatter. It's never happened before.

As if that isn't strange enough, catch this: Platform Faith doesn't stand on the bottom. The ocean floor there is way too deep for that. Mostly it floats on gargantuan pontoons. But to keep it stabile Faith is moored to the bottom by cables attached to huge, reinforced concrete footings.

Not long after it was set in place. Platform Faith's stainless-steel cables, which are four inches in diameter, started shearing off, apparently easy as a knife going through butter. Not just one, but several of them.

It gets even weirder.

The reinforced concrete footings? They are sitting on the bottom, full of holes like a collection of overgrown Swiss cheeses.

Isn't it obvious? Somebody (besides yours truly) or something very powerful doesn't want Clearsea drilling for oil.

As for Clearsea? The word is they cut off all outside contact for their employees on Faith — the better to cover up the catastrophe in the making.

CEO Gonzales, it's time to come clean.

What's going on down there? What is Clearsea — or should I say Dark Sea — up to and what kind of trouble is it in?

Chapter 17

The Above: New York, New York

Ten minutes after Noah Reiner posted the newest entry on his blog revealing the problems at Clearsea Energy's massive offshore oil platform in the Pacific, a young oil industry stock analyst at Bloomberg in New York read it and exclaimed, "Holy Shit!" She printed it out and literally ran, heels clicking on the floor like a staccato accusation, to show her supervisor.

Breathless, she said, "Bob, you've got to see this," and handed him Oil Foil's latest blog.

Over half-glasses, her supervisor — a cynical, middle-aged former New York *Times* crime reporter — said, "Calm down, honey," and began to read. His demeanor changed from cynicism to surprise. "This is good shit… if it's true," he said and handed it back to her. "Call Clearsea and get a comment. I want to go with this."

Ten minutes later she was back.

"They say they know nothing about it, that it is false, and that this blogger is just an anti-industry gadfly."

"And are they pumping any oil from Platform Faith?"

The young woman smiled. "I asked that."

"And?"

"They say not as yet. But they are right on schedule."

"Did it sound credible?"

"No."

"I want you to do two things. First, talk to the blogger and see what more you can get out of him. Check him out. See if he's trustworthy. Then run it by some technical types and see if they agree that the story holds water and that Clearsea's drilling schedule is off. Get a quote and then we'll go with it. I want you to give the blogger his attribution by name. That way, the lawyers won't be on our case if it turns out to be bullshit."

"Okay," she said. "Wow."

He laughed. "This is what we live for. Now go to work!"

— «» —

Gonzales spoke slowly and deliberately into the phone.

"You are to give them a general denial. Is that clear? Then I want you to get a hold of the Editor-in-Chief over at Bloomberg and see if you can get the story killed."

He hung up, shaking his head slowly. The other man in the room — tall, handsome, and lanky — sat quietly in front of his CEO's desk and waited.

Gonzales finished reading the blogger Oil Foil's *Sludge-Gate?* piece. He felt rising rage and something more — an acidic little jab in his solar plexus that was the first physical manifestation of what he had rarely known in his life: fear. Outwardly, though, he betrayed none of his inner turmoil and seemed, as always, totally in control.

"Cute," he said. "What do we know about this guy?"

"Some little Jew leftist peckerwood from Sacramento..."

Gonzales held up a finger and shook his head. "We'll have none of that, Bobby."

"Oh yeah, right, boss. Sorry about that..." responded the man in a thick Texas drawl. "You'll have to forgive me. You know I'm just a good ole boy from up in the Panhandle."

Bobby Smith wasn't sorry, and Gonzales wasn't angry. The two men had met when Gonzales was elected Texas Attorney General and Smith was a Texas Ranger assigned to command Gonzales's protection detail. Across the vast gulf of culture and ethnicity dividing them, they quickly recognized they shared the ruthless ambition of smart boys who learn early in life what it takes to escape the hardscrabble poverty into which they are born. Smith was the only person in the world Gonzales truly trusted and, over the years, the men had grown so close they knew each other's thoughts. A look, a nod, or the movement of a hand often said it all. When Gonzales took over Clearsea, he brought Bobby over as his new Chief of Corporate Security.

"Where did this kid get the information?" asked Gonzales.

"We don't know yet, but it's totally accurate," responded Smith.

"So, it has to come from someone on the platform. Didn't we already cut off Internet access to Faith?"

"Yeah, yesterday."

"Okay, you need to investigate this. I want you to come up with a shortlist of potential leakers. I want a squeaky-clean investigation. We don't want to compound our problem."

"I get it."

"Bobby, batten down the hatches. This is going to be very rough."

"Yeah, so I figured."

Smith stood, meeting Gonzales's eyes and nodding, before quietly turning to leave.

Gonzales picked up the phone and called his Vice President of Corporate Operations.

"Assemble the crisis team. And get our lawyers and every elected we have on the phone to try and get that story killed."

— «» —

Although it was getting late in the day, for whatever reason — perhaps resentment at Clearsea's high pressure tactics or because of its inherent newsworthiness — Bloomberg's editors put a rush on the story and it went live ninety minutes before the New York Stock Exchange closed. Within minutes, there was a sell-off of Clearsea's shares. When the final bell rang, the company had lost ten percent of its value.

Meanwhile, Noah Reiner's story was in the process of going viral. The most hits he had ever gotten previously were just over two hundred and fifty on the day BP's platform in the Gulf exploded. This time, by midnight, his blog had been read by over one hundred thousand people and he was getting emails from journalists all over the world asking for more information.

The next morning, he received a phone call from a producer of a documentary series on the Discovery Channel called *Science Unknown* asking whether he thought that the situation on Platform Faith was caused by extraterrestrials.

"There's nothing 'extra' about it," Noah replied, a comment far more prescient — and less flippant — than he could have ever imagined.

Chapter 18

The Below

When the He'e *gather together as one in the Great Dream, they sense the life pulse of the creatures that dwell around them — those close and those far. All creatures have a pulse unique to their kind, the male different than the female, some stronger, some weaker, some so distant they have no name because they dwell far beyond eight-eighths of arms. Their arms flash deep purple and black in trepidation because the new life's pulse travels not through the sea, but along hard tongues that come from the Above and sink their heads, made of rock and metal, into the sand and grit of the seafloor. The pulse travels more slowly and more faintly along the monster that eats rock and creatures alike but has no life pulse of its own. What is this thing whose life is not there, but along whose parts the life pulses of other creatures travel? P'heen thinks that the life pulse controls the thing of metal and stone that attacks the He'e, but is not part of it.*

P'lad'ep, the Ancient One, whose skill at sensing the life pulse is a gift, is the first to feel this new pulse. It is faint, but if the He'e gather together to feel the pulse, it is made stronger and all sense it.

The He'e pulse back as one. There are two threads of the pulse, then three, then more — some stronger, some fainter. One or two are stronger than others, and so they pulse back, modulating it, sensing the response, and pulsing again.

"Creature," they pulse together, strongly, "leave this place or you will all die!" They join in thought, swaying as one in the sea of the Great Dream. "We do not harm your fry. Why do you endanger ours?"

No new pulse comes back, though the pulse coming down the tongue changes and so the He'e know those above feel the pulse.

Chapter 19

The Above: Platform Faith

Gusman was hot with anger. How could that SOB cut off their communications? They were stranded out in the middle of the Pacific for months and needed email and the Internet to keep in contact with their spouses, children, girlfriends, and boyfriends — not to mention their bill collectors, porn sites, chat rooms, and online dating services.

He marched over to Drake's office and banged on the door with his fist.

There was no answer.

Gusman tried the handle. To his surprise, the door was unlocked. Should he go in? The answer was obvious: of course not.

Gusman entered anyway.

"Drake," he called, his voice loud, its pitch a tad too high. "Hello?" He was attempting to establish plausible deniability; what came out sounded hopelessly theatric, like the moment just before something very bad is about to happen in every low-budget horror movie Gusman had ever seen.

"Anybody home?"

No answer.

"Fuck it," he muttered to himself and proceeded to walk behind Drake's desk, his heart pounding out a clear warning to his brain that he had already crossed over the plausible deniability line and was entering the land of instant termination.

Drake's desk, like his conscience, was neat and free of clutter. There was the photo of the blond trophy wife, a cut-glass paperweight etched with the company's logo bearing a congratulatory message, and a leather cup that held a pair of scissors, a matching leather-handled letter opener, and a few pens. Sitting in the middle of his desk was Drake's laptop. Everything was laid out in perfect symmetry: the edge of the computer was perfectly parallel to the edge of the desk, the photo of Mrs. Drake was placed at a precise forty-five-degree angle to the corner of the laptop, and the leather cup was the same distance from the other corner of the computer. Gusman, who was not particularly well organized, found this sort of neatness obsessive and disturbing. It evoked in him a mixture of envy and contempt. If nothing else, Drake was a study in form over substance — with some other negative characteristics, such as cunning, arrogance, and aggression thrown in for good measure.

Gusman opened Drake's laptop and it came to life — without the usual login screen. He found this odd and surprising. It was a clear breach of the company's security policy for a management employee to leave a computer on and accessible when he or she left a room. Drake not only left his computer unattended but forgot to lock the door to his office. In what state of mind would a man so obsessed with detail depart so absentmindedly that he forgot the most basic measures to protect the company's secrets?

And then it hit Gusman.

A trap.

Could there be any other explanation for a door left unlocked when it locked automatically (unless someone went out of his way to set it to stay open) or for an unlocked laptop left in the middle of his desk?

Gusman looked around wildly — for what, he wasn't sure. Security cameras? For that big lumbering asshole of a security chief, Morrissey, to come barreling into the room to place him under arrest?

He stood silently, holding his breath. When nothing happened, Gusman calmed down, although the nausea he felt did not pass entirely. If it was a trap, the trap was sprung, and it was too late for him to do anything about it.

He was now all in.

As if to put a coda on the point, a large drop of sweat from his forehead landed with a plop on the keyboard of

Drake's laptop. Gusman wiped it off as best he could with the tail of his shirt.

The screen showed the basic home page, but one email was minimized. He brought it up.

In the subject line, it said: "Analysis of Events. Secret. Destroy and remove from Server."

Bingo.

The email was from Gonzales to Drake.

Drake:

We have performed a thorough analysis of the available evidence. There is no known technology (civilian or military) that could have produced the damage that occurred.

We are sending a scientific and security team to Faith. They are scheduled to arrive at approximately 0900 tomorrow. You are to give them complete freedom of access and cooperate fully in their investigation.

Take the following immediate steps and await further instructions:

All evidence regarding these events is to be collected, copied onto a single data storage unit, and removed from all other computers. The data storage unit shall be known to you only and shall be kept in your safe.

Internet access by the crew is to be temporarily shut down. This will be done remotely by our IT staff. You are to inform the crew that access will be restored as soon as possible and that the problem is related to technical issues affecting the company's Comsat.

Drilling activities shall be suspended until further notice.

All email communications regarding this are to be destroyed and wiped from your computer.

You are to institute Security Status 1.

Gonzales

Gusman held his breath while he read the email and, when he finished, something — shock, nerves, fatigue — caused him to swallow a big gulping breath of air, which took his dry throat by surprise and set off a huge coughing fit. Gusman tried to contain it by putting his hand over his mouth. His involuntary reflexes, however, were refusing to cooperate and he coughed so hard he blew saliva through his fingers right onto the screen of Drake's laptop computer.

His hands were shaking, but he groped in his pants pocket for his key ring and tugged it out. Thousands of miles from nowhere, he still had his apartment key on the ring next to the key to his cabin on Faith. There was also a stubby thumb drive on which he kept bits and pieces of his life. Looking around nervously as if Drake would step in any minute and catch him in the act, he plugged the thumb drive into a port and copied the email message onto it, then hurriedly shoved it back in his pocket. Done. Another thing that would get him fired — or worse — if Drake or Morrissey found out. He had no idea what he intended to do with the information. "Insurance," he mumbled under his breath. He was about to leave when he noticed that, where he had coughed on the laptop screen, there were streaks of his spit half-dried.

"Sweet Jesus," he said, and tried to wipe off the computer screen once again with his shirtsleeve, which just made a smeary mess. Drake would know someone was tinkering with his computer if he saw great swaths of half-dried bodily fluids on his laptop screen. He looked around for something to clean it. *Oh, yes*, he remembered, Drake had a little bathroom in the corner of his quarters. Gusman walked over to the metal door of the bathroom and tried to open it. The door opened only a few inches and then hit an obstruction on the floor. Gusman tried to push the door open farther but it wouldn't budge.

"What the fuck?" he mumbled.

He bent down on one knee and tried to stretch his hand around the crack in the door, pushing with his shoulder, but the crack in the door wasn't wide enough for him to feel around. Perhaps out of frustration or fear, Gusman put his shoulder into the door. There was a thud and the door lurched open another inch. From inside the bathroom, it smelled powerfully of human feces. Gusman could now reach his hand through the crack. He groped with his fingertips and strained them to reach farther — when he felt something soft and moist with his fingertips.

He felt around some more.

Hair and an earlobe.

Gusman yelped and pulled back his hand. Blood covered his fingers. In his panic, he wiped his hands on his pants, smearing blood all over them. With his head spinning and nausea surging, he put his hand on the doorframe to steady himself.

It didn't help.

Gusman vomited, seemingly everywhere: on the bathroom door, on the floor, on himself.

He knew who was on the other side of the door.

— «» —

Morrissey looked at Gusman with disgust so deep that even the hoods over his eyes were in a tactical retreat. "Jesus Christ, Gusman, it stinks in here. What the hell happened?" he said, as he walked into Drake's office, all two hundred and twenty-five pounds of big man confidence, looking around, trying to make sense of the situation. He sniffed, his nostrils flaring aggressively as they vacuumed in the odors — Gusman's sweat and vomit, the smell of feces, the acrid coolness of recycled air, disinfectant, and death. Morrissey stopped in mid-stride as he registered the strange combination of odors. It was a graceful move, speaking of the man's athletic life, now concealed by the extra weight he carried around his middle.

Gusman sat behind Drake's desk, slumped in his chair. "I puked on myself," Gusman said, his voice flat. He nodded his head in the direction of the bathroom door.

"Over there. Drake."

The door was open four inches, light showing through the crack, revealing vomit and blood — not only what Gusman managed to smear over the walls, but a thick, dark puddle that had migrated under the doorframe and was turning the carpet black.

"What?" Morrissey boomed in his big man voice.

"Over there," said Gusman wearily. "Drake is in there, dead." Then, raising his voice as if Morrissey was deaf, he repeated. "Morrissey, I'm telling you, Drake is dead."

Morrissey went over to the bathroom, holding his breath against the odor of vomit, spilled blood, and shit. He tried to push the door open but couldn't budge Drake's body. So, he put his shoulder into it and managed to shove the door open a few more inches, enough for him to peek into the bathroom.

"It's Drake, all right," said Morrissey calmly. "Throat slit from ear to ear. The poor bastard."

Morrissey pulled his head out of the door, which nearly closed with the weight of the corpse wedged behind it.

"Gusman, what happened here?" asked Morrissey, his voice now soothing and soft. The grimace he had worn after seeing Drake's body was wiped from his face, replaced by an expression that was, as Gusman saw it, no expression at all. Morrissey sounded concerned.

Gusman wasn't fooled. Morrissey was starting to do what he done for most of his life, first as a homicide detective and then as an FBI agent: investigate murders.

"I came to talk to Drake. I knocked and there was no answer. The door was open, so I came in. It seemed weird to me that he had unlocked his door. I mean, we all keep them set so they lock when you leave. So, I walked over to the bathroom and tried the door thinking maybe Drake was hurt or had a heart attack or something. When I tried to open it, I could feel something against the door, blocking it. I opened it enough to slide my hand in and felt the body. When I pulled my hand out, there was blood all over it."

"And that's when you puked?"

"Yeah."

"Then what?"

"I don't know. I figured it must be Drake. I slid my hand through and turned on the light in there. I could see his wrist on the ground, with a big, fat Rolex on it. So, I knew it was him."

Morrissey cocked his head. "The light was off?"

"Yeah."

"Are you sure?"

"Yes. Definitely," replied Gusman, his voice rising slightly in frustration.

"Weird," muttered Morrissey, more to himself than Gusman. He walked back over to Gusman, put a reassuring hand on his shoulder, and said, "Gusman, you're a mess. Go get cleaned up then come back here. I've got to get this situation under control, then get Drake's body out of there and on ice."

"Okay," said Gusman quietly.

"One more thing. Put your clothes in a plastic bag and bring them back here."

Gusman looked up.

"They're evidence. Oh, and one more thing before you go." Morrissey pulled a small pocketknife from his pocket. "I need to scrape out what's under your fingernails."

"You think I killed him, don't you?"

"Probably not, son."

— «» —

Gusman stared at his reflection in the little mirror above the sink in his cabin. Framed in stainless steel, the face staring back at him was pale and bloated — like the last half-rotten piece of fruit left in the bowl, too far gone to consume. His eyes were sunken, and the rings underneath were so dark they were nearly black. There was a smear of blood — dead man's blood — across his forehead. Other bits of unidentified detritus had taken refuge in the creases of his face and in his hair. A menacing plug of semi-dried snot hung ominously from one of his nostrils, like an avenging angel sent by the god of embarrassment.

He turned on the water and let it run long and hot before he splashed it on and began to wash away the filth. But the self-loathing, bitterness, and exhaustion that stared back at him in the mirror could not be cleaned off with soap and water.

Gusman splashed his face with hot water, then stirred the shaving soap with the brush, massaging the lather into his face in slow circles, luxuriating in the heat and steam. Then he slid the razor across his face — an old Gillette Adjustable he found among his father's things when the old man died — letting the heavy weight of the razor do the work.

When he was finished, he looked again at himself. Still battered, but perhaps looking a little less beaten. And then something totally strange happened. For a fraction of a second, he did not recognize his own face. It was his face, but every feature was subtly different: his eyes were darker, his nose longer, and the turn of his mouth something he had never seen. It was his face but not his face — something unrecognizable, alien.

He closed his eyes and shook his head. When he opened them, his face had returned to normal.

Same old Gusman.

"Wow," he said, out loud. "Keep it together."

It was time to go back and find Morrissey.

— «» —

Drake's body was laid out on one of the stainless-steel prep tables in the galley. He was still wearing his blood-soaked clothes, but his face and throat had apparently been cleaned. A long, deep slash crossed his throat from ear to ear. Morrissey was standing there staring intently at the wound.

"Oh, Jesus," Gusman exclaimed.

"Throat slit," Morrissey said, without looking up.

"What?" Gusman said, nearly yelling, shaking his head, not quite comprehending. "He cut his own throat?"

"Well, you said he was locked in the bathroom when you found him. Right?"

Gusman nodded. "When I got the door open enough to look in, his body was leaning against it. Like maybe he closed the door, sat down with his back against it, and then, you know... did it."

"With this?" Morrissey picked up a bright yellow steel utility knife, smeared with blood. He held it with a paper towel by the handle.

"Where'd he get that?" Gusman asked.

"They're all over the place," replied Morrissey brightly. "There must be dozens of these on board."

Gusman shook his head, disbelief replacing incomprehension. "I don't get it. How could anyone cut his own throat? Why? And why Drake? That guy seemed like the last candidate to put out his own lights. And in such a weird way. Morrissey, you were a cop. Who slits their own throat?"

"Well, you know, Gusman, in my time I investigated quite a few homicides — and some suicides for that matter — and, frankly, if it were a homicide, there would have been signs of a struggle. There are no defensive wounds. Hell, there wasn't enough room in that bathroom for two people. Blood spurted everywhere as he bled out. It would have gotten all over the assailant and there would have been tracks. If he was killed somewhere else and dragged there, then there wouldn't have been so much blood in the bathroom and his body would not have been in that position. On the other hand..."

Morrissey reached down and put his latex-gloved hand under Drake's neck and, with his other hand, pushed back on his forehead, opening the wound so they could look inside his throat.

"Oh, God," Gusman said, gagging.

"Don't be a baby, Gusman. Look, you see? His trachea and esophagus are cut nearly through. The wound is a full inch deep — deep as the knife's blade. The cut is smooth, not ragged. It would take tremendous force and strength to pull a knife through like that. It is almost unimaginable that a person could do that to himself."

Morrissey removed his hands and Drake's head relaxed, closing the wound. He then paused and cocked his head, a nasty little smirk on his face. There was a long silence while Morrissey snapped off the gloves and tossed them into a trashcan.

"Suicide? Maybe. Murder? Maybe. Pending further investigation, the only guy with any of Drake's blood on him was you. You didn't kill him, did you, Gusman? I mean you and he were not exactly best buddies."

Gusman laughed, but then immediately realized that Morrissey was only half joking.

"No," he said, trying to sound dismissive. "Come on, Morrissey. I didn't like Drake very much, but I didn't want to murder him. Anyway, everybody hated the guy. You know that."

"True," Morrissey said, almost to himself.

"Now what?" Gusman asked.

"We put him on ice until a proper autopsy can be performed. I have to report this to the FBI. They have jurisdiction over crimes — or possible crimes — that occur on a US-owned facility in international waters."

"What about corporate?"

"I will go file a report with them right away."

"There is no Internet access. That's why I went to Drake's office in the first place."

"Yeah, I know. I'm the one who cut it off." The friendliness in Morrissey's tone was gone.

"Why?"

"Gusman, never mind about that. Help me put Drake into a body bag and put him in the walk-in freezer. I'll take the knife with me."

Morrissey searched one of the cabinets and found a zip-lock plastic bag and dropped the utility knife gingerly into it.

When they were finished moving Drake's body to the walk-in freezer, Morrissey turned to Gusman and said, "Thanks. And by the way, I'm sealing Drake's quarters off. Nobody goes in or out of there. I've got his laptop under lock and key, Gusman. So, don't get any more smart ideas about searching through it."

Gusman felt the bite of Morrissey's words, but chose not to respond.

— «» —

The Below

Life is precious to the He'e, who kill for food or defense but take no pleasure in killing. The dead are empty, lifeless shells. Their carrion is sustenance for those living. In the He'e's universe of danger, humor tames the fear of death and paints the corpses of their dead with permission to become food for the next generation.

Drake, his name made real in the Dream by P'aldil, is, in death, just meat; though meat that is far beyond the reach of any He'e. But Drake did not die because the He'e wished to consume his meat. He died because, like any threat, he had to be scared away. When he wouldn't scare, he had to be dealt with like any enemy.

"Too much dying," P'aldil had said when Drake had ended and become no more. "Too much."

No He'e had disagreed. Drake had seemed to be a thinking sort of life and none of the He'e were happy when he had passed into whatever Dream connected his kind. A dull saffron glow of regret and sorrow lit the arms of the He'e gathered there. This death, they knew, was needed, but not unmourned.

To kill a creature, however threatening, that you did not see was new and upsetting. But P'heen reminded them that in the Dream of the faraway He'e, it had happened before, many eight-eights of Hungers away.

Chapter 20

The Above: New York, New York

"Dead, sir."

"What did you say, Morrissey?" Gonzales' supremely confident tone was gone, and from where Morrissey sat, the man staring back at him on the computer screen looked like a guy who was about to lose it.

Somewhere off camera, he heard another voice say, "Ah shit," in the unmistakable Texas drawl of Bobby Smith.

Gonzales said, "I have Mr. Smith here as well."

"Of course you do. Anyway, Mr. Drake's dead, sir," Morrissey repeated slowly so they would understand. Morrissey was trying to sound grave, but he feared it came out a bit too bright, betraying the part of him that enjoyed putting these supremely arrogant and powerful men into a state of near panic. The security man thought, *Watch it.*

"How did he die, Mr. Morrissey?" asked Gonzales.

"Well, sir, that's a bit unclear at the moment. His body was found in his private bathroom by another crew member. And well… brace yourself, sir… he apparently died from a large knife wound to his throat. Pending an autopsy, I'd say it's pretty obvious he bled to death."

Then Smith's craggy face came to the picture. "Are telling us his throat was slit?"

"Well, yes. Slashed quite deeply, actually, would be a more accurate description."

Two or three very long seconds passed.

"Any evidence of… foul play?" asked Gonzales.

"Of course," responded Morrissey, momentarily losing his deferential tone. "His throat was cut. So sure, it could have been a homicide, but, on balance, the evidence would support suicide."

"For Christ's sake, what the hell does that mean?" Bobby Smith interjected.

"Well, sir, it means this: Gusman, our engineer, found Drake in the bathroom in the office part of his quarters, with the door closed and Drake's back leaning against the door. The bathroom is very small, hardly big enough for one person to turn around in. His throat was apparently sliced with a utility knife, which we recovered at the scene."

"I'm not sure I know what you mean by a 'utility knife,'" Gonzales said.

"You know those tools that hold a retractable single-edged razor blade? They use them in construction a lot. We have them here."

"Yeah. Yeah. Now I know what you mean. I have one at home. Go on."

"Well, he apparently used that to inflict the wound."

"Okay, I understand, but what's the evidence that it was anything but suicide?"

Morrissey cleared his throat. "Do you really want me to go into this kind of detail? It's pretty grisly."

"Mr. Morrissey, remember I was a prosecutor. You don't have to worry about offending my sensitivities. Just give it to us straight."

"Okay. Well, when I examined the wound, the cut was deep — to the one-inch depth of the fully extended blade for the entire length of the wound, practically severing his trachea. I just don't see how a wound of that nature could be self-inflicted. It would take almost superhuman strength to do that. On the other hand, the circumstances do not support homicide. The blood was pretty much contained to the bathroom. There was no sign of struggle. No other marks or bruises. No defensive wounds."

"You're also not a coroner, Morrissey," said Smith.

Morrissey clenched his jaw, trying not to betray his anger. "That is true, but I investigated plenty of homicides when I was a police detective and then an FBI agent, so I know a thing or two about murder."

"Did he leave a suicide note?"

"Nothing that has been found so far."

"Well, then, Mr. Morrissey, isn't it possibility that Mr. Gusman might be involved in some unnatural way?" asked Smith.

"It's possible, I suppose," responded Morrissey. "They were not at all on good terms, but Gusman doesn't seem like the homicidal type."

"Maybe, maybe not," said Smith.

Gonzalez interrupted. "Is the rest of the crew aware of what happened?"

"Only a few members. I've asked them to keep it confidential, but you know how it is, sir. It's gonna get out."

"Yes," said Gonzales, the words slow and deliberate. "I suppose that is inevitable. Okay, here's what we need to do. First, you are to call the crew together and tell them that Drake has died, but I would appreciate it if you told them he died of a heart attack. Can you do that?"

"Yes. But shouldn't we just tell them the truth? People kill themselves. It happens."

"No. I would prefer that you do not do that. We have enough problems. Just tell them he died suddenly of natural causes. That's true, correct?"

Morrissey cleared his throat. "I guess so, sir. And what about Gusman? What do I tell him?"

"You will just have to tell Gusman it is imperative that he keep the facts confidential while we sort this thing out."

"I'll do my best to be persuasive. Meanwhile, I assume reporting Drake's death to the authorities and the next of kin will be handled on your end."

"That's right," responded Smith. "We'll handle that."

Chapter 21

The Below

In the Chamber *of Decision of the Eight-Eights, the He'e roil in the news that one of the enormous worms from Above has once again descended, this time into a kula where the fry are gathered to learn from the knowledge of the old He'e. The worm descended and bored into the seafloor, striking the kaimana shell and exploding. Although the kaimana shell stopped the descent of the great metal worm, the force of its descent shifted the kaimana and six fry are no longer, having lived barely an eight of eights of hungers. The explosion has torn them apart and now they live no more. It has been many eights of hungers since so many have died in such an attack.*

"It is not a muhe that did this," says P'omanuaa, arms intertwined with M'omanuaa for comfort. They have lost one of their fry in this attack and wish to make an end of it.

"No," says P'heen. "It is a creature very different from any we have seen before. It has an appetite for the rich bath of the soul sea beneath us and is not dissuaded by the shell we have placed there."

"These worms descend again and again from the Above. No matter how many we destroy, more keep coming. They are very hungry beasts."

"It is not a beast," says P'heen. "It is something constructed; fashioned from the same shaped metal as the ancient object with ray's wings that hangs in the Chamber of the Strange. It is not alive as we are alive. Something has made it."

And the Eight-Eights are silent at this. Although many suspect the same thing, they are nonetheless shaken by the thought that there might be other beings not of the He'e with powers of thought and manipulation great enough to fabricate such a massive and destructive thing of metal.

M'noda, who is alone — her mate P'noda having long since gone to the Dream — and is the oldest of the He'e in the gathering of Eight-Eights, flashes a call for attention, a flicker of brightest command along her arms, saying, "Although the ancient teachings tell otherwise, some of us have long thought the Above does not go on endlessly upward. We have thought there must be an end to it and asked what is above the Above. When metal constructions descend and act as if they are living creatures, attacking the substance of the soul sea, it is a time for asking what and why they are. When their biting radula shatter against the unparalleled hardness of kaimana we have placed to shield the urb, it is time to wonder of what these worms are made. We all see it is fashioned from inert metal and driven somehow to us. But when it attacks our fry, the time for wondering is past."

"We must know," says M'toktai with P'toktai next to her. They have lost no fry, but fry of theirs were at the kula where the others died and became no more. If some fry are attacked, they know others can be as well, and their arms ripple with the orange glow of fear.

"Yes, we have to know," says P'heen. "We have long dreamed of going up to see what is in the Above, to see if anything is beyond. Now with fry lost to us, we have a reason." P'heen calls upon P'aldil, who has seen the worm descend from far Above and pierce the seafloor and burst apart against the kaimana shell. P'aldil along with his mate, M'aldil, are of the travelers who go from vent to vent along the seafloor visiting other urbs of the He'e.

P'heen taps P'aldil and M'aldil and asks, "If I wish you to, will you gather yourselves and go up to explore the Above and seek the place where these worms come from?"

And P'aldil, though the oddity of the question troubles him, is honored by the trust placed in him and says, "Yes, of course," and gathers M'aldil to him. Together, they ask how to plan this venture into the Above. And P'heen says he will consult with all the Makers among the He'e who might know how to rise in the water to the heights of the Above. But away *from the sight of the others, M'aldil turns red and purple because she fears they will lose their lives in such a quest and be no more and that their fry will not know them. P'aldil caresses M'aldil with his arms in the rhythm that only they know so she will not feel such fear. M'aldil's arms flash slowly yellow as she is calmed by her life mate.*

Sometimes P'aldil stares at M'aldil when her concentration is elsewhere, in another Dream. They have known each other their entire lives; they are bound one with the other, and he feels tenderness toward her in these thoughts and great comfort. And there is pride: M'aldil is a healer among the He'e and much respected throughout the urb for her wisdom and skill. She has knowledge of all the healing properties of creatures and plants and the fluids that seep from rocks and smokers, but it is her touch that enables her to understand why there is pain and makes her much respected among the He'e.

— ‹› —

In the Great Dream, which is the collective Dream of all the He'e, P'aldil sees the plan for the shape of the construction that will carry him and M'aldil to the Above. Every fry knows there is stone from the depths of the vents that when cut free from the ocean floor will forcefully rise until it is out of sight and beyond the range of clicks, having vanished into the lightless murk Above. M'audbil is among the thinkers of the He'e who know why the stone will rise. She rests for a moment, arms exploring the seabed near her. She raises an arm to stretch straight up into the dark waters and says, "It is like the sponges, a lattice of stone full of hollows. Deep below us is a heat so great that when the stone below the seafloor becomes soft, it flows almost like water itself. In that heat, the water that seeps down and some of the constituents of the stone itself cannot hang together as solid substance or even as liquid-like water, but as elementals so hot and fast moving they would expand to nothing were it not for the great weight of the sea pressing from the Above. When the liquid stone cools and becomes solid rock again, the holes inside it remain with the ghosts of the hot elementals inside them in turn. They displace a greater weight of water than the remaining stone weighs."

"Yes!" adds P'aldil. "And so the stone will rise." He sees it and in the Dream they all soon see it, blocks of the sponge-like stone inside a net woven of worm fronds, a tighter weave of basket slung below it, the empty hollow stone tugging the net and basket eagerly upward into the Above.

— «» —

In the Dream, P'aldil again senses one watching them, one who is not of the seafloor and who seems at home in the emptiness. As if through his eyes, he sees the stupefying brightness, the choking absence of water, and feels the heat that seems as fierce as that from a vent. He feels that which the pulse has touched, feels the uneasiness that comes back along the pulse from the Above. A pang of terror shoots through P'aldil. Shivers of confusion course up his arms. Is that what is above he Above? The absence of everything; an emptiness like the hollows in the frozen rock? How to conceive of this emptiness, of an existence without the waters or the seafloor? How to conceive of others in the empty Above, far different from the He'e — though with a kind of intelligence of their own — with eyes that see in a different light and have segmented arms for grasping? Is that what is above the Above?

P'aldil tries to explain it to M'aldil, but it is inexplicable.

Chapter 22

The Below

P'aldil and M'aldil *rise, the fry and the grown He'e sending them off, pulsing a bright cascade of color, a language rich with fear and excitement and anticipation. What is Above has forever been a mystery — the waters of the sea darkening into nothingness with only the rare lights of the creatures that swim in it over the seafloor flickering in the great dark. Around the lip of the basket, they have placed a ring of mindless luminescent worms that give them a dim light. They don't need it. They click and touch to define their reality as well as light can. But the illumination is a sort of comfort, a reminder of home so far below. It is cold away from the vents and they wrap their arms around each other in the basket as they rise. In the bottom of their basket is a cage of crabs for their meals and beside it in a great clam's shell is a paste of tubeworm flesh, bitter tasting but sustaining.*

The basket is a cozy cup in which they rest comfortably. Above them is a net full of volcanic stone blocks tugging them upward. At the base of the basket are large, heavy stones from the seafloor, each suspended in its own small net as ballast so their journey upward is gentle and smooth. P'M'kauka, the chief healer of the He'e from P'M'aldil's urb, warns that their journey to the Above is an unknown and they should not allow themselves to rise too rapidly.

"We know that the press of the water is less as you rise because more of its weight is below you," P'kauka says. "We know that the sustaining substance in the water that your gills take into your blood grows more abundant as you rise. As the press of the water recedes, the press of this substance

will assert itself and may try to burst out of your blood in the same way that the stuff in the hollows of the buoyant stones tries to burst out and by doing so makes them rise. So, our advice, and that of the Dream, is to take care not to rise too swiftly. The stones around the basket are made to be a drag on it. Release one if you rise too slowly. Release a buoyant stone from the net above you if you rise too fast."

M'kauka feeds them a broth of the tiny animalcules too small to see that live on the surface of the giant deep-sea amoebas, bottom dwellers an eighth of an eighth of an arm across. The broth has a sharp taste and M'aldil makes to regurgitate it, but P'kauka warns her not to. "From those who have gone part way to the Above, we have learned that the waters' lessening press brings one's mind to a muddle of confusion that will not resolve quickly when you are back here again. Also, as you rise, minute bits of the sea's water will penetrate the tiny structures that make up the meat of your muscles and they will not fold as they should. Pain and an end of life would come. But the essence of the creatures that come with the amoeba broth will pull the water away and the structures will fold as they should. It will also harden the surface of your body's cells, so they will not soften and break apart as the water's press recedes. Your minds will stay sharp."

In the Dream, P'M'aldil see it is so — that those who take these precautions as they ascend to the Above will not be affected by the lessening press of the waters. Their thoughts will remain focused and their bodies will function as well as at the sea's bottom.

They ride their basket toward the Above. In the dark of the deep around them, they sense little life. "The Dream says this is a sterile stretch of water," P'aldil says. "But farther up in the Above there is abundant life, though it might be strange."

M'aldil doesn't ask how long they will be in the basket. In her mostly timeless life, duration is a subjective thing. The only true constant is the persistence of a heartbeat's flicker on her arm or the urge to eat. The former, the He'e measure in heartbeat flicks; The latter they measure in hungers. Their longest sense of time is of their lives, which last many hungers. This journey to the Above will take perhaps eight hungers.

They eat. The number of crabs diminishes in the cage, marking the time since their last meal. Half an eight of meals later, the press of the waters seems noticeably less. It remains dark, but their clicks return images of an array of creatures from tiny to immense.

Out of the dimness comes a fish the size of a tubeworm. There is no question what it is — a figment of the Dream or a memory makes it familiar: a mano-niuhi, not big, but viciously toothed and with flashing eyes. It's very quick, with skin as rough as a He'e's tongue. P'M'aldil would be afraid, for the Dream sings of this fish as ferocious and very dangerous. It is one that dives deep and eats fish such as the fry in a single gulp — a nightmare that can bite a chunk of flesh out of even the largest creature. The Dream also speaks of the mano-niuhi's larger cousins, the true niuhi that are big enough to take one of the He'e in a single bite. But the true niuhi do not dive so far down as they are now. It prefers living in the waters further in of the Above. The Dream speaks of how generations of He'e have fought the mano-niuhi. So, neither P'aldil nor M'aldil has any fear of it, because they know what needs to be done.

The sound of it is a rush and a whisper of its rough-skin through the water. It has seen the glow of the luminescent ring around the basket's lip, their light reflected in the niuhi's eyes, and it has come to investigate — its big eyes bright but dead-seeming, no sense there but hunger — its mouth half open, a nest of sharp, triangular teeth. The mano-niuhi is half as long as one of their arms and comes forward in a flash toward the faint taste of He'e in the water. It pokes its blunt nose into the basket, mouth opening, aimed at M'aldil's arm, mouth now open wide to bite it off entirely. But she snatches it back as the mano-niuhi darts forward, retreating across the basket as it follows her. P'aldil's ink sac convulses with a gush, spewing ink that contains an essence of terror, and the mano-niuhi convulses, darting back and forth — unhinged in the dark water — then hangs, vibrating, consumed with the ink-generated fear. P'aldil jets upward, wrapping his arms tightly around the now-insensate niuhi.

The muscular fish thrashes, whipping about in the water. In front of it, M'aldil's body flickers with a fast, continuous run of light up her arms as she vibrates her mantle in a mesmerizing thrum. The fish stills, hangs uncertainly in the water above the basket, caught mindlessly in the ink and flashing, throbbing beat in the water. P'aldil pulls it close and bites; the digestive juices flow there, and the venom rushes quickly into the mano-niuhi's blood. The fish's heart pounds for a moment. It shudders, gills no longer pulsing. P'aldil remains wrapped around it until its motion ceases. The two He'e find the mano-niuhi's flesh to be succulent and they scoop it out of the rough skin, tearing it away with their beaks, eating their fill and leaving only the unappetizing skin and hard shafts of the fish's cartilage to drift slowly away from the basket and downward into the black depths of the Below.

As they continue to rise, the sea brightens; a dim glow suffuses the Above, outshining the ring of luminescent others on the basket's rim, which blink in numb confusion and finally cease to glow.

After half a hunger, they float up alongside the same thick metal cables that the He'e had broken away from the seafloor and which are now slack and moving fractionally in the sea's current. Around the He'e, the sea is full of life as they ascend. They see cuttlefish familiar from the Dream and small versions of the shrimp they know below. Here, fish are everywhere: lightfish, bristlemouths, and flat-nosed bigscales half as long as the He'e's arms. Many other sorts the Dream has not told them of also swim there. For benthic creatures like P'M'aldil, used to the scarcity of life on the deep-seafloor except near the vents, the variety of creatures at this depth is stunning.

—— «» ——

For two hungers, the sea above them has been brightening. P'M'aldil's eyes, evolved for the midnight darkness of the deepest Below, ache in the growing glare. Their eyes pull back of themselves into their mantles, leaving only the smallest opening for the light to enter. Around them, the sea is a storm of creatures, finned and scaled. The shape shifts of a vast school of tiny, silvery fish and larger predator fish mesmerize M'aldil.

P'aldil recognizes one from the Dream, a Big Eye Ahi. Larger even than the mano-niuhi, it is a fish that does not *go far into the Below but does hunt in the waters deeper and colder than most of the other creatures of this layer of the soul sea. It, too, is a predator fish, and when it explores close to the basket, P'aldil aims a squirt of terror ink at the Big Eye and it jitters away in a frenzy of fear.*

"I would have liked to taste that," says M'aldil in mock disapproval as ripples of mirth move up her arms.

The residue of terror ink in the waters has scattered a school of tiny sardines, which dart away in an exploding cloud in the water around them. P'aldil snags one at the end of an arm, pulls it to his beak, and takes a bite. The taste is rich and strange, warm to one from those colder waters of the Below.

They continue to rise, though at a slower pace. Gradually, a dark patch appears in the sweep of paralyzing brightness Above.

"It is as if something eats a hole in the center of the light," says M'aldil, who can find no context in the Dream or in her own experience to explain the image.

The dark patch grows larger, still bright, but far less glaring than the vast stretch of brightness that roofs all the sea above. Like M'aldil's, P'aldil's thoughts are chaotic and he wonders if they should abandon this exploration, cut away the net of volcanic rocks and let the basket plunge down into the dark of the comforting Below.

M'aldil hears his thought in the Dream and answers, "No, the He'e wish us to find what is troubling our lives. We have come near to what seems to be the source of those troubles. I want to go on."

P'aldil says she is right, tells himself to be stolid, to do the bidding of the He'e. And so, the craft continues to rise toward the dark patch in the waters Above.

— «» —

They burst up into a brilliance, eyes pulled tight into their mantles, a sudden sense of lack as the waters utterly vanish around them. Nothingness. The basket rests on the surface of the waters. A surface in some ways like the seafloor, the light shining from it as brightly as that from overhead. A side-to-side motion tugs at their craft. There is sound, though attenuated in a medium nothing like the waters of the sea.

Into this strange, waterless medium, P'aldil clicks. His clicks come back as whispers, telling him of a great life presence, something as large as the entire urb of the He'e.

He senses creatures like large fish moving in this new medium above him and around him, emitting wild sounds. It is hard for P'aldil to concentrate. Brightness tears at his eyes, sending a fierce pain into them. He wants to suck water through his gills, but what is here at the end of he Above is nothing like water. Instead, they are surrounded by something as thin as the gases that bloom from the smoky vents in the seafloor. But this gas is not in a flume like the gas that spews from the vents and heats the waters. It is everywhere and nowhere like the soul sea itself. It is painful — a searing heat in their gill slits. A savage grinding noise comes closer, a vibration in the sea into which they dip some of their arms as if for reassurance that the waters are still there. In his thrashing, P'aldil splashes water into his gill slits and the pain abates. In the Dream, he tells M'aldil of this, and they labor to keep their gill slits moist. The panicky choking fear abates, but it is painful still.

There are other noises, articulated as if from a voice, though nothing like the voice of anything Below. The sounds are surprisingly regular and seemingly have meaning — "Got it." "Looks like a damn hot air balloon." "What the hell? "Octopuses" "Jesus fucking Christ."

P'M'aldil sense the great fear these creatures exude.

P'aldil risks the slightest relaxation of his mantle, letting in a faint sliver of light. Large creatures loom, more like halos than real things in the intense glare, somehow with eyes looking back at him. One stretches a sort of spear-like arm toward him, pushing him, and suddenly fierce pain fills one of his arms. He shrieks, though the noise is lost in the thinness of the medium around him. P'aldil grabs M'aldil tightly. The pain grows and P'aldil, beyond terror now, does what he can to defend himself. He thrashes as M'aldil's ink sack spurts the fear essence. There is more thrashing and another burst of sounds, but he can make no sense of meaning, just a sort of bellow. Now, a loud bang erupts from a thing pointed at them by one of the chattering creatures and then something fierce strikes the volcanic stone that bobs around them. It hits at the junction between the waters and the emptiness above that is not water. The stone, full to bursting with the volcanic essence and jolted this way, gives up its essence all at once with a resounding detonation that sends a blast of shattered stone against the two He'e. Others of the stone blocks now explode in a great secondary detonation with a noise past understanding. A shock of pain rips through one of P'aldil's arms. The sound, even in the strange, thin medium of the not-sea, is deafening. Something grasps at P'aldil and, in his own terror, he empties the repellent from his ink sack in a gush. There is another screeching sound. "Fuck, it sprayed me!" And then only a fierce high-pitched keening.

P'aldil has had enough. Grasping M'aldil by an arm, he slips off of the basket, back into the water, and pulls free one of the heavy stones hanging in the nets from the lip of the slowly sinking basket. The water enfolds them again with coolness. Water sucks through their gills. The glare dims and P'aldil lets go of the basket. Arms together, wrapping around the stone, the He'e plunge back down into the waters, seeking the darkness and the comforting chill of the Below.

Chapter 23

The Above: Platform Faith

As they did every week, weather permitting, Dennison and Babitch lowered one of the Zodiacs into the water for a routine structural inspection of the enormous pontoons that supported the platform. The purpose of the inspection was to look for hairline cracks in the welds and take samples of the bivalves, seaweed, and other marine species that clung to the metal. Since they rarely found anything significant, Babitch often took along his fishing gear. As anyone who has ever worked on an oil platform knows, there is no better fishing than close to a platform's structural supports which are encrusted with barnacles, clams, and a hundred other species of invertebrates which attract fish. It is an artificial reef surrounded by the vast, empty sea; a complete ecosystem rich with the great diversity of the ocean.

Done with the inspection, they tied onto a cleat on Support Number Four.

Dennison wasn't much into fishing, but loved seafood, so he was happy to go along. Babitch laughed and said, as he did every time they went fishing, "He who helps the fisherman partakes of the catch."

Babitch was in the middle of a cast when Dennison, pointing to the west, said, "Do you see that?"

"What?" responded Babitch without looking up from his rod, which he was just setting.

"What the fuck?" and then "Oh, my God, Frank. Look!" Dennison tapped on Babitch's shoulder without taking his eyes off what he was looking at.

"What is it?" asked Babitch, sounding irritated, but finally looking up.

Perhaps twenty-five feet away, bobbing in the low surf, was a large assemblage of floating rocks — almost a perfect circle about ten feet in diameter — wrapped in a heavy woven net. The stone was jet black and looked to have the texture of pumice. In the center of the net were two enormous octopuses, bright pink in color, streaked with blue and black.

The creatures were looking at them.

"What are those?" asked Dennison, reflexively lowering his voice to a near whisper.

"The look like octopuses to me," Babitch whispered back.

"Jesus fucking Christ," said Dennison, "they're giant."

"I've never seen anything like it."

"What should we do?"

The creatures were moving now. Waving their tentacles.

Babitch grabbed his two-way and called the control room. "Hey, Luke, do you copy?"

"Yeah," came a voice through the radio. "I copy."

"There's something really weird here."

"What is it?"

"Well, there's these floating rocks covered by a net or something with these really large, pink octopuses on them."

"What the fuck are you talking about? Is this a joke?"

"No, I'm serious."

"Where are you?"

"We're at Four."

"Okay, I'll get a camera on it."

"What should we do, Luke?" asked Babitch.

"Just stay still until I can focus on them. Don't scare them away."

"Okay, will do." Babitch turned to Dennison. "He says to stay still."

"Well, duh," responded Dennison, the fourth grader in him emerging under stress.

"They're getting closer. Luke, do you copy?"

"Yeah. Calm down, Dave, we've got it on visual... Wow, that is really weird."

"No shit. They're getting closer. What do we do?"

"Just don't do anything."

The array of rocks was now no more than fifteen feet away. The creatures were moving, undulating, their color turning from pink to blue with angry purple and black stripes and splotches.

"Do you see that? They're turning color."

"Yeah, and they're getting too close."

"I don't like this," said Babitch, loudly now, tremulous panic in his voice.

"Fuck, untie us, Charlie. I think we better get out of here."

Dennison started fumbling with the tie line, but he kept looking over his shoulder at the creatures. The rope was wet, and his hands kept slipping. "Shit," he said repeatedly.

It was like a slow-motion horror movie. The current was driving the octopuses into the humans. The octopuses weren't doing anything hostile, but they were moving their arms around, which was frightening enough.

When the octopuses got to within five feet, Babitch — overcome with fear — picked up the fishing pole with the intent of pushing them away. In his nervousness, he missed, and the tip jabbed into the flesh of one the octopuses, which let out a sound that was something between a whoosh and a guttural scream. Bluish-colored blood spurted from the wound. The other creature, moving with amazing speed, reared up and squirted black ink at Babitch, who immediately dropped his fishing pole, screeching, "It sprayed me." But his words were swallowed up by a wail of pain as he began to feel intense burning wherever the inky liquid touched his exposed skin.

Dennison, now in full flight-or-fight mode, grabbed the first weapon he could find: a flare gun kept in the Zodiac for emergencies. He took aim at the cephalopods from a distance that would be difficult to miss and pulled the trigger. In his nervousness, he nearly did miss, but managed to hit one of the floating rocks inches from one of the creatures, which whipped away its enormous arms. The rock detonated with earsplitting thunder as if it were made of some sort of explosive, sending fragments everywhere and severing one of the creature's arms.

And then it was over as quickly as it started. The creatures, still making their weird noises, simply slid off the rock into the sea and were gone. The only thing that was left on the ocean surface was a few of the device's rocks, bobbing gently in the current, with the severed arm of the octopus lying in the netting, thrashing and oozing blue blood.

"Help me! Help me!" screamed Babitch, welts forming everywhere the ink had touched him, writhing in agony on the bottom of the Zodiac.

Chapter 24

The Below

Their descent is *swift, a rushing down into the colder depths, the light fading into an enfolding darkness and a heartening coolness that restores their calm. M'aldil presses an arm tip onto the stump where half of P'aldil's arm had been ripped away and from where the savage pain had come.*

"It is gone," she says. "As if bitten off. Is it painful?"

"It is," P'aldil admits. "But what bit me had no poison. See? The seep of my blood has already stopped."

P'aldil pushes the stump of his severed arm to her beak. Arms, sometimes seeming to have minds of their own, are sometimes lost. Many dreams ago, P'aldil lost one of his in a battle against the dumb predators of the deep; and many, many Dreams ago, in battle against other He'e. Such fights are not fought any longer. Not a few of the He'e have lost arms, and the Dream contains methods to soothe them — especially with the black hinu — though it cannot immediately restore what has been lost. But half an arm lost is no disaster to P'aldil. It will grow back. M'aldil wills a shift in the makeup of her saliva, a change from venom to analgesic, and her rough tongue ever-so-gently presses into the torn flesh of the stump as she lets the saliva flow. She feels P'aldil relax, the fine tremor of ache diminishing.

They fall farther into the darkening waters.

"What was it we found in the Above?" M'aldil asks when P'aldil seems calm again and in less pain. "It was unlike anything I know. Not even in the Dream have we seen such."

"You felt it, too, na'au?" he asks tenderly, using the term for everlasting. "I thought it was the substance of the Dream. The waters were not there, nor was the press of them. It was…"

*He can find no words for it or even any way to conceive of it. It was not. Not water, not mud or stone, not flesh as of some creature. It was just **not**. Then he knows. "It was like the spaces without any substance in the bubbles in the stone, only hot and bright."*

"Those… creatures… They spoke, didn't they? That was not just the bellow of a mindless thing. What they struck you with was a weapon, something very sharp like a barb on a hard tongue?" M'aldil asks, her words coming slowly as she tries to puzzle through something so seemingly impossible.

"They spoke," P'aldil says. "I'm sure of it."

"They are not creatures of the sea, are they? They were not in the sea, but on it, in something like our basket. How can that be?"

P'aldil doesn't know. He enters the Dream, but for once, it has nothing to offer him, so strange was their experience in the Above.

And then, from the Dreams of the old ones, many eights-of-eight Dreams ago, P'aldil thinks of the dead creatures without gills that were imprisoned inside the metal carapace with broken fins that hangs in the Chamber of the Strange, though the bodies of the creatures have long since dissolved. Above, in the strange place, even though the light was searing, he saw the creatures that had attacked them had the same soft brown eyes — though much smaller — as the Mala-t'uee, the largest of the swimming creatures, whose enormous tails flap up and down, not side to side, and who have no gills. It is said the creatures that came down in that metal carapace had such eyes. They are the eyes of creatures that know things.

Could they be the same creatures as in the ancient Dream? They have always wondered about the carapace, which was made — not grown — of thin metal, like the blocks of structures the He'e build in the voids beside the sea vents. And that has always frightened them because in the Great Dream, of all the creatures, only the He'e can make things.

P'aldil says nothing to M'aldil. She has seen enough, and he does not wish to cause her skin to change to the color of worry again.

— «» —

They descend very fast now without the buoyant stones to slow them. Both hunger and so it comes as a pleasure rather than a threat when another many-toothed mano-niuhi approaches them, rushing at them out of the gloom. P'aldil lets go the heavy stone and turns to face the mano-niuhi. M'aldil again uses the strobing flash of her arms to stun this fish. P'aldil pulls the shuddering fish toward him, bites it and injects his venom, holding the brutish thing with his uninjured arms until its thrashing stops. They eat.

More slowly, without the stone to pull them down, they continue to descend. A hunger later, they catch a toothfish nearly as large as the mano-niuhi — muscular, too, but without the fight the large predator fish had given them. That is all they catch in the darker and deeper waters, but it serves to hold their hunger at bay. They drop into the deepest of the Below, back to the seafloor where the taste of the waters tells them they are only a few eights-of-eights away from their home.

P'aldil looks at M'aldil and flushes. He thinks, "She will always be in the Dream with me. There is no other." He feels joy at the throb of her hearts, her na'au beating.

Chapter 25

The Below

In the Chamber *of Decision, the elders listen in awed silence to P'M'aldil describe their ascent to the Above and their amazing encounter with the noisy creatures of four arms and stumpy heads with gaping orifices.*

P'aldil says, "They live in a gaseous miasma of blinding light that is everywhere but comes from nowhere."

"How can any living thing survive there?" asks P'heen.

"We do not know," says M'aldil. "But they are as comfortable in their gaseous sea as we are in our watery one. To be there does not affect them as it does us, but we did not die in that awful place, though it was very painful there."

P'aldil adds, "We quickly discovered that as long as our gill slits remained wet, we could survive — though it was laborious."

"And the creatures you encountered, are they thinking creatures, like the blow-holers, or dumb predators, like the mano-nuihi?" asks another elder, the ancient M'paunee, her arms still flashing a bright blue despite the many generations of fry whose birth she has witnessed.

P'M'aldil think long and then P'aldil gives their answer. "It is complicated. They did not try to eat us like the mano-nuihi, which can think of nothing else. They seemed as frightened by us as we were by them, but they did not try to swim away. The bladder that held them from the sea was a made thing and contained many made things of use to them, but of mystery to us. Things that were not alive, all with a purpose — like the thing that caused the eruption that severed my arm."

P'aldil, held up his shorn limb. "One of the creatures, though in evident fright, pointed the thing at us with a concentration of effort which was anything but mindless."

M'aldil says, "The bladder which held them on top of the soul sea was attached by tethers to the great metal structure from which the metal worm's radula bit into our urb. It is all one connected thing that stretches from the bottom of the soul sea up into the gaseous miasma of their world. They make things that are dead — but can come alive — out of bone or stone that has been stretched or bound or twisted together. They are tool creatures like we are swimming creatures. It is their essence."

There is great murmuring among the He'e, which rises to a roar. The implications of this are clear.

There is more than one Dream.

Chapter 26

The Above: New York, New York

Morrissey is listening, but not saying much. He used to think that after a lifetime in law enforcement he'd seen it all. But, after the last few days, he wasn't sure about anything anymore. First came the bizarre suicide — or murder — of Drake and then some kind of weird alien encounter. New York was in full-scale damage control mode.

"Now listen, Morrissey," said Gonzales, "We've decided there is only one course of action given the circumstances and we have taken steps to put it in place. Tomorrow morning, a team will be arriving out there consisting of a doctor, a medical inspector, a marine biologist, and an FBI agent."

"Pardon me?" Morrissey asked.

"The FBI has requested that an agent be sent to investigate Drake's death to rule out a homicide."

"I understand. And what are the others there for?"

"The doctor — actually he's a forensic pathologist — is going to perform an autopsy on Drake. The marine biologist is on contract with us. We want her to figure out what went on with the encounter with those... sea creatures. You have the recovered limb on ice, right?"

"Yes, sir."

"Please give the FBI agent your full cooperation, but let's keep him as far away we can from any information regarding our other problems."

"Understood."

"I'll also be sending out a temporary replacement for Mr. Drake until we can make a final selection."

"And who will that be?"

"I haven't made that decision."

"Yes, sir."

"That's all, Morrissey."

The computer screen went dark and Morrissey shook his head. He wondered to himself: Could this situation get anymore fucked up?

— «» —

After terminating the call with Morrissey, Gonzales looked up at Bobby Smith whose tall, lanky body was sprawled loosely on one of the leather chairs that faced Gonzales' desk.

"Pack your bags, Bobby. I'm sending you out to Faith."

"Why didn't you tell Morrissey?"

"Until you get out there, the less anybody knows on that platform, the better."

Chapter 27

The Above: Platform Faith

Morrissey and Gusman stood near the helipad, looking east. The midday sun was bright and they both shaded their eyes with their hands. They heard the faint thumping of the helicopter's blades before they saw it.

"Right on time," said Morrissey.

"Yeah," responded Gusman.

"My fucking head is killing me."

"Really?"

"Yeah, I've had a splitting headache for that last two days and I just can't get rid of it."

"Yeah, me, too… since the moment I arrived back here."

Gusman pointed at a little orange dot on the horizon. "Look, I see them." Then, after a pause, he asked, "Did you take anything for it?"

"Huh?"

"For your headache."

"Yeah, everything. Tons of aspirin. Then I switched to Advil. Didn't do shit."

"Did you drink coffee? Caffeine sometimes helps me."

"I always drink coffee."

"Oh. Maybe it's allergies."

The orange dot was growing steadily bigger and they could just make out the contours of the Beast.

Morrissey waited a few seconds and then said, "Allergies? What's there to be allergic to on this tin can? The smell of crude oil?"

"Could be, except we're not pumping any."

"Good point."

Gusman put a hand to his head. "I was sick coming out here and I still don't feel right. I've been having headaches, too. And I've had these weird fucking dreams. Some of the other guys have told me the same thing."

Morrissey turned to Gusman, his head cocked. "Yeah, same with me. Shit, I guess they'll have to add 'sick oil platform syndrome' to Epstein-Barr, fibromyalgia, and the other diseases on the shortlist of favorites for malingering neurotics at the workplace."

Gusman laughed grudgingly, not sure if he liked agreeing with the security man or not. "They'll be here in a couple of minutes."

"Speaking of headaches, there's something I need to tell you about Drake."

"You don't still think I did it, do you?"

"Not unless you wrote this and stuck it in Drake's safe."

"I don't know the combination to his safe. Hell, I didn't even know he had a safe."

Morrissey reached into his front pants pocket and pulled out a piece of lined yellow paper, carefully unfolded it, and handed it to Gusman.

Gusman studied it. Each line was numbered, one to twenty-five. The first line was written in neat block letters, the last in barely legible scrawl. Each line said exactly the same thing.

"Stop the pain."

"Wow. This is so weird. He must have been going insane. Maybe he had a brain tumor."

Morrissey nodded in the direction of the now clearly visible orange helicopter closing in on the platform. "We'll find out when they get here."

Gusman did not respond for a few seconds. "I saw him the night before he died. He didn't seem crazy to me."

Morrissey laughed. "You mean he was his normal asshole self."

"Exactly."

Gusman handed the paper back to Morrissey, who carefully folded it and put it back in his pocket.

"What's going on here, Gusman?" asked Morrissey.

"I don't know."

They lapsed into silence as they watched the helicopter make its final approach.

— «» —

The first one out was a young man wearing a blue windbreaker emblazoned with the shield and gold and blue wreath that formed the seal of the Federal Bureau of Investigation. He wore aviator-style Ray-Bans, which, to Gusman, gave him that self-important cop look. The rest of his outfit was a blur of neatly pressed khaki and polished leather. When he reached the bottom of the cargo ramp, he looked around and waved at Morrissey and Gusman.

Gusman waved back.

"You know him?" Morrissey asked.

"No. But given who he is and my situation, I thought I'd try being friendly."

"Well, I do. His name is Harple. Charles or Calvin. Something like that. He started just as I was leaving the Bureau. By-the-book type."

"I'll settle for fair."

Next out of the helicopter was a man followed immediately by a woman. Gusman figured one of them must be the forensic pathologist who was supposed to autopsy Drake's body and the other was the biologist who was there to examine the severed arm of the creature that Dennison and Babitch encountered.

The last to emerge was a tall, lanky figure. He wore a gray felt Stetson hat — which he took off as he emerged from the helicopter. His tailored western-cut suit and finely tooled cowboy boots hung well on his lean frame.

Gusman's stomach took a turn. "Isn't that Bobby Smith?" he muttered.

Morrissey merely growled his assent, then tapped him roughly on the shoulder and said, "Come on, Gusman. Let's go say 'hello' to our guests."

They walked toward the helipad.

Bobby Smith thrust his hand out as the two men approached in a way that announced he was in charge.

"Mr. Morrissey," he said, pumping Morrissey's hand.

Then he turned to Gusman, looking him directly in the eye. "Mr. Gusman?" he said, without much enthusiasm and offered his hand.

"Yes, sir," replied Gusman. "Nice to meet you."

Smith was one of those men who always seemed to squeeze just a bit too hard. Gusman hated that. He felt a tinge of something rise up in his stomach. Fear? Maybe it was the small, dark eyes, or something hidden in the infinite crags on the man's face. Or the way his coffee-stained teeth looked — the canines came to a sharp point, revealing malevolence when he smiled.

"Gentlemen, allow me to make the introductions," said Smith, his Texas drawl making his words sound long and hard. "This is FBI Special Agent Harple."

Up close, the FBI agent looked older than he did from a distance. Maybe late thirties or early forties. Gusman was immediately struck by his eyes, which were an intense shade of blue, suggesting a frankness that made him look smart and trustworthy. His jaw was strong, and his smile reserved, cool, and wry.

Nodding toward Morrissey, Smith said, "This is Joe Morrissey, our security officer, and this is Gusman, our Chief Engineer.

Harple smiled more broadly and said, "Mr. Morrissey and I have met. It's good to see you again, sir." He shook his hand and then turned to face Gusman. His smile went from genuine to polite.

Gusman tried his best to smile back. It felt forced and fake. "Welcome to Platform Faith, Special Agent Harple," he said, thrusting out his hand.

Taking Gusman's hand, Harple responded matter-of-factly, "Nice to meet you, Mr. Gusman." He stared into Gusman's eyes a split second longer than necessary, taking his measure.

It made Gusman feel even more edgy than he already was.

As if he was intervening to prevent an embarrassing social gaff, Smith moved his body in close to Gusman and the FBI agent. The Texan turned to the two scientists. "Now, let me introduce our two other guests. "This is Dr. Campos. She is a fisheries biologist we have retained to examine the remains of the thing that your folks ran into."

"Nice to meet you, gentlemen," she said, shaking hands with Morrissey and Gusman. Her handshake was firm and her smile genuine. She had long, jet-black hair tied back in a tight ponytail. Her face was unlined and her eyes brown and large. "As you can imagine, I am very excited to begin my investigation."

"And this is Dr. Howard Schwartz. He is a pathologist on contract with the US Coast Guard."

Schwartz, a small, powerfully built man, thrust his hand forward and shook hands with the two men.

"Gentlemen, it's very nice to meet you, but I'm anxious to get started. Can someone take me right away to the body?"

"Are you sure you don't want to get settled first, Dr. Schwartz?" asked Bobby Smith, with an unctuous smile and an even more extreme Texas drawl than usual.

"Actually, no. I want to get the autopsy started right away."

"Yes, sir," replied Smith, obviously bemused.

Chapter 28

The Above: New York

It was nearly midnight and Enrique Gonzales stood staring out the large window of his office. The lights of Manhattan's skyscrapers illuminated the night sky. He had just finished reading the chemical analysis of the soil samples taken from the entrance to the borehole at Platform Faith. It was stamped 'highly confidential.'

At first, what he read was unremarkable: bits of carbon steel from the shattered drill bit, granite and calcium carbonate, the skeletons of dead microorganisms, the constituent elements of the fluid used to lubricate and cool the borehole.

And then there was the finding that, in the understated language of scientists, the report described as "highly anomalous."

Buckminsterfullerene, (C60), Superdiamond variant.

Knowing the report was intended for a lay reader, the author had included a description pulled largely from Wikipedia:

Buckminsterfullerene (or "buckyball") is a spherical fullerene molecule with the formula C_{60}. It has a cage-like, fused-ring structure (shaped like a truncated icosahedron) that resembles a soccer ball, made of twenty hexagons and twelve pentagons, with a carbon atom at each vertex of each polygon and a bond along each polygon edge.

Buckminsterfullerene was first intentionally prepared in 1985 and its discoverers were awarded the 1996 Nobel Prize in Chemistry for their roles in the its discovery and the related class of fullerene molecules. The fullerenes are named after Buckminster Fuller, as C_{60} resembles his famous geodesic dome. Buckminsterfullerene is the most common naturally occurring fullerene molecule, as it can be found in small quantities in soot. Solid and gaseous forms of the molecule have been detected in deep space.

As noted, while fullerenes are extremely rare, they do appear in nature. The fullerene molecule in the sample, however, is what scientists have called the "Buckyball Superdiamond Variant." To our knowledge, this molecule has never been found in nature and has only recently been produced in a laboratory. Chemically, the Buckyball Superdiamond Variant is composed of C_{60} arranged in a lattice with the gaps in the molecular structure filled in with another carbon compound, xylene. When extreme pressure is applied to the compound (@320,000 atmospheres), a part diamond, part buckyball crystalline structure is created. The resulting molecule is the hardest substance in the known universe. Indeed, the process of creating the Buckyball Superdiamond molecule dented the diamond used to apply the pressure needed to create it.

The report concluded that it was possible that the drill bit had come in contact with an as-of-yet undiscovered, naturally occurring form of the Buckyball Superdiamond, which could be a plausible explanation as to why the drill bit had shattered.

The implication was clear: Platform Faith stood atop the source of what might be the most significant discovery since the development of the nuclear bomb — a source of the hardest substance in the universe.

Gonzales' training was in law, not materials science, but he knew well enough that the pressure of the ocean where this substance was found was a bare fraction of what it would take to make such a superdiamond. So its provenance was an enigma — hell, impossibility — but its value was beyond measure. And Gonzales wanted it.

Chapter 29

The Above: Platform Faith

Gusman dropped his head on the pillow and stared up at the ceiling. Sleep did not come, and he felt restless. He looked toward his feet. He was naked and lying on top of his bed, which struck him as odd, since he usually wore an old T-shirt to sleep in and slept between the sheets. He wanted to get up but felt too exhausted to move. The lights were on. He should turn them off.

Then he noticed something else odd. It was absolutely silent in his cabin. The usual hum of the ventilation system was absent. He could not even hear his own breathing. A wave of anxiety passed over him. He felt entombed. Was he even alive?

He closed his eyes.

Time passed.

He opened his eyes.

Someone had turned off the lights. The only illumination in the room was the pale green indicator light on his laptop, which was sitting on his desk, charging.

"Who are you?" said the voice, which came from somewhere in his head.

"I'm Gusman," he responded, though not with his voice. He was somehow able to speak with his mind.

"Gusman?" the voice asked.

"Yes, Gusman."

"Hello, Gusman."

"What is your name?" Gusman asked.

"P'aldil."

"P'aldil?"

"Yes, P'aldil."

"Hello, P'aldil," said Gusman, trying to get used to the strangeness of the name.

There was silence. Gusman wondered if the voice was still there.

"P'aldil, are you still there?"

"Yes, I am here."

"Where are you?"

"In the Dream."

"This is a dream?"

"It is always the Dream."

"P'aldil, what do you see with your eyes?"

"I see M'aldil, the fry, the smoker. I see my arms. But not all of them."

"How many arms do you have?"

"I have eight, but one is partly missing."

"Missing?"

"Yes, it was injured when I went to the Above."

"Are you in pain?"

"I am no longer."

Silence followed.

"Gusman?"

"What?"

"Do you have arms?"

"I have two arms and two legs."

"There are only arms, Gusman. Do you have four arms?"

"I suppose. Two are for movement. Two are for holding things."

"Ah. You are like a crab. You have two arms for walking and two arms for grabbing."

"Yes, that's right."

"You must be very awkward with so few arms."

Gusman laughed. "Perhaps I am."

More time passed.

"Gusman?

"I'm still here."

"What do you see where you are?"

"It's dark, so I can't see much. I'm in my room, on my bed. I see the ceiling of my room and the walls. I see my feet. I see a little green light on my computer."

"I don't understand this place."

"Do you sleep, P'aldil?"

"Yes."

"This place is where I sleep."

"Are the waters cool or hot there?"

"There is no water here. Only air."

"No water. That is strange. Like the Above. I have been to the Above."

"What is 'the Above?'" asked Gusman.

"The place above the water."

"I think I live in what you call the Above. In a structure above the water."

"Gusman?"

"Yes, P'aldil?"

"What is air?"

"Air is what I breathe. Without air, I will die.'"

"Is air the gas that is in bubbles?"

"Yes, that's right."

"Is air the heated gas of nothingness that is everywhere in the Above?"

"I think so."

"Gusman, do you live in the metal creature that sends its long arm to eat stone at the bottom of the sea?"

"I don't know. I live on an oil platform."

"Oil?"

"Oil is a thick, black fluid that comes from the earth."

"Is oil a fluid that cannot be mixed with water?"

"Yes. That describes two of the properties of oil."

"Does it combust when it comes in contact with flowing lava?"

"Yes, it can burn."

"Gusman, I think what you call 'oil,' we call *hinu*. It seeps from the rocks under the sea and flows slowly into water. It has special properties and is sacred to the He'e. It is a fluid, yet it does not mix with water. However, when it is heated it spreads rapidly within water. It can mix with the stuff of life in the water, and with enough heat it can combust. Its heat of combustion is paltry though compared to the great store of heat in the rock below the smokers.

But when it is cold, it becomes solid — but never hard like a rock. It is a deadly poison and cannot be eaten by any creature — except for the tiny kahi kino — tiny single-bodied creatures — that gather in great yellow colonies and devour it. Yet when it is rubbed on a wound, it has healing properties."

Gusman laughed. "Our whole world runs on what you call hinu. It is not sacred, but it might as well be. Without it, our civilization would come to a halt. Many people — that is what we call ourselves — hate hinu, but love what it does for them. Our kind's appetite for hinu is without limit. My job is to find new sources of hinu."

"Why? Do you eat it? Do you heal yourselves with it?

"Mostly we just burn it for its energy."

There was a silence, as if a great question hung there for P'aldil to consider. Finally, he said, "The hinu is a marvelous source of stuff to enrich living. And you combust it?"

The question lay there, until Gusman, embarrassment rising, finally admitted, "Yes, we combust it."

"And you have sent your monster claw into the gathering of the He'e just to find hinu?"

"Yes."

"Even though it will kill our fry?"

"Who?"

"Our progeny, Gusman. Don't you have progeny?"

"Yes. Well, not me, personally."

"That is sad. All living creatures should have fry. Why do you not have fry, Gusman?"

"Well, I never found the right woman to have fry with."

"'Woman' that is a female, like my M'aldil?"

"Yes."

"Does your kind stay with one female or have many?"

"It could be either or both."

"That cannot be. Since the first Dream, when all creatures were created, there are only two ways to have a mate. One way is to mate for life like M'aldil and me. We have been together for many eights of dreams and she has borne all my fry. And we have watched those fry grow in dream after dream and take mates and have fry for seven generations. The other way — for the lesser creatures — is to mate with anyone. There is no both.”

“It is that way here — in ‘the Above,’ as you call it — for all creatures except for us. We are called humans.”

“Gusman?”

“Yes?”

“I have seen humans. One tried to harm us. That is how I lost my arm.”

“Now I understand. I am sorry, P’aldil. He was frightened.”

“It will grow back.”

“I’m glad. He did not intend to hurt you.”

“He seemed frightened. It was hard to see because of the intensity of the light.”

There was silence.

“Gusman?”

“Yes, P’aldil?”

“Why did you not leave when I asked you to do so before?”

“You asked me to leave?

“Yes, but you did not respond. You remained silent and then I could not see you in the Dream anymore.”

“I’m sorry.”

“Gusman?”

“Yes.”

“The humans must not be allowed to destroy our dwelling places. Tell them to leave.”

“It is not that simple.”

“Yes, it is.”

Gusman started to answer, but P’aldil interrupted. “Gusman, I must go. One of the fry is too close to the smoker.”

“Okay.”

Gusman opened his eyes and sat up with a start. He was drenched in sweat, although the air was cool. The light in his cabin was on. The ventilation system hummed. And then, in a sudden rush, he remembered his dream of a creature named P’aldil as if it had just happened. It was not a fragmentary memory like in a typical dream, but the memory of a real conversation, a memory like the memory as intense and recent and real as his conversation with Morrissey on the helipad a few hours earlier.

"What the fuck?" he said in a voice loud enough to startle himself.

— «» —

The Below

P'M'aldil rest in their shell chamber. Close as they are to the smoker, the waters carry a small bit of heat, alive with the energy of it, far different from the comforting cold of the waters around them. In that faint heat, P'aldil's arms curl and writhe restlessly. All over him are the shifting specks of violet and gray that speak of deep thought.

"We are not alone," he finally says, saying it slowly, the thought itself almost beyond belief. "We have never known other thinking life. Life that uses its mana'o — its brain — to fashion its environment."

M'aldil wears a startled white on her arms. "You are right, my kuu kane, my love. The He'e' have talked before, in our lives and in the Dream, about finding others that also have thoughts. Now we have found them and..."

"And?"

"And I am ashamed, thinking that the thing we should do is destroy them. Yet they are dangerous."

P'aldil's arms lash anxiously, "I think the same. Sadly, I do."

"Even the one called Gusman?"

"I don't know. I hope not."

Chapter 30

The Above: Platform Faith

When Gusman entered the library, Special Agent Harple was already there. He was seated at the table in the middle of the room facing the door, his hands clasped neatly in front of him.

Off to the side of the table, a small video camera sat on a tripod. A red light on the front indicated that it was recording. The only thing on the table was a small remote control.

Agent Harple smiled slightly but did not extend his hand.

"Hello, Mr. Gusman. Please sit down."

"Thanks." Gusman pulled out the chair. It squeaked loudly, which made him wince.

After he sat, he didn't know what to do with his hands. So he clasped them in front of him, in a mirror reflection of Harple's. Then he wondered if Harple would think he was mocking him and quickly put them in his lap.

They stared at each other for a few seconds and then Gusman said, "Okay, now what?"

"Well, Mr. Gusman, I will ask you some questions about the events that transpired here."

Gusman nodded at the recorder. "Why are you recording this?"

"It is standard procedure to videotape witness interviews. It is for your protection."

"I bet you guys say that to everyone," Gusman said. It came out sounding cynical and defensive and he immediately regretted it.

The FBI agent just stared at him with an expression somewhere between mild disdain and feigned empathy.

"Sorry," Gusman mumbled. Then he cleared his throat and sat up more stiffly, as if to reset the conversation. "So, is this a formal interrogation?"

"Well, Mr. Gusman, I suppose all interrogations are formal."

"What I mean is, am I a suspect?"

"In what crime?

"In the death of Drake."

"Do you think Drake was murdered, Mr. Gusman?"

"Not by me."

"Then by somebody?"

"I don't know if he was murdered or not."

"You found him, correct?"

"Yes."

"When was that?"

Gusman held up his hand. "Mr. Harple, before we go any further, I need an answer from you."

"Okay. What is the question?"

"You see, I had an uncle who was a criminal defense lawyer in Chicago. He told me that you should never talk to the police if they think you are a suspect. So, I'm asking you again, Special Agent: am I a suspect?"

"No, not at this time."

"But I could become one?"

"Yes, you could become one."

"Then why aren't you reading me my rights?"

"Look, Mr. Gusman, the answer to your question is this: we read someone their Miranda rights when they are under arrest or preceding what is called a 'custodial interrogation.' You are not under arrest. You are free to go at any time. I am interviewing you as a witness. All I want to do is find out what you know. I will be interviewing other members of the crew. As far as Mr. Drake is concerned, the cause of his death has not been established, let alone has a determination been made that he was the victim of a homicide. So, you can just relax and tell me what you know."

Gusman stood.

"I'm sorry. I know this looks bad, but I won't talk to you until I've been ruled out as a suspect."

For a brief second, something sharp flashed across the FBI agent's eyes before they returned to their state of nonjudgmental blandness. In the same calm, emotionless voice, he asked, "Do you have something to hide?"

"No, and I had nothing to do with Drake's death. But plenty of innocent men have gone to jail because things they said were misconstrued."

Harple shook his head once slowly and sighed, as if he pitied Gusman's foolishness but was resigned to it. Then he said, "Well, then, Mr. Gusman, I suppose this concludes our interview."

He picked up the remote control and pressed a button. The red light on the video camera went dark.

"Can I go now?" Gusman asked.

"Yes."

Gusman stood and walked to the door. He felt embarrassed and humiliated and wanted to say something to justify his conduct. He stopped and turned.

"Look, I'd be happy to talk to you, but not if I'm being set up to incriminate myself."

"You don't owe me an explanation. That is your right. But I must say, Mr. Gusman, your failure to cooperate in this situation is quite inexplicable to me."

"When you rule me out as a suspect, I'll be happy to talk to you."

"I know. You already said that."

— «» —

It was clear that Bobby Smith was one angry Chief of Corporate Security. His jaw was clenched, and his lips were tightly pursed. He rubbed his chin and looked over at Morrissey. Morrissey acknowledged Smith with a nod, his face a mask.

Gusman looked around the office Smith had commandeered. It was windowless and featureless. Just a metal desk and a few chairs. In the background were the constant companions of the crew on Platform faith: the hum of the electrical system and the antiseptic smell of recycled air that left its residue in everyone's throat.

Smith turned his gaze on Gusman. When he spoke, his words were slow, his Texas drawl deep and menacing. "Son, I don't know you and I already damn well wish we'd never met. But I got to say, that was the dumbest God damned stunt I've ever seen. Telling an FBI agent investigating a suspicious death you wouldn't talk to him until you were 'cleared as a suspect.' What in the hell got into you?"

"Look, Mr. Smith. Here's what I know. I know I was the one who found Drake. I know Agent Harple is here because somebody thinks Drake may have been murdered. I know I'm under investigation and that I could be falsely accused. And I know my rights."

The Texan looked at Morrissey again and shook his head. He locked on to Gusman's face and stared at him for what seemed an eternity. Gusman could see his jaw muscles tense.

"Rights? You're looking at two former lawmen. Yeah, you have rights. But rights don't mean shit if they suspect you. The reality is, if you stay silent, they *will* use it against you."

"I know how it looks. Anyway, I found the body. Given the circumstances, I don't see how I'm not going to be a suspect. I'll tell them everything as soon as I know they don't think I murdered him."

Morrissey said, "That's a very high-risk strategy, Gusman. Plenty of innocent men have been convicted of crimes because they didn't cooperate when they should have. You're being stubborn for no reason."

Gusman paused before answering. Maybe they were right. He knew he was innocent. Yet he was following the advice of a long-dead uncle he idolized. "Maybe you're right and maybe you're not. But I've made my decision and I'm going to stick with it."

"Well, then, I have no choice but to suspend you from your duties pending the outcome of the criminal investigation and our own internal investigation," said Smith.

"What?" Gusman said, his voice rising. "I've done nothing wrong."

"We asked you to cooperate with the FBI and you refused. That's insubordination in my book. There's no presumption of innocence in the employment relationship and our company has the highest ethical standards."

Gusman stood, his face flushed with anger and humiliation. "This is outrageous."

"Really. And your conduct isn't?"

Gusman brought himself to his full height, adjusting his shoulders and fixing his gaze on the two men, attempting to project dignity and strength that he did not feel. "If there's nothing else, I'm going."

Without waiting for a response, he turned and walked out of the room.

Morrissey laughed and said to Smith, "If I didn't think he was innocent, I'd say he was acting like a guilty man."

"What makes you so sure he's innocent?"

"Well, for one, that crazy suicide note I found in Drake's safe."

"Yep, maybe."

"By the way, did you hand that over to Harple?"

"Sure did," replied Smith.

Smith was lying. In fact, he had destroyed the note. It didn't fit in with his plans. The fact Morrissey knew about it was a problem.

Chapter 31

The Above: Platform Faith

When the door to Smith's office closed behind him and Gusman saw that he was alone in the corridor, a wave of nausea overcame him. He bent over, placing his hands on his knees to steady himself.

And then he heard a voice, at once close and distant, strange and familiar, call his name.

"Gusman?"

He stood and looked down the corridor in both directions. There was no one there.

He heard it again.

"Gusman?"

He stood still, his head cocked like a dog that hears a strange sound, waiting for the voice to say something else.

But there was only silence.

He began to walk down the hallway, slowly at first, then more quickly. He needed air.

Gusman didn't know what to do now. He was relieved of his duties and free to roam the platform, yet he felt like a prisoner. It was as if he were between two worlds: one free, one shackled.

Since he had discovered Drake's body, he noticed that when he greeted other crew members, there was a hesitation before they greeted him back. Did they suspect? Perhaps he was just imagining things.

Imagining things.

From the moment he had arrived on Faith, it was as if reality itself had shifted. The strange dreams, the people who did not seem like themselves, and the death of Drake had sent his sense of reality into a wobbly orbit. All he wanted to do now was get the hell off Faith and return to the mainland. He was resigned to the fact he would now almost certainly lose his job and probably get blacklisted in the industry. And there were the deeper fears. What if the FBI concluded that Drake had been murdered and he was the killer?

Gusman decided it would be best if he avoided other members of the crew, so he decided to go to lunch late.

It was well after 2:00 p.m. when he entered the mess hall. To his relief, it was empty. Gusman sauntered over to the serving line, where the kitchen crew left out an assortment of sandwiches and snacks for the stragglers. Gusman didn't have much of an appetite. He grabbed a hard-boiled egg and a couple of those little individual boxes of cornflakes. He sat down nearby and began to peel the egg.

"Mind if I join you?"

Gusman looked up, startled. It was the scientist. She smiled at him. Her eyes were dark and very expressive. There was intelligence and humor in them. She was beautiful, but the sort of woman who didn't flaunt it. She didn't need to.

Gusman clumsily started to stand, but only managed to get halfway up. "Oh, Dr. Campos. Yeah, sure, please join me. I'd love the company."

"Okay. Let me just get something to eat."

Gusman slid back down into his chair and watched her walk toward the counter. She had a natural sway to her hips. Her black hair was in a thick braid and, as she walked, it moved with her body, which was lithe and athletic.

When she turned around to return to the table, he looked down, fiddling with his box of cornflakes. Did women know when men were watching them? They seemed to know everything else, so why not that, too?

"So, how's your work going, Dr. Campos?" he asked as she got herself settled. She had a glass of iced tea and a yogurt.

"Well, first of all, you can call me Anna."

"And you can call me Gusman."

She frowned. "Don't you have a first name?"

"I do, but no one calls me by it. It's always been that way."

"Excuse me for saying this, but that's really weird. Even your wife and your mother?"

"Ex-wife, actually. Yeah, she called me Gusman or just 'hey, you.' My mother's been dead for years, but she used to just call me 'son.'"

"Interesting," she said, obviously bemused.

"Well, Anna, at this stage, my first name sounds as foreign to my ears as if someone called you by your middle name."

"I don't have a middle name."

"Well, I guess you're just lucky."

She laughed. Her high cheekbones flushed a little. She looked down and pulled off the foil from the top of the container of yogurt and stirred it.

"So, have you started your examination of that thing?"

"No, not yet. As you can imagine, Dr. Schwartz's autopsy was the first priority, so I haven't even been able to get into the examination room until now."

"Examination room? I didn't know that we had such a thing."

"Well, I guess I should say 'improvised examination room.' It's supposed to be behind here somewhere, next to the kitchen. Actually, I was on my way find it."

"I know where they must mean." Gusman pointed to a door. "You go through there and turn right. There are walk-in freezers in there and a big prep table."

"Yes, that sounds like it."

"Is the autopsy done?" Gusman tried to sound matter-of-fact, but he was curious and worried. He hoped that his voice did not betray his anxiety.

"I believe so. Just a little while ago."

She raised the spoonful of yogurt to her mouth and slowly ate it. Something about the way she did it seemed sexual. Or was he just being a jerk?

"Do you know what they found out?" he asked.

"I have no idea. That's none of my business." The way she said it made it clear she thought it was none of his business either.

"So, if you don't mind asking, how did you wind up being invited to our little paradise in the central Pacific?"

"Well, I'm a marine biologist at Scripps. I study the ecosystems that develop around offshore oil platforms. Over time, they become incredibly rich places, a sort of vertical artificial reef — although on a platform like this one, which floats, that is much less the case. Anyway, I am often called in as a consultant when there are incidents that may impact the critters living in and around oil platforms. This is my first time working for Clearsea."

"Congratulations," he said, dryly, wondering if she'd catch the sarcasm.

"Thanks," she responded.

"And they have briefed you on everything that happened here?"

"Well, you'll have to tell me. They sent me the videos of that incident with your two crew members. I'm an expert in cephalopods — octopuses and squids — and those creatures that your people encountered appear to be some kind of large cephalopod."

"And what did you make of that incident?"

"I have many more questions than I have answers. Like what those creatures were doing on that thing they were floating on? It looked like it was..." She paused, searching for the right word.

"Made?" Gusman interrupted. "As in, made by intelligent life for floating to the surface of the ocean?"

"Well, that's what it looked like in the video."

"Are octopuses smart enough to do that?"

"They are quite intelligent, certainly capable of guile, mischief, and planning. Like popping the top of aquarium tanks and escaping. Making and using tools is quite another matter. There is one species we are aware of — the veined octopus from Indonesia — that gathers coconut shells and arranges them to form a shelter. There is debate in the scientific community as to whether that can truly be called using a tool."

Gusman interrupted. "Well, what we recovered looked like a sophisticated raft. Three large pumice rocks filled with gas that made them buoyant with a net attached to form a basket so those things — whatever they were — could sit in the middle. It was like an ocean-going hot air balloon. To make something like that involves a hell of a lot more than guile and mischief. It involves knowledge of physics, managing materials, and advanced planning. I'm not sure even chimps could do something like that."

"No, I don't think they could."

"So, what do you make of it, Doc?"

"I'm not sure what to make of it and I'm going to reserve judgment until I complete my examination of the severed limb."

"Can I help?"

"Are you serious?"

"I'm dead serious."

Dr. Campos's eyes narrowed. She stared into Gusman's, a thin smile crossing her lips.

"I don't want to take you away from your other duties."

Gusman lied. "It's my day off."

"Well, I suppose I could always use an assistant," she said, still looking at him.

He stared back into her eyes, the hardness of her stare demanding something — honesty perhaps — and he looked away, unable to keep eye contact. Perhaps it was the shame of lying or the shyness of attraction or something else. When he looked back, her head was cocked, and her smile had grown.

"Try not to get in the way, okay?" she said.

Gusman raised his hand to his brow and saluted. "Yes, ma'am," he said crisply and stood up at mock attention. "Shall I lead the way?

"Please do," she replied.

— «» —

The creature's limb lay on the stainless-steel kitchen prep table illuminated by the halogen work lights that had been placed there for the autopsy Dr. Schwartz had completed earlier in the day.

As Anna Campos busied herself setting up her microscope and dissection equipment, Gusman bent down low to look at the thing. It was thick, perhaps twelve inches in diameter where it had been severed and almost five feet long. It was a bluish gray color with pink and white splotches. Underneath were a series of suckers that ran along its whole length. When he looked at them closely, he could see they were covered with tiny spiky hairs.

Gusman touched it. It was cold and very firm, the skin rougher than he had imagined.

"Not so fast, partner," said Dr. Campos as she came up next to him. He drew back quickly as if he had been caught with his hand in the cookie jar. "Some species of cephalopods — one of which we are presuming this limb belongs to — have poison glands. So, go wash your hands thoroughly and don't touch that thing again without wearing these."

She handed Gusman surgical gloves, a Plexiglas face mask, and a pair of blue scrubs.

"I'm sorry," he said. "I guess that was pretty dumb."

"You guess right. Now get going," she said. "I'll wait for you."

"Do you really think it could be poisonous?"

She laughed. "Well if you've been exposed to poison, we'll know because you'll start convulsing pretty soon."

When Gusman returned, Anna Campos was holding a scalpel in one hand and a petri dish in the other. She was staring intently at the wounded end of the severed limb.

She looked up.

"You're still alive." Her voice was slightly muffled behind the face mask.

"Yes, it appears so."

"Well you're either fine or it's a slow-moving toxin."

"Is that a joke?

"Yes, Gusman, it's a joke," she said as if he were the village idiot.

"Okay, fine, so my sense of humor is a bit compromised." He lowered his mask and came around the back of the table and stood next to the biologist. "Okay, Doc, what have we got?"

"Well, not to belabor the obvious, we have the severed arm — technically, a leg, but why fight popular culture? — of a very large cephalopod; an octopus. Given the size and configuration of this specimen, I would guess this was severed at about half of its length. I'm not aware of any known species of octopus this large. Therefore, I think we are looking at a previously unknown species."

"So, now what?"

"Well, the first thing I want to do is take some tissue samples. I'm going to examine some of them under the microscope and send the rest back to the University of Hawaii for radiocarbon dating and genetic mapping."

"Radiocarbon dating? Isn't that how they date fossils?"

"Yes, and fake religious objects like the Shroud of Turin. But we now also use radiocarbon dating to determine cellular age of living creatures. In fact, the only reliable way to know the age of the creature this was attached to is to perform Carbon-14 dating of its cells."

"How old do octopuses get?"

"Well, that's an interesting question. Octopuses are what we call 'semelparous.' That means the females die after they give birth. Humans and most other advanced creatures are 'iteroparous,' meaning they survive the birth of their young. Semelparous species, like the octopus, are very short lived. They usually die after one or two years. The only iteroparous octopus species we know of is the Pacific Striped Octopus. If there are others — like this one appears to be — we haven't found them yet. One of the amazing things about the octopus is that they are so intelligent yet have such a short lifespan. We've often speculated what would happen if they lived five or ten or twenty years or even longer — long enough to learn and teach their young."

She bent down low and looked at the ragged flesh of the severed arm.

"You know, they can grow these things back when they fall off."

"Really?"

"Yes, really."

"So, now what?"

"I start cutting."

She moved in close to begin her work. As she made her first cut, Gusman felt a stab of pain in his head so sharp that he let out an audible yelp and brought his hand to his temple.

Anna Campos looked up.

"What was that?" she asked, sounding irritated.

"I don't know. I just felt this sharp pain in my head."

"Are you okay?"

"I think so," he said, massaging his right temple.

"Well, does it still hurt?"

"No. It was just for an instant. I think I'm fine now. I'm really sorry," he added, embarrassed.

"Are you sure you're okay?"

"Yeah, I'm good. Sorry."

He waved her off with a shrug and a crooked smile. She looked down at the octopus arm and put the scalpel to the flesh again.

As the knife sliced through flesh, Gusman screamed out again in pain, this time falling to his knees.

Dr. Campos put down the scalpel, tossed off her face mask and knelt next to him. She placed her arms around his shoulders.

"Are you all right?" she asked, this time clearly concerned.

"I don't know," he said.

"Is the pain still there?"

"Not anymore, but I feel really nauseous."

She patted his back gently and murmured, "It's okay. Sometimes people get squeamish at these things."

"No," he protested, his voice sounding ragged and breathless, "that's not it. Every time you put that damn scalpel into that thing, I get this stabbing pain in my temple."

"Gusman, do you really think they're connected? That hardly seems possible." Her brow furrowed and she sounded irritated again.

"I don't know. I'm just telling you what happened."

"Well, then, let's see."

She rose, carefully reattached the face mask and walked over to the arm. She picked up the scalpel and said, "Turn around so you can't see what I'm doing, close your eyes and tell me if you feel anything."

She did nothing, and after a second or two said, "Did you feel anything?"

"No."

Again, she did nothing. "What about now?"

"No, nothing."

She pushed the dull handle of the scalpel gently into the severed limb.

"Yes, a very slight sensation."

She poked the skin in another place, this time harder.

"Yes, that hurt more, but not anything like before."

"Okay," she moved around the table to the back. She stuck the business end of the scalpel sharply into the solid interior flesh of the torn arm.

"Ow," Gusman yelled, again reaching for his temple. "Stop!"

She placed the scalpel down on the table, then pulled off the face mask and set it down. She put her hands on her hips and looked at Gusman.

"Turn around."

He obeyed her command, his fingers still rubbing his temple.

"What?" he said, sounding a bit like a petulant teenager.

"'What' is right. What's going on here? Is this a joke, Gusman?"

"No," he said. "I don't know any more than you do. All I know is that when you poke that thing, I get a stabbing pain in my head."

"That's impossible," she said.

"No, it's not, because it just happened."

Her expression softened. "Is there something you know about this that you are not telling me?"

"Well," he said, lowering his voice to just above a whisper. "Kind of."

"What do you mean, 'kind of?'"

"Do you really want to know?"

"Yes, if it helps me understand what just happened."

"I don't know about that, but strange things have been happening on this platform."

"You mean besides your boss being found dead with his neck slit from ear to ear — apparently by his own hand — or the fact a pair of giant octopuses surfaced on some kind of ocean-going craft and had a stare down with your coworkers?"

"Well, yeah, but other stuff, too."

She cocked her head and gave him the once over. "You're not bullshitting me, right?"

"No. Fuck, I'm scared, Anna. Why would I lie to you? To make myself look crazy? A bunch of weird stuff has been happening to me, stuff I haven't told anyone."

She put her hands up. "Stop. Okay, here's what we're going to do. You go as far away from here as you can so I can collect my samples, hopefully without sending you into a seizure. I need to get those samples on the helicopter when they send Drake's body back to the mainland. When I'm done, I'll find you. Where can we talk privately?"

"My cabin or yours."

"All right, you come to my cabin at 6:30," she said. "And try not to be seen."

"Yes, ma'am," he said, attempting a smile, but only managing a wince.

She shook her head again. It was not unfriendly. "You run along, Gusman. I'll catch you later."

He nodded and turned to walk away, wondering how it was that his male brain, recovering from searing pain and mind-numbing confusion, still managed to feel such strong feelings of sexual attraction. How would he explain *that* higher primate psychological phenomenon to the disembodied consciousness that called itself P'aldil the next time the two met up in one of his fevered dreams?

— ‹› —

The Below

The jab is nearly as fierce as the blow that had severed P'aldil's arm all those hungers ago. In that renewed pain, the Dream brings him an image that flares and dies with it. The image is of what Gusman had called hands, poor substitutes for the tips of a He'e's richly supple arms. The hands are not Gusman's. They are smaller, smoother looking, and more slender. One holds a long thin bit of metal that Gusman had once described as a blade. Unbidden comes the word 'scalpel,' perhaps from Gusman's own Dream.

The hands touch the scalpel to the end of P'aldil's detached arm. It is like the severing ala eha snap of a biting fish, sudden, sharp, and strong. In it P'aldil sees through eyes that must be Gusman's. An explosion of pain. A voice cries out. Gusman's? The hands pull the blade away and the pain fades.

There is talk between Gusman and the one the hands belong to. There are other jabs, an even stronger flare of hurt, a touch almost painless, another, stronger jab, several hardly perceptible, and then nothing. P'aldil has pulled away into a sublime painlessness. Gone is his touch with Gusman's thoughts. Gone, the fleeting connection with the other, the one wielding the blade. For a long time P'aldil sits, only the ends of his arms moving minutely, as if with their own life, in the sand on the floor of his and M'aldil's shell home. When M'aldil returns from tending fry at the crèche he tells her of the pain. It is a pain of the mind, he says, a pain that M'aldil cannot produce an analgesic to ease. In that pain, P'aldil finally allows himself to understand how thoroughly he and the Gusman creature are now connected.

Chapter 32

The Above: Platform Faith

Gusman approached the door of Anna Campos' cabin quietly, making sure no one saw him. It was a futile gesture, as he knew that there were security cameras everywhere and, if anyone was paying attention, they were observing him stop, compose himself, and knock gently at her door.

He heard a faint shuffling. His pulse raced. Whether it was fear or attraction or some other emotion, he could not say. He was a mess of emotions: weariness mixed with nervous energy; a sense of feeling trapped like a caged animal colliding headlong with the equally animalistic desire of a male on the scent of a female; fear mixed with bravado.

She cracked open the door and, when she saw it was him, opened it a bit wider and gestured with her chin for him to come in. Her cabin was dimly lit, the only source of illumination the little light built into the wall above her cot that served as a reading lamp. It cast a small circle of light on the cot and left the rest of the little room in shadow.

"Hi," he said quietly and a bit shyly.

"Hey," she responded, her voice soft. She gestured to the desk chair. "Please sit down."

He sat, Anna opposite him.

Her almond-shaped eyes looked even larger and her cheekbones higher in the dim light. Her jaw was square and angular, adding to the overall impression of strength. Her lips were neither thin nor thick, but sensual in the way of Latin women. Her full and somewhat unruly hair was down now, hovering over her shoulders.

Gusman tried not to stare.

"So," he said, "I suppose you want to know if I felt anything when you took your samples?"

"Well, yes, I do."

"I got as far away as I could. All the way across the platform. I felt a faint tugging three or four times in my head, like something was pulling at it. Not painful, but a little uncomfortable."

"I don't even know what to say about that. I think the only way to try to get to the bottom of this would be to measure your brainwaves, pulse, blood pressure, et cetera, when the creature's arm is touched."

"I'm game," he said and laughed.

"Well, we don't have that kind of equipment out here. But I'll tell you what. I think we could both use a drink."

"That's strictly *verboten* out here. You can get your ass fired for consuming alcohol aboard one of these tin cans."

"Well, guess what, Gusman? I know it's forbidden, but I brought a bottle of wine with me. Care to take a risk and join me for a glass?"

"Is the Pope Catholic?" he responded.

She went over to the other side of the little cabin and rummaged through her bag, emerging with the bottle of red wine. She handed it to him.

"Just a sec," she said and went into the little bathroom.

She emerged a few seconds later with two plastic cups. "Well, these will have to do."

"I would have been fine drinking it straight from the bottle."

She tilted her head ever so slightly. She was drawing some conclusion from his last statement. Perhaps he was just a bit too uncouth for her taste. She held the bottle out to him. "Will you do the honors?"

"With what?"

"Oh, yes. A corkscrew. I actually have one." She dove back into her suitcase and came up with one of those red Swiss Army knives, holding it up triumphantly. Gusman wondered whether anyone in the Swiss army ever actually used one of those.

She handed it to him.

He pulled out the cork and poured some wine into the two cups.

"*Salud*," she said, and they touched glasses.

The wine tasted good. There was a pause while they looked down into their glasses, neither knowing quite what to say next. As often happens at such moments, they both spoke at once.

Their laughter broke the ice.

"You go," he said.

"No, you," she replied.

"All right. Where should I start?"

"At the beginning?"

"Okay. When I returned here last week... My God, was it only a week ago?" He laughed, shaking his head slowly in near disbelief. "Anyway, I wasn't feeling well. The flu, I guess. I was running a slight fever. Almost immediately, the dreams started. Weird, disturbing dreams."

"Nightmares?"

"No, they weren't frightening like a nightmare. They were vivid and matter-of-fact, like normal reality, just a bit strange and twisted."

"Can you describe them?"

"Well, yeah. In the first one, I fell asleep in my bed and then I dreamed — except that it didn't feel like I had been dreaming — that I woke up a few hours later. I was in my bed just as it was when I went to sleep. Everything was the same. I was wearing the same T-shirt I wore to bed. The cup of water I drank before I fell asleep was where I left it on the desk. It even had the same amount of water left in it. The book I was reading when I fell asleep was also on the bed where I placed it. I got up and walked down the hall to the elevator. Nothing was out of the ordinary, except when the elevator door opened, there was this blinding light. Then I woke up for real and I realized it was a dream. I felt completely disoriented. Like reality was indistinguishable from my dream."

"Well, I've had hyper realistic dreams, too. They are very disturbing, but not really so out of the ordinary."

"Anna, that was just the first dream of many. It gets weirder." He raised his cup. "Here's to the unpredictability of life."

She laughed and clinked his cup. They downed their wine.

"Another round?"

"Why not?" she responded. "But only if you tell me more about your dreams."

He refilled the plastic cups.

"The next dream was kind of like the first. I dreamed that I woke up just before dawn and decided to watch the sun rise from the platform deck. When I reached the rail, I saw something strange moving just below the surface of the ocean. It was lit up."

"Bioluminescence," Anna whispered.

"Yes," he said. "And swirling wildly, like sharks attacking their prey. Then this thing rose up from the water and flew toward me. It was like a snake with a face. It was white and was moving incredibly quickly, so quickly I didn't have time to move. Anyway, I couldn't move; it was like I was paralyzed. It stopped a few inches from my face and spoke to me."

"Do you remember what it said?"

"It said, 'Creature, leave this place or you will die.'"

"Jesus," she said. "Then what happened?"

"It plunged back in the ocean and I woke up."

"That's so weird."

"And there was something else."

"What?"

"In my dream, I woke up at 5:32 a.m. Then when I actually woke up, it was 5:32 a.m."

"That's very odd, but certainly explainable."

"Maybe. But let me tell you what came next."

"Do tell," she said, a little loudly.

He took another big gulp of his wine. He was starting to feel it, too. "Well, you won't think I'm crazy, will you?"

She reached across and touched his arm. It was a warm and encouraging gesture. "I'm a scientist. I more or less see everything as part of the natural world."

"How does craziness fit in?"

"It is just another state of consciousness. I won't judge."

"All right. Here goes."

He took a deep, audible breath. "In the last dream, I heard his voice. He talked to me. We had a conversation."

"Who talked to you?"

Anna's voice had taken on the quiet earnestness of a parent attempting to calm an upset child. Or perhaps, Gusman thought, the tone a psychiatrist uses with a mentally disturbed patient.

"That thing that surfaced, the giant octopus," he replied as if it were obvious.

She nodded slowly. "And your conversation was in English?"

"Yes, but he taught me some words in his language, and he didn't understand some words in mine. It sounded a lot like some of the Hawaiian words I've heard on the Islands. Anyway, we weren't speaking. It was like the words were flowing between us without the need to speak."

"Telepathically?"

"Well, yeah, I guess so."

"Okay," she said, stretching out the word.

"He told me his name. P'aldil. He is the one who lost the arm."

"How do you know that?"

"He told me. And he also told me that it would grow back."

"He's probably right about that." She laughed. "Wait, what am I saying? It was a dream. What else did he tell you?"

"He asked why we are here, and I told him we are searching for oil. He seemed to know what that was and had a word for it. '*Hinu*,' which I just happen to remember. He said they just wanted us to go away and leave them alone."

She nodded. "You can hardly blame them. What else?"

"That he has fry and a mate and that they have been together for a long time."

"Really? That's interesting. Did he say how long?"

"I think he said for seven generations. So, depending, I guess, on how often they reproduce, it could be years."

"That could be decades. The carbon dating should give us a good idea of its age. If that were true, then they would be a new species that is iteroparous."

Gusman paused, trying to remember what that meant. She put her hand on his knee.

"That means that the females live after they give birth."

"Oh, right," he said distractedly.

"Anyway, it seemed so real. Like the other dreams, but more matter-of-fact."

"Dreams can be so strange sometimes."

"He spoke of dreams as if dreams were the basic state of their reality. He said something about the 'first' dream. It was almost as if dreams were a measure of time."

"How did it end?"

"He said something about how one of his fry was getting too close to what he called a 'smoker' and that he had to go."

"Wow," she said quietly.

"I don't want this to sound crazy. But is it possible that the creature was really communicating with me?"

"Not in any way that can be explained by the present state of science. But then, you seemed to react when I poked something sharp into the creature's severed arm. That can't be explained, either, but we know that it happened."

He locked his eyes on hers.

"Anna, I'm really scared that I'm losing my grip on reality."

She reached across the space between them and put her arms around him. He hesitated for a second then put his arms around her, surrendering to the embrace. It was a gesture of pure human kindness and it comforted him in a way that he had not felt for a very long time.

Chapter 33

The Above: Platform Faith

Anna walked into the mess hall and headed for a table in the back. She carried her laptop and planned to complete her report on her examination of the creature's severed arm. Given all that had happened, she was debating how open she should really be with her opinions. Should she say anything about Gusman? The possibility she might be the first scientist to document the discovery of a new and important species of intelligent life was thrilling. She hardly dared think about it: the book deals, the fat research grants, the job offers. Hell, why not the Nobel Prize and her own research institute? On the other hand, it felt as if a pervasive aura of fear infected every corner of Platform Faith. She saw it on the faces of the crew and on Gusman's face as well. She knew in her bones that the death of Drake was somehow linked to the appearance of the creatures, but she had no idea how.

Distracted by these thoughts, she didn't notice the three crew members sitting at a table near the door. They were young and had the hungry, predatory, and resentful look that men sometimes get around attractive — and off-limits — women.

She sat at a table in the back and opened her laptop, then got up to go make herself some tea. As she walked back, she saw that one of the crew was now sitting at a table near hers staring at her. She hadn't notice him come in. She felt uncomfortable, exposed.

"Hi," she said, trying to sound calm and unthreatened. *The games of dangerous higher primates*, she thought.

He suddenly moved his chair out, blocking her. The chair leg made a loud screech as it slid across the floor. He was tall and strongly built. He was also good looking and, by the expression on his face, he knew it.

"Why would you want to sit there all by your lonesome when you could sit with me?" he asked, his smile crooked and forced.

She felt fear in pit of her stomach, the fear every woman lives with when she crosses a deserted parking lot or passes by a group of men who stop their conversation to stare.

Anna tried to remain calm, but her adrenalin was running. She was scared.

"I'd love to, but I have work to do. If you'll excuse me."

To her own ear, her voice sounded shrill and loud. She tried to walk around the man, but he stuck his arm out.

"Please, let me pass," she said in a monotone.

The man licked his lips. It was a frankly and obscenely provocative gesture. Anna's mouth went dry as her fear exploded.

"Why are you so stuck up? That ain't the way Mexican girls act where I come from."

He laughed, and the others did, too.

She knew she had to run, but as she turned to do so, he put his hand firmly on her shoulder to yank her back.

Then someone out of her view yelled, "What the fuck are you doing?"

The big man let go of Anna's shoulder and turned around just in time to meet Gusman's fist with his chin. There was a sickening thud and the anger vanished from his eyes as he teetered like a drunk and staggered back onto the table, his hand cradling his chin. The other two men seemed to shrink back into their chairs like they were trying to melt into the wall.

The man stood up and shook his head. "Shit, Gusman, why'd ya go and do that?" He sounded genuinely hurt.

"What the fuck is wrong with you, Jones?" asked Gusman, pushing past him and draping his arm over Anna's shoulders. She was shaking.

Jones looked at them with a puzzled look in his eyes as if he had never seen Anna Campos before.

"Who's she?"

"Are you shitting me?" Gusman said. "You must be punch drunk."

"Well, I don't know who she is, that's all."

"She's working here now."

"Okay, but why did you hit me?"

"Because you were harassing her. I had to stop you."

Jones looked puzzled. "I don't know what you're talking about. I never saw this lady before."

Jones sounded sincere.

Anna said quietly into Gusman's ear, "Let's get out of here."

—— «» ——

"Drink this," Gusman said, handing Anna a shot glass of whiskey.

She was seated on the edge of his bed, looking not at him but straight ahead, her legs pressed together defensively. She was fighting the urge to cry, from fear and humiliation caused by the encounter, and the sudden escape from it.

Anna took the glass, grimaced at the thought of downing it, and then, with her eyes closed and her head tilted up, drank it in one quick gulp.

She coughed, and her face turned bright red.

"Awful," she said, shooting the hand that held the shot glass straight out, elbow locked, waiting for Gusman to take it away.

He obliged.

"Oh," she murmured as the alcohol hit her stomach and, then "Oh" again, this time a little louder as it began to be absorbed into her blood and hit her brain.

"I guess you don't drink much."

"Not that kind of thing."

"It was a special occasion."

"You told me that you weren't allowed to have alcohol here," she said.

"That doesn't mean I don't keep some around for emergencies," he replied.

She laughed — the first time since the incident with Jones.

He sat down next to her on the bed and gently put his arm around her. She let him.

"Are you okay now?"

"I think so," she said quietly.

He removed his arm. He didn't want her to take it the wrong way. But she moved her body in a way that made it clear she wanted him to leave it there.

"You know what the weird thing is?" he asked.

"There's only one?"

"Okay, let's just say one of the weird things. Jones is a nice kid, a real gentleman. It's way out of character for him to act like that."

"How about you? Is it in character for you to come to the aid of a maiden in distress by slugging a guy twice your size?"

"Not really. I just saw what was going on and reacted without thinking."

She turned and kissed him on the cheek. It was more than a mere peck; it was longer and firmer. A swell of emotion surged up in him, not lust but the stirring of something he had not felt in a long time: that thing you feel when you are falling for someone.

It took him completely by surprise and left him feeling utterly off balance, which seemed to be his normal state lately.

He turned to face her, hesitating before he spoke. "May I kiss you?"

She gave a little laugh and said, "So formal, Gusman. You surprise me." She closed her eyes and then reopened them, the way people do to reset the moment. "Yes," she said quietly.

He bent over and kissed her tenderly. She tasted of whiskey and mint tea. Her lips were soft and full. He kept his eyes open and looked directly into hers. Perhaps they both needed to verify this was really happening — Gusman certainly was having trouble believing it.

Their kiss was awkward and halfway to passionate. They sensed the humor in it and smiled as they parted.

They kissed again. This time they got it right, all the way to passionate and beyond.

Gusman felt good for the first time since he had arrived on Platform Faith.

— «» —

"Gusman?"

Gusman opened his eyes and sat up. Anna was asleep next to him, her breath slow and steady. For a split second, he felt disoriented. What was she doing in his room? Then it came flooding back: the passion, the tenderness — that strange, long-dormant feeling of surrender to overwhelming emotion, the pushing and pulling of their bodies. He leaned over and kissed her gently on the shoulder. She stirred but did not wake.

"Gusman?" The voice was everywhere but nowhere.

"I'm here, P'aldil," Gusman replied. He was not speaking; it was just in his head. *How?*

"You are with another creature like you."

"Yes. How do you know?"

"Gusman, I see what you see."

"Oh, wow. How weird is that?"

P'aldil ignored the question. "Is it a female?"

"Yes. Her name is Anna."

"Anna," P'aldil repeated slowly, pronouncing each sound as if he was savoring it.

"You have tender feelings for this female."

"Is that a question, P'aldil, or a statement?"

"I don't understand."

"Forget it."

"She is already part of your Dream."

"What dream? What are you talking about?"

"The Dream you share with this female called Anna."

"Whatever." Gusman sounded irritated. If P'aldil noticed, he did not let on.

"Gusman?"

"Yes."

"You mated with Anna, didn't you?"

"Um... yes."

"How long will it take before your fry are born?"

Gusman laughed.

"With any luck, P'aldil, there will be no fry."

"You mate, but then hope no fry are born. You are very strange creatures."

"No, we're not," said Gusman, sounding childish even to his own ears. "Well, maybe we are."

"Gusman, I have something to tell you."

"What?"

"Your kind must leave our kind alone or the Dream will fill with death."

— «» —

Gusman woke with a start. Anna was asleep next to him. He leaned over and kissed her gently on the shoulder. He felt odd, like he had done that exact same thing before, like déjà vu.

Chapter 34

The Above: Platform Faith

Gusman stood at the safety rail, not far from where he and Nancy had stood less than a week earlier. It seemed like a lifetime ago. The sky was cloudless and blue, the sea calm and flat to the horizon. His stomach was anything but calm; he felt jittery and on the edge of panic.

Maybe even over the edge.

Any way he looked at it, he was fucked. Minimally, he could kiss his career goodbye. Undoubtedly, the company would toss him for refusing to cooperate with an FBI investigation. How that arrogant son of a bitch from the FBI would handle it was anyone's guess. But getting indicted for murder was a distinct possibility.

At least there was one bright spot. Anna. She was smart and beautiful, and he was supposed to meet her in fifteen minutes.

He watched some albatrosses do dive bombing runs near the edge of one of the enormous pontoons that kept Platform Faith afloat. They were awkward when they tried to waddle on land, but extraordinarily graceful in flight. He wondered how they acquired their nickname 'gooney bird.'

Suddenly, he sensed a shadow at the periphery of his vision and a change in air pressure. It made the hair rise on his neck.

He turned.

"Andy?" he said, startled.

Andy Noguchi was walking rapidly toward Gusman, a far-off look in his eyes. He did not respond to or even seem to notice Gusman. He was barefoot, unshaven, and his clothes were disheveled. As he came up next to Gusman, the overpowering odor of Noguchi's unwashed body invaded his nostrils.

"Andy," he said again, "are you okay?"

Noguchi did not slow down or turn his head. He locked his hands on the rail, holding on so firmly that his hands turned red. Then Noguchi started to pitch forward.

Gusman realized what was happening and tried to grab him.

"Andy!" he screamed, the "eeeee" sound stretching as Noguchi's body accelerated forward. He managed to grab hold of one arm and the fabric of Noguchi's pants leg.

It was too late.

Noguchi tumbled over the rail, his legs locked, his body stiff. He uttered some guttural word Gusman could not understand. Then Gusman lost his grip on Noguchi's arm. He held onto his pants for a split-second longer, which began to rip as the full weight of Noguchi's body became committed to the fall.

Then Noguchi was airborne, pulling Gusman hard to the rail and breaking his grip.

Noguchi fell, flipped once, and landed on the pontoon with a sickening thud, then slipped into the ocean. Immediately, his body was set upon by a school of sharks, as if they had been waiting there, anticipating the arrival of food. They tore at the corpse and the water near Noguchi turned briefly pinkish amid the swirling frenzy.

Gusman stood transfixed, watching in disbelief. He shook his head slowly back and forth, then turned and faced the empty platform.

He began to bellow the word "Help" in a deep, guttural cry.

Over and over again.

Chapter 35

The Above: Platform Faith

Chuck Harple's mouth was dry and butterflies had settled in his stomach. He reached for the bottle of water on the desk and finished it, crumpling it up and throwing it toward the wastebasket. He missed. He sighed and stood up, picking the plastic bottle off the floor, and carefully dropping it this time into the wastebasket. Somehow, the moment seemed pregnant with meaning. Reaching both hands to the small of his back, he massaged his spine, which was stiff and sore. He closed his eyes and swung his head in circles, first clockwise, then reversing directions. He felt little cracks and pops in his neck.

His mouth was already dry again.

Harple had felt out of sorts the moment he landed on Platform Faith. At first, he thought it was jet lag. Then after the first few days, he thought perhaps it was stress. Now he was wondering if he was coming down with something. In any case, he seemed to be feeling worse with every passing hour. To top it off, he wasn't sleeping well, and he was having these wild, disturbing nightmares.

He sat down and stared at the blinking icon on his laptop screen. The situation was a complete mess. When he arrived, there was one dead body; now there were two. He couldn't believe Gusman was a murderer, let alone a murderer so brazen that he would kill again after law enforcement had arrived to investigate the first possible homicide. Yet there was strong circumstantial evidence tying Gusman to both possible homicides.

First there was Drake. Although the evidence was confused and inconclusive, there were only two stark choices for the cause of death: suicide or homicide. Gusman had motive — he loathed Drake and Drake loathed him — and access. His conduct had been erratic. He refused to talk.

Then there was the death of Andy Noguchi.

He glanced at the yellow legal pad lying next to his laptop. Line after line of his small neat writing: the chronology of events, the questions to be answered, checklists of things he needed to do. There were no doodles, no cross-outs. He was a neat and orderly man trying to make sense of one very disorderly world.

Harple pressed the icon that played the video clip from the security camera. For something like the hundredth time, he watched the black-and-white image of Andy Noguchi walking up to the rail next to Gusman, Gusman engaging Noguchi in a brief conversation, and then appearing to push Noguchi over the rail. Unfortunately, the image of the two men was at the far corner of the camera frame, partly obscured by shadows from the platform's superstructure. The image needed enhancement and his laptop did not have that capability. That would have to wait for the technicians at the FBI's laboratory.

Harple pushed the top of the laptop down and stood again. He knew what he needed to do. He had cleared it with his superiors. But he couldn't help but feel it was wrong.

He sat heavily on the bed, his weariness so profound it made his shoulders feel like weights were resting on them. He lay back, not even bothering to take off his shoes. Sleep came fast.

And then the dreams began.

He awoke with a start, disoriented, expecting to be in his bed in his apartment, momentarily confused as to where he was. The last images of the dream were still there — the strange undulating creature named P'aldil calmly talking to him — urging him... no, *all of them*, to leave Platform Faith. Then, in the rush of retuned consciousness, the dream images faded, and he was in his reality.

But the name — P'aldil — stayed in his head.

Who was P'aldil?

He looked at his watch. Two hours had passed. Shit, he

thought, he needed to find Morrissey and confront Gusman. How could he have let himself fall asleep?

He stood up, perhaps too quickly, and had to steady himself on the desk with his hand. He looked down at the yellow pad, and in large letters scrawled across the bottom of the page in his own writing were the words 'go away.'

Chapter 36

The Above: Platform Faith

Gusman felt a wave of dizziness and cupped his head in his hands. His temples were tender to the touch.

"You need a glass of water, son?" Morrissey asked, patting his shoulder.

"No, I'm okay. Just give me a few seconds."

Nobody said anything. They were waiting for Gusman's signal that he was ready to start.

Perhaps a minute passed, then Gusman slapped his hands onto his thighs and lifted his gaze to face his interrogators, inhaling a big gulp of air.

"Alright, I'm ready."

Agent Harple said, "Mr. Gusman, I'm afraid that this time I am going to have to read you your rights."

"Okay," Gusman responded quietly.

The FBI agent removed a small card from his pocket and began to read. *"You have the right to remain silent. Anything you say can and will be used against you in a court of law. You have the right to an attorney. If you cannot afford an attorney, one will be provided for you. Do you understand the rights I have just read to you?"*

Gusman cleared his throat. "Yes," he said quietly.

"With these rights in mind, do you wish to speak to me?"

"Yes."

"All right then. Mr. Gusman, tell us what happened with Mr. Noguchi?"

"He walked up next to me and jumped over the side. That's what happened."

"You didn't push him?"

"No, I did not," Gusman responded.

"Take a look at this." Harple opened the laptop that was sitting on the table. When it lit up, the frozen image of Gusman at the Platform's railing came into view. He turned the laptop so it faced Gusman and started the video.

As Gusman watched the video, Morrissey and Harple stared at Gusman's face, which twitched once but was otherwise drawn and expressionless.

When it was over, Gusman looked up.

"It's not what you think."

"You pushed him over, Gusman. Why did you do it?" Harple's tone was urgent, but without anger.

"Look, you have to believe me. I did not hurt Andy Noguchi. There was something wrong with him. He jumped."

"We also know that you were in his cabin last week. One of the crew members walked by and heard you arguing."

Gusman stood, his face now flushed red. "I've had enough of this. I'm leaving."

Morrissey rose, positioning his large frame between the Gusman and the door.

Harple said, "Sit down, Mr. Gusman. You're not going anywhere."

"I'm not free to leave?"

"No, you are not."

Morrissey said quietly, "Come on, son. Sit yourself down." He touched Gusman on the shoulder softly, but firmly.

Gusman sat.

"It's time that you tell us what happened with Drake and Noguchi."

Gusman looked at Morrissey. "Do you think I did it, Morrissey?"

"It doesn't matter what I think," he responded quietly.

Gusman shook his head from side to side then looked up at Agent Harple. "Fine. Then I have nothing more to say until I can speak with a lawyer."

Harple and Morrissey did not respond. In the heavy silence that followed, all that could be heard was the sound of breathing and the ever-present hum of Platform Faith.

Finally, Harple said, "That's your right, Mr. Gusman. However, I'm going to have to place you under arrest. You will be held in a secure cabin until I can arrange your transportation to the mainland."

The FBI agent rose again and walked behind Gusman.

"Well, Mr. Gusman, do you wish to continue?"

"I'm done here."

"Have it your way. Please stand so I can search you."

Gusman stood, shooting Morrissey the dark and frightened look of a man who feels betrayed.

When Harple was finished relieving Gusman of his personal possessions — wallet, keys, a scrap of paper, his watch — he brought his hands behind his back and, with a pair of black plastic handcuffs that he seemed to produce from nowhere, bound Gusman's wrists together.

His humiliation was now complete.

Chapter 37

The Above: Platform Faith

Gusman paced the room like a caged animal. They had locked him in a secure room in the infirmary. The room was empty except for a hospital bed, a chair, a sink, and a toilet. Within fifteen minutes of being locked up, he was bored out of his mind, not to mention angry, frustrated, and frightened. Couldn't they have left him with a book or a magazine to help pass the time?

Eventually he lay down on the bed and fell asleep, exhaustion and boredom taking over.

He began to dream.

— «» —

It was Morrissey's idea to place a small hidden camera in the room where they were holding Gusman. Initially, Special Agent Harple opposed the idea, concerned that a court might find any evidence they obtained would be tainted and ruled inadmissible — the fruit of the poisonous tree. But he relented. Although Morrissey did not say it, Harple had the distinct sense that Morrissey thought Gusman was innocent. Despite the mounting evidence, so did Harple — and maybe that's why he agreed to the camera.

Harple and Morrissey took turns watching the monitor. He had already crossed the line when he allowed Morrissey, who was no longer a law enforcement officer, to participate in an interrogation. He knew he was compounding the error, but Harple rationalized it away because Morrissey was ex-Bureau and promised not to act without his express approval.

It was Harple's turn to watch Gusman on the laptop they had set up in Harple's improvised little office. There wasn't much to watch. Gusman was asleep. He lay on his back, his mouth slack and slightly open, breathing deeply and regularly. Harple thumbed through some old magazines, looking back occasionally at his sleeping prisoner.

Then Gusman began to talk in his sleep. Harple dropped the magazine and stared intently at the screen, pushing the ear buds he was wearing deeper into his ear canals. Most of what Gusman was saying was unintelligible, but it was clear from the gaps between sentences and the inflection of his voice, that Gusman was having a conversation with someone.

Harple heard Gusman say something that sent a bolt of electricity through his brain, causing him to sit upright in his chair.

It was one word and it wasn't in English.

P'aldil.

Later Harple would replay the video over and over.

The single word 'P'aldil.' Or, rather, as Harple well knew — the *name* P'aldil.

Chapter 38

The Above: Platform Faith

Anna Campos looked everywhere for Gusman, but it was like he had vanished. She went to the mess hall and asked several of the crew members if they had seen him. One of them smiled and with a smarmy grin said, "I'm sure he'll turn up for *you*, darlin'."

Asshole.

She went to Morrissey's office and knocked on the door.

"Come in," came a booming voice from inside.

She opened the door and Morrissey looked up from his desk, his face puffy and thick, like he'd had a rough night. His jowls slowly transformed into a smile. His eyes were hard and gave lie to the smile.

"Hello, professor. What can I do you for?"

"I'm looking for Mr. Gusman. I can't find him anywhere."

Anna was trying to sound matter-of-fact, but Morrissey wasn't buying. His smile widened into something genuine, if entirely predatory. A thousand interrogations told Morrissey that this woman was soft on Gusman. He'd bet his fat federal pension that the two of them had slept together.

"I haven't seen him, either. Why?"

"He is assisting me in the lab and he never showed. I've looked for him everywhere and I can't find him. Ever since that poor guy, Mr. ...?"

"Noguchi?"

"Yes. Ever since Mr. Noguchi fell over the side, I've been worried. I mean what if something happened to Gusman?"

"Have you seen Gusman since that incident?"

"No. That's what I'm saying. He didn't show up. It's like he disappeared."

"He's fine, Dr. Campos."

"Where is he?" she asked.

"I'm sorry. I cannot discuss that with you."

"What have you done with him?" She stepped forward and put her hands on his desk, leaning in. The move was aggressive, and Morrissey was taken aback. His smile vanished.

"Little Missy, you need to calm yourself down."

"Don't patronize me, Mr. Morrissey. Just tell me what I need to know. Where's Gusman?"

Morrissey leaned back in his chair and crossed his arms. She was a hard case and Morrissey had grudging respect for tough women.

"You need to talk to Special Agent Harple."

"Thanks," she said flatly, turning quickly for the door.

She didn't see Morrissey smile and shake his head in admiration.

Fiery little thing, he thought.

— «» —

Anna Campos finally spotted Special Agent Harple outside the communications room. Even from fifty yards, Harple was unmistakable: blond crew cut, blue windbreaker, pressed khaki pants. She had been all over the platform, and by the time she found him, her anger and frustration were at a fever pitch. She wanted answers and she wanted them now.

"Hey!" she yelled.

She closed the distance between them with long, purposeful strides, her runner's muscular frame propelling her forward like an angry predator.

Harple turned around and, seeing Anna Campos coming at him, unconsciously brought himself to his full height. It was a defensive move.

She stopped, shook her finger at him, and said, "Where's Gusman?"

"Excuse me, Professor Campos. Is that how you talk to people?" Harple was trying to sound calm but he was put off balance by her aggressive stance and they both knew it.

"Spare me the bullshit. Where's Gusman? Morrissey won't tell me, and he says you know."

"Ma'am, all I will tell you is that Mr. Gusman is in custody. Beyond that, there is nothing more I can discuss with you." He turned around and started to walk away.

Out of desperation and a wild guess, Anna blurted out, "Hey, Agent Harple, how's your friend P'aldil?"

The FBI agent stopped in mid-stride and whipped back around. "What did you say?"

"P'aldil, Agent Harple. Have you met him?"

"What do you know about that?" he said in a quiet, terse voice.

"A lot," she replied, lying.

"You need to tell me what you know."

"Not until you let me see Gusman." It was Anna's turn to play hardball. She turned and walked away.

"You come back here, Dr. Campos. We're not done."

She stopped and turned around, laughing. "What are you going to do, arrest me? You take me to see Gusman and then we'll talk about the voices in your head."

Anna Campos once again turned her back on the FBI agent and strode down the hall, a smile on her face.

Hooked.

It was a wild guess, but somehow it had worked.

— «» —

Special Agent Harple and Anna Campos stood outside the door of Gusman's improvised holding cell.

"Dr. Campos. Please empty your pockets. I will need to pat you down."

"Oh, good God," she said, rolling her eyes. But she complied.

When the pat down was done, Harple said, "You have ten minutes."

"Fine," Anna answered.

"When I knock on that door, you will come out. No arguments."

She leveled her gaze at him, unintimidated. "Okay. I get it."

Harple knocked on the door. "Gusman, this is Special Agent Harple. I'm opening the door. You have a visitor. Please stand back."

Given their earlier confrontation, Harple's courteous tone sounded odd to Anna.

When the door opened, Gusman was standing there, exactly where he wasn't supposed to be. Harple started to say something, but just shook his head and stepped out of the way as Anna swept past him into Gusman's arms.

Special Agent Harple quietly closed the door behind them, locking it.

Their embrace was long and tight, and they forgot everything for the moment: the deaths, the inexplicable events, the murder accusation. They forgot everything but the intensity of their feelings toward one another, which had developed with amazing velocity. They barely knew each other, but they were going through an ordeal together and it had sped everything up. Their embrace lasted longer than it should have and ended only when Gusman whispered in her ear — another surprise — "I love you."

She pulled back and looked in his eyes. "Do you?" she asked.

He seemed startled by what he had just uttered. "I think so," he responded and they both laughed at the craziness of it all.

Then they hugged again, and he kissed her tenderly, stroking her long, black hair.

"Are you getting enough to eat?" she asked, laughing.

"No, that's not what you're supposed to say. What you're supposed to say is, 'Here is a birthday cake which you can eat later.' Of course, there will be a file baked inside of it."

"I did that. I baked a cake with a file in it, but our FBI friend became suspicious and said, 'No baked goods.'"

"Darn," he said. "I'll have to figure out another way out of here."

They laughed. He sat down on the bed and patted it, motioning her to sit next to him.

She sat down, and he put his arm around her, whispering in her ear, "There's a camera behind us in the corner and they're recording this, so watch what you say." Anna nodded and then kissed him on the cheek. It was a light and fluffy little peck, utterly unmatched to the gravity of their situation and, perhaps, in open defiance of it.

As she pulled away, she whispered to him, "Harple has met P'aldil."

— «» —

Chuck Harple sprinted back to his makeshift office to observe Gusman and Anna Campos. He took out his key, but when he placed his hand on the handle, it was unlocked. Entering, he found Morrissey sitting in his chair, feet up, watching the screen. Bobby Smith stood behind him, his cowboy hat back on his head, staring at the screen.

They both looked up.

Harple stopped mid-stride.

"What are you doing here?" he asked. It was more an accusation than a question.

"Settle down, Special Agent," Smith growled. "This is our oil platform and we have every right to be here. The better question is, why are you letting that woman talk to your prisoner?"

Harple did not speak immediately but cocked his head ever so slightly — like a dog picking up a scent and not liking what he smelled.

"Sir, I am asking you to leave now. Both of you." His voice was a slow burn.

"Come on, Chuck," Morrissey said affably, waving his arm loosely to show they meant no harm. "There's no need to get upset. Hell, we're not trying to take over your investigation. But as long as we're here, we'd like to see what Gusman has to say to the girl."

The FBI agent was having none of it. He opened the door and motioned for them to leave.

There was an ugly silence that followed while they all waited for someone to blink. Finally, Smith stood up slowly. He turned his hooded eyes to Harple and then smiled in a way so malevolent that Chuck Harple felt a lump of bile rising from his stomach. The words that followed came out slow and low.

"Son, we're going to do as you ask. But I think you have very seriously mishandled this situation. You need to think about that."

"Yes, sir," Harple said, standing his ground.

The two older men swept past him. Bobby Smith made no eye contact, but Morrissey did. He winked.

Harple shut the cabin door and locked it behind him. He sat down to watch Gusman and Dr. Campos. But all he saw was their backs. They were whispering to one another quietly. After a few minutes, Gusman turned around and, looking up at the camera, said, "Hey, Harple, you can come back and let Anna out now."

— «» —

The Below

"What has happened to Gusman?" P'aldil wonders.

"They have sequestered him," M'aldil says. It is an odd word, one from far back in the Dream. It carries the sense of casting out, an old He'e punishment from the far-gone time when some He'e acted in ways harmful to others. "I don't understand. Has Gusman harmed others? Does he need to be kept away from the rest of his urb?"

P'aldil says nothing for an eighth of a hunger. His arms lashing in worry tell the story. Finally, he looks at M'aldil. "The creatures in the Above seem pupule, not possessed of a full mind."

"To me they all seem pupule. Will they harm Gusman?"

P'aldil says nothing. His arms again thrash as if to say for him that we He'e must do something before another hunger passes.

Chapter 39

The Above: New York City

Enrique Gonzales wanted answers. Real answers. And he wanted them now. Things had spun out of control so quickly that the homicides or suicides or whatever the hell was happening *on* Platform Faith seemed to pale in comparison to the bizarre reports he was getting about what was happening *beneath* his oil platform.

He had just finished reading the preliminary report from the biologist, Dr. Campos. What had emerged from the ocean and interacted with his oil workers was, incredibly, a new species of giant octopus. The report also suggested intelligence, not just the ordinary mental and physical dexterity all octopuses display — but a much higher degree of intelligence than had ever been observed in an aquatic, non-mammalian species. The report — though carefully worded — suggested this new species of octopus behaved in a manner that demonstrated that it was "fully self-aware, on a par with the most intelligent mammals on the planet." Self-aware! Smart as whales or elephants or chimps! Perhaps even as smart as humans? That two of the creatures ascended in what appeared to be a manufactured craft was evidence of an advanced social structure. As if this wasn't enough, the carbon dating of the tissue samples from the severed limb of the cephalopod indicated that it was somewhere between twenty-seven and thirty years old. Much older than the lifespan of any known cephalopod species. Old enough for it to develop advanced intelligence and gain experiential knowledge and then pass that knowledge on to others of the species.

Gonzales feared — no, he knew — that that information itself, were it to become known to the public, would bring drilling activity on Platform Faith to a grinding and indefinite halt as legions of scientists and journalists would invade Platform Faith to study the creatures, write about them, and make endless documentaries. And it would, no doubt, give the environmentalists a new *cause célèbre* with which to beat the oil industry over its collective head.

Though the tone was dry and scientific, it was hard to miss the underlying excitement in Dr. Campos' report. Gonzales winced every time she used the adjectives 'major,' 'important,' and 'new.'

The report was a problem. Dr. Campos was a problem.

Gonzales looked at his watch. It was time. He walked over to his desk, flipped up the screen of his laptop, and keyed in the password that initiated the secure video conferencing line. The craggy face of Bobby Smith appeared on the screen.

"Hello, boss," Smith said.

"Hi, Bobby," replied Gonzales in a monotone. "I've read the report of that biologist we sent out there."

"So have I. It's a problem." Smith's voice was low and gravelly.

"An enormous problem. We can't afford any further interruptions in the flow of oil from that platform. It cannot become public that there's some new species down there."

"It would be a media circus."

"And then there's the matter of the buckyball findings."

"Yes."

"I've ordered a manned submersible be brought to Platform Faith with orders to descend to the seafloor and deal with the situation."

Smith did not immediately respond as the implications of Gonzales's words hit home. "Who is the contractor?"

"Ironstone."

Smith smiled. He knew them well. Ex-navy SEALs. Very quiet, very tough, hard as nails. Useful for sensitive missions. They had contracted with them once in West Africa to eliminate a piracy problem. In and out in one week, problem eliminated.

"They will take care of it," said Gonzales.

"Understood."

"There is another matter. The biologist. Obviously, we need to obtain an agreement that she will keep the information in strictest confidence."

"Didn't she sign our standard confidentiality agreement?"

"She did, but we are asking her to sit on the discovery of a lifetime. What are we going to do? Sue her? The blowback would be unacceptable."

"So, what are we supposed to do?"

"I'm sending you an addendum to her agreement. It will ask her specifically not to reveal any information about those creatures. We will be offering her a lot of money to buy her silence."

"And if she refuses?"

"That is not an option."

There was a long pause while both men took stock of the situation.

"How far am I supposed to go?" Smith asked.

"As far as necessary," Gonzales responded. There was no hesitation.

"No bright lines?"

"None."

Smith paused before he spoke. "Understood."

"Anything else?" asked Gonzales, clearly wanting to terminate the conversation.

"Well, actually, there is something else."

"What more could there possibly be?" Gonzales asked, incredulous.

"I think the FBI agent could be a problem."

"What kind of problem? I thought he was completely under control."

"He was, but I don't think he is any longer."

"Goddamn it, Bobby!" Gonzales was yelling. "You need to get the situation on that fucking platform handled. Do I make myself clear?"

The screen went blank before Bobby Smith had a chance to answer.

Chapter 40

The Above: Platform Faith

Chuck Harple stood outside the door to Dr. Campos' cabin, trying to compose himself.

Try good cop.

He held his fist up to the door to knock, then reconsidered and rapped gently with one knuckle instead.

"Who's there?" she said.

"Dr. Campos, it's Chuck Harple." He tried keeping his tone light and friendly.

She wasn't buying it. "You woke me up."

"I'm very sorry..."

"I bet," she said acerbically.

"Dr. Campos, please open the door. It's important I talk to you." He heard her emit a hard, frustrated breath and then she opened the door. Without saying a word, she stood to the side and gestured for him to come in.

"Thank you," he said. "I appreciate that." He swept past her, then stood uncomfortably in the middle of the small cabin, stooping slightly because of his height.

She pulled out the desk chair and sat down.

He had no choice but to sit on the bed, his legs in front of him and his hands resting on his knees. It was an awkward, childlike posture. It had the effect of placing him at a physical disadvantage, as if he were a naughty schoolboy waiting to be reprimanded. He had the distinct impression that she knew exactly what she was doing.

"So, what do you want?" she asked in a tone that made it more of an indictment than a question.

"You know very well what I want to know, Doctor Campos. I held up my end of the bargain and now you need to hold up yours. Before we start, there's something I need to say to you. I'm not here to railroad Mr. Gusman or falsely accuse him of a crime."

"Then why is he under arrest?"

"That's a fair question. There is sufficient evidence — probable cause — to believe Mr. Gusman may have committed a crime. But that doesn't necessarily mean he is guilty or will ever be charged. In fact, what you say could be exculpatory evidence that could lead to his release." He kept his tone level and tried to smile benevolently.

"So, what do you want to know?" she asked.

"Who or what is P'aldil?"

"One of the creatures that surfaced — the one that lost his arm. At least that's what Gusman says."

"How does he know the creature's name?"

"I know it sounds crazy, but he says that he's been having these dreams in which P'aldil communicates with him."

Anna noticed that Harple seemed to physically recoil at the word 'dreams.'

"And you believe that?" he asked.

She stared at him straight in the eyes for a long time before answering. "Well, if you'll bear with me, let me try to answer that by telling you about something that happened when we were examining the severed arm of the creature. Every time I touched the flesh of the specimen with my scalpel, Gusman felt pain."

"What did you say?"

"Well," she repeated slowly, "Gusman felt an extreme pain in his head every time I poked the scalpel into P'aldil's arm."

Harple drew back, cocking his head.

"I don't think Gusman was faking the pain he felt, nor do I think he is lying about the dreams he's having."

"Tell me about his dreams."

"Well, he said that he has been having dreams about P'aldil in which the creature communicates with him."

"I know that you have developed a..." Harple paused, choosing his words carefully. "Personal relationship with

Mr. Gusman. But I must ask you: in light of what you have just told me, do you think he's mentally stable?"

"Well, he is under a lot of stress, but he has not acted irrationally around me. The point is, there are many phenomena in the natural world that we don't understand, and it is pure hubris to think otherwise."

"Yes..." Harple said, the word trailing off into silence.

"May I ask you a question?"

"Go ahead," he responded.

"Chuck... may I call you that?"

"Yes," he said, knowing full well that allowing her to call him by his first name changed the balance of power between them.

"Have you seen P'aldil in your dreams?"

Agent Harple looked down at his lap. He didn't answer for a while and Anna waited in silence, the ever-present hum of the ventilation system filling the void.

Finally, he said, "Yes."

Chapter 41

The Above: Platform Faith

Harple stared at the image of a pacing Gusman on the computer screen. He had spent the past several hours in vigorous debate with himself, but had finally decided he had to confront Gusman. He turned the camera off and watched the screen go dark.

Harple headed for the infirmary and Gusman. He took a circuitous route, not wanting to be seen.

He knocked on the door of Gusman's improvised jail cell.

"What is it?" asked Gusman, his voice angry and tremulous.

"Mr. Gusman, it's Special Agent Harple. I'm coming in. I need you to sit on the bed with your hands out in front of you."

He waited. "Are you sitting on the bed, Mr. Gusman?"

"Yeah," replied Gusman loudly.

Harple could tell from the way Gusman's voice sounded that he was away from the door.

"Stay where you are, I'm coming in." The FBI agent unlocked the door and carefully entered, locking it behind him. Gusman was sitting on the bed, as directed, staring at Harple. He said nothing.

Harple pulled a paperback book out of his jacket pocket. He tossed it on the bed. Gusman made no effort to pick it up.

"I thought you might be getting bored," he said, conjuring up a crooked smile.

"I told you I'm not talking to you without a lawyer."

"I understand that, but I have a question that has nothing to do with Drake or Noguchi. This is off the record. Are you willing to answer it?"

Gusman nodded as if to say, "Ask away and I'll see."

"Who is P'aldil?"

Unexpectedly, Gusman laughed. "He's my special little friend."

"It's a serious question, Mr. Gusman. I've talked to Dr. Campos. I know what happened during the examination of the creature's arm."

"What do you mean?"

"Dr. Campos said you felt pain when she prodded the arm with her scalpel."

"Yes," he responded ambiguously.

"The creature's name is P'aldil, correct?"

Gusman did not answer the question, but asked one. "What else do you know?"

"That you had dreams in which you had conversations with P'aldil and that it was his arm that was severed by the flare gun."

"And what else?" Gusman smiled, as if he *knew* already what Harple was about to say next.

Harple started to speak, then hesitated. He began to speak again, but could not utter the words. Then he stayed silent for perhaps thirty seconds, staring at Gusman who stared right back.

"Spit it out, Harple," said Gusman in an acid tone. "You can tell me. I'm your friend. Anyway, I already know what you're going to say."

Harple nodded and cleared his throat. This time, he could get his words out, although they were barely above a whisper. "I dreamed about P'aldil."

"I bet you did. And what did he tell you?"

"To go away."

"Sounds like good advice," Gusman said, laughing.

"Gusman, what is going on here?"

"I don't know. You tell me, Special Agent. You put me in here. You must think I'm a murderer."

"I'm not talking about that. I'm talking about the dreams. I'm talking about the fights. The people are on edge. I've talked to other crew members. They all feel it; there is something happening. What is it, Gusman?"

"Look, everything I say can be used against me. Maybe you're just playing me. Now you're just trying 'good cop' with me. Why should I trust you?"

"That's a fair question. You have no reason to trust me. I'm not your friend and I'm not trying to be. If the evidence proves that you killed Drake or Noguchi, I will do everything in my power to see that you are prosecuted and punished for your crimes. But if the evidence proves that you are innocent, I will be fair to you and you will be freed. That's all I can offer you."

Again, Gusman lapsed into silence. Finally, he said, "Okay, what do you want to know?" He gestured with his chin to a spot high on the wall behind Harple. "I assume you've turned your stupid little camera off."

Harple smiled. "It's off."

"Thank you for not lying to me."

"I didn't think lying would work."

"All right, then what specifically do you want to know?" asked Gusman.

"Who or what is P'aldil?"

"Who do you think he is?"

"I think he is one of the creatures that surfaced last week, the one who lost the arm."

"I agree," responded Gusman.

"And what does he want?"

"They want Clearsea to stop drilling into the middle of their habitat."

"They've stopped, right?"

"For now. The creatures have been able to deploy something down there that is shattering our drill bits."

"Really? Do you have an explanation for it?" asked Harple.

Gusman laughed. "Me? No, I haven't the faintest idea what they could use that would cause a hardened carbide steel drill bit to shatter upon contact. Whatever it is must be very hard — on the order of diamonds. And it would be worth a lot to get a hold of it."

Harple cocked his head. "Hmm," he muttered.

Gusman thought he looked like the old RCA Victor dog listening to his master's voice through an antique gramophone.

"What do you know about a firm called Ironstone?" Harple asked, leveling his gaze.

"I've heard the name but have never dealt with them. I think they do 'sensitive missions' for the industry in the security area."

"What does that mean?"

"Can't you just ask your FBI friends?"

"Yes, but I'm asking you, Mr. Gusman."

"I only know what I hear. They're the guys who clean up the messy shit. When you drill all over the planet, you confront problems — criminal gangs, crooked cops, pain in the ass environmental groups, indigenous people — you know, that sort of thing. Firms like Ironstone know how to play rough but keep it on the down-low."

"They're coming here," said Harple.

"Really? Why?"

"They're sending a submersible down to the bottom. I don't know much beyond that."

"I have a feeling P'aldil and his friends are not going to like that very much."

Chapter 42

The Above: Platform Faith

Smith, Morrissey, and some of the crew members stood at the railing as the converted US Navy minesweeper dropped anchor a quarter mile from the platform. It was painted a shade of gray so dark the ship looked almost black. It had no flag or name painted on its hull. Shooting out from on top of its bridge was an array of antennas and parabolic dishes. Behind the bridge, the deck was flat all the way to the stern of the ship. Near the stern was a marine crane with two large submersibles tethered next to it. They were painted the same dark gray color as the ship. The image it evoked was militaristic, not scientific. Crew members in black jumpsuits moved about the ship with deliberation, ignoring the giant oil platform next to them.

Special Agent Harple walked across the deck to the railing and joined the others. Bobby Smith noticed, but merely nodded coldly. It was the first time he and Morrissey had seen the FBI agent since he had ejected them from his makeshift office.

"Mr. Smith, what's going on here?" Harple asked. "What ship is that?"

"It's an operational matter, Special Agent Harple. I wasn't aware that was within the purview of your investigation."

"It's not, but it would be helpful if you were to let me know if any crew members arrive or leave."

"They are not coming aboard now. If that happens, we'll share the roster with you. If you'll excuse us, Special Agent, we need to get back to work." Smith turned and walked away, Morrissey and the others following him.

Harple felt like he had the plague.

Chapter 43

The Below

M'dat'maunee is no more. She who has been called 'maunee since long before her mate became no more; who — with her mate, P'dat, and now without him — has seen more cycles of fry, more eight-eights of hungers, more descents into the Dream's depths than any other of the He'e in this conurbation, is gone. Why? Because what comes is a thing the length of twice two arms' span, its body like the biggest of true fish, a hard metal like the hardest of the shells the great clams produce.

It swims down from the Above. If it has eyes, none can tell. Its skin is black, like the smokers, and it can barely be seen in the depths of the ocean. Piercing it are transparencies clear as the clearest of the great clams' diamonds, which emit a light so fierce none of the He'e can endure its shine long enough to view what is in the innards of the fish. P'M'aldil has encountered such light in the far, far Above. Their eyes ached for an eight of hungers when P'aldil and M'aldil had returned. The hard, black fish seems as clumsy and obdurate as the stupidest of the muhe'e. It doesn't seek to eat or even attack the He'e. It doesn't even take notice when the most inquisitive of the fry emerge from their seafloor crannies to watch it. It swims without a flick of fins or any jet of water. Something whirls at its tail end, throwing a current backward, and shell-hard fins flex at its sides for it to turn or rise or descend.

P'M'aldil, as Examiners of the Strange, are the first to approach the thing that is not a true fish and watch it traverse the He'es' seafloor conurbation.

"It is of them, isn't it?" M'aldil asks. "Of the ones from the Above. It is not living, but a tool of theirs, in the way we might *take the metallic waste that is filtered by the giant clams living by the smoker called kälä ke'oke'o and shape it with heat to pry or crush."*

"I think so," says P'aldil.

"It is all constructed. None of it grown, is it?" M'aldil asks.

Again, P'aldil says, "I think so." He senses, as if from the Dream, that the huge, false fish has a way of speaking to the ones living in the Above, perhaps not unlike the way he has spoken to the creature called Gusman. He senses that, though it appears blind, it in fact has eyes of a sort and, through those eyes, those Above are watching as it swims among the He'es' dwellings. An orange flicker of his unease runs up P'aldil's arms. M'aldil sees and her own arms flicker. He senses a danger not named or defined. The orange betrays his unease and spreads like an infection among the other He'e observing from their places of concealment. What is this thing? Why has it come?

It noses among the He'es' dwellings, grasping and pulling at them with its strange, angular, metal arms, tearing away chunks of them, baring the once comfortable interiors where the He'e shelter and rest.

At a spot closest to the upwelling hot waters of the smoker is one of the oldest of He'e dwellings, that of M'dat'maunee. In her life of countless eights of hungers, M'dat'maunee has been a collector of the odd and curious. She scoured the ocean bottom for many eights-of-eights travel from the smoker, gathered the shells of rare and beautifully colored benthic snails and bones of the pelagic cuttlefish with their intricate warp of ribs and pure whiteness, objects of glass and now-corroded metal that show signs that they were not grown but fashioned, and of other articles so strange and scarce he had many times asked her to lend them to the Chamber of the Strange. So, she does not move when the fish-thing approaches, senseless and obstinate in its motion toward her and the smoker. In its mindless fashion, an arm of the fish-thing reaches out and grasps at one face of M'dat'maunee's dwelling and begins to pull.

M'aldil sets up a rattle of alarm; her arms thrash, sending up the muck and gravel of the ocean floor, her arms pulsing scarlet, calling, "She is in danger." The other nearby He'e take up the call and the thrashing of alarm until the entire ocean floor is agitated and its muck rises into a cloud above the bottom. In it, the thing moves like a shadow from the Dream. M'dat'maunee will not move and the fish-thing comes on, going irresistibly forward. M'aldil calls to M'dat'maunee, but the elder will still not move. The fish-thing presses into M'dat'maunee. Its force is far beyond what she can resist and all she can do is grasp its nose. Then it pushes forward more until it begins to move out over the up-rushing scald of the smoker. Searing black waters engulf her and the nose of the fish-thing. In the boiling smoke, the nose of the thing bobs upward, pulls back, and swims away. The sweeping upward path of the black smoke feathers out in the cold bottom water — and in it is M'dat'maunee. She is no more, but is one now with P'dat'maunee and the Dream. Beyond what once was P'dat'maunee, the fish-thing circles in the unlit waters seemingly unaware of what damage and death it has caused.

A rushing of arms and a wild rallying cry come from the He'e who still are. Among them, anger is rare. But they are angry now. The push and flash of their horror and fury rides with them as they swarm the fish-thing, rip away its arms, smash clamshells into its whirling tail to stop the motion, and tear away the things the Dream says are its eyes.

They repeatedly drive spiked shafts of kaimana into the bright eyes located on the body of the fish-thing until there is a resounding crash as the eyes disintegrate and the water bursts into its empty insides.

"It's hollow," P'aldil says, a flash of pink wonder on his arms. "The eyes were strong and held out the pressure of the waters. So strong." Inside the fish-thing, the water is hazy with pink clouds that are the leaked fluids of the two creatures inside it. Their life has been crushed out by the pressure, but P'M'aldil can see what they once were, creatures of the Above, of the hinu-seeking platform that rises from the waters into the emptiness Above.

So furious at M'dat'maunee's end that anger overwhelms rationality, the He'e thrash chaotically on the ocean floor. P'M'aldil alone seem to know that the ones inside guided the fish-thing and that it had seemed to be trying to turn before plowing into M'dat'maunee.

"They were trying not to touch her," P'aldil says. "They didn't want to harm her. They were just exploring here as we explored the Above." But in their agitation and anger, none of the He'e except M'aldil hear him or understand.

He knows he must enter the Dream with the one who calls himself Gusman.

Chapter 44

The Above: Aboard the research vessel *Ironstone III*

It happened so fast the crew in the control room monitoring the submersible did not have time to react. In the glare of the powerful lights mounted atop the submersible, the cameras picked up only quickly moving shadows.

Seconds later, one of the two crew members on the submersible yelled, "We're under attack!"

Then they heard the banging noise of something hitting the thick glass of the submersible's small window.

"Oh, God," the other crew member yelled.

Those monitoring from up top watched in slack-mouthed horror as water exploded into the compartment. The two crew members reared up, screaming in agonizing pain as pressure crushed them.

Everything went black.

"The signal's dead. There's no power."

"What are you saying?" asked the other.

"They must have sunk."

Chapter 45

The Above: Platform Faith

Smith and Morrissey sat grim-faced as the captain of the *Ironstone III* finished his report. From New York, Gonzales watched what transpired on the video feed. The captain, Haig, had the square face and hard-set jaw of a military man. His report, delivered in a dispassionate monologue, told of the loss of the submersible and what must have been the instant and horrid deaths of two of his crew members. He had seen death many times; it came with the territory. But beneath the restrained control of the man, there was something in his voice: fear. Raw, unthinking fear. The fear of the unknown.

Morrissey turned his gaze away from Haig to watch Gonzales's reaction. His mouth was tightly drawn and dark lines of stress had formed under his eyes. He looked angry and older than his years.

Gonzales cleared his throat. "Captain Haig, can you send your second submersible down there and deal with it?"

"Come again?" the captain responded, looking genuinely shocked.

"We need the situation dealt with," Gonzales repeated.

"Precisely what do you mean by 'dealt with,' sir?"

"Whatever it is down there... those creatures are dangerous and need to be destroyed. Isn't there an explosive that can be used to neutralize them?"

"We have the capacity to perform underwater demolition, but those things, those octopuses, would be ready for us this time and might be able to move our device away from their habitat. I'm not even sure how we would acquire targets or insure the mission would be accomplished. Essentially, you're asking us to destroy the habitat of a creature we know very little about. We don't know where they live, how protected their habitat is, how many of them are down there, and whether they have the ability to defend themselves."

"For Christ's sake, Captain. They are just big goddamned octopuses. How dangerous can they be?"

"Sir, they are dangerous enough to sink my vessel and kill two of my crew. I'm not aware of a situation where multiple sea creatures have intentionally coordinated an attack on a submarine or other submersible. These creatures penetrated the hull. We have no idea how they did that."

"Mr. Haig, I understand your concerns, but I think you are exaggerating the threat. So, here's what I want, and you tell me whether you can do it. I want you to drop the explosives necessary to destroy everything within a quarter mile radius around the borehole."

"To cover an area of that size, we will need to be resupplied from the mainland. And a quarter mile is way too far. I'm no physicist. I would need somebody to calculate how big a bomb we would need to do any real damage more than five miles down. I'd say anything much smaller than a nuke would have to be right on top of the target."

He saw Gonzales' eyes widen at the mention of a nuclear weapon. "We don't do nukes, sir. Countries do them, we don't."

"Got it," Gonzales said, maybe a bit ruefully. "So, what can you do?"

"Pinpoint it. Hit them dead center with enough charges fast enough to overwhelm them. Planning that will take a couple of days. All of this is contingent on you dealing directly with headquarters and getting their buy-in."

"What kind of damage *can* you do down there?"

"Essentially what we will be doing is dropping the equivalent of depth charges on the ocean floor. Close in, the concussion should kill most anything within the blast radius."

"That's what I want."

"Sir, I think you need call my CEO. I do not have the authority to authorize this kind of an operation."

"I will do that. In the meantime, get your other submersible ready to go."

"Yes, sir."

"And when you complete this operation, your mission for us will be done. You will then leave the area immediately."

A thin smile appeared on the captain's face. "Without delay."

Chapter 46

The Above: Off Platform Faith

Resupplied and orders clarified, the crew of the *Ironstone III* worked steadily through the night adding the necessary modifications to their remaining submersible. Welding sparks flew when they rigged racks on sides that would allow them to deploy explosives. The charges were packed into surplus NATO naval mines, which looked like flattened beer kegs. They had time fuses so that after they were dropped, the submersible could be well out of range of the shock waves when they detonated.

The last step, which the crew finished just as a reddish sun rose over the horizon, was to load the four mines onto the submersible. The mines, designed to sit in a static position on the ocean floor, were extremely heavy and had to be winched in place. The fuses were then attached.

At 0700 Captain Haig gave the orders for the two-man crew to board. There was no joking, no backslapping. Nearly everyone on board was a combat veteran and, since the loss of the first submersible, the mission had taken on the gravity of a wartime operation. Indeed, so fearful was the captain of another attack that he ordered the *Ironstone III* to drop the mines from a full 150 meters above the seafloor and then surface immediately.

The crews of both the *Ironstone III* and Platform Faith stood at their respective railings as the crane lifted the submersible over the side and lowered it slowly to the surface. The swells were gentle and, when the submersible was untethered, it bobbled for only a few moments on the surface before it slid silently under the waves.

Everyone returned to their duties. Aboard Platform Faith, the loss of the first submersible was a closely guarded secret. No one knew about it except Smith and Morrissey. It was a different story on the *Ironstone III* and the crew waited anxiously while the second submersible descended to the bottom.

Three hours later, the crew of the submersible reported that they were in position. Captain Haig hesitated. His gut told him that this was wrong, that dropping explosives was a huge mistake. That something terrible would result. He knew from a lifetime of confronting danger that his gut was rarely wrong and that he ignored it at his own peril. Still, he could find no justification to abort the mission, so he gave the order for the crew to commence.

The two men aboard the submersible followed their orders with precision, releasing the mines as close to the borehole as possible.

With their ordinance dropped, the submersible immediately began its long ascent to the surface.

So far, so good. The sense of relief was palpable aboard the *Ironstone III*.

The mines were scheduled to detonate in precisely sixty minutes.

Chapter 47

The Below

There comes a *second fish-thing and while the first seemed to have no evil intent, killing only by accident — or so P'aldil insisted to the He'e gathered together in the Chamber of Decision — the second shrieks of danger, as if poison runs through its soul and evil pours even into the Dream. Many of the He'e scatter, snatching up their fry and moving many eight-eights of arms from where it descends into their urb. Many stay, filled with a deep and abiding fury that another of the fish-things should descend upon them. And then from legs attached to its belly, the intruder drops what looks like the egg sack of the largest of the mano-niuh — the one that is gentle and feeds on the tiny ones through its huge mouth. It is black and curved and solid, and when it drops hard on the seabed, its weight causes the rocks and sediment to fly up. The mother fish-thing, dark of skin with its lighted eyes, moves up and away. Some He'e explore the things and it seems that, perhaps, they are inert and harmless. Many He'e return to their dwellings.*

Then there is a concussive rippling in the water and the Dream explodes in front of the He'e's eyes. A shock and the seafloor boils with clouds of muck rising and with pieces of He'e dwellings. Many He'e, bashed into the broken shells of their own dwellings, are no more. Others drift, dazed by the shock in the ruins of their urb among the broken and drifting pieces of the creatures that provide light to the urb, still glowing with a soft fluorescence. Those who fled are unhurt, among them P'M'heen and many of the elders. The Dream records shocks far more titanic than this, when the whole seabed shook and rocked. Such concussions are nothing to the He'e, who live in a benthic habitat in the profoundest pressures of the deepest of the Below.

In time, the survivors among the elders gather to consider what path the He'e must take.

"Do you say that this time, too, the creatures were not trying to harm us, but only killing by accident?" P'heen asks P'aldil. P'heen's arms flash a caustic, rolling yellow.

"No," says P'aldil. "They meant to make us not." His thoughts are deeply wounded. Could this have been the one from the Above he knows as Gusman? Would he have instigated such an awful wrongdoing? He cannot believe it is so. P'aldil reaches into the Dream to ask, yet the Dream is silent.

The He'e rage now even more than when the first fish-thing had attacked, but this fish-thing, having laid its grim eggs, has flown full-tilt toward the Above, vanishing rapidly into the deepest of the dark above the He'e. Those who give chase soon return. "It fled from us in a cowardly escape. It knows what it has done, yet flies from us so shamefully," says one of the pursuers who speaks for all.

— «» —

In the conurbation, there is sorrow such as not seen before in any of the lives of the He'e now here; sorrow not seen even in the worst of the Dreamtime. More than two eights of He'e are not anymore, gone now to live only in the Dream. All stops as the surviving He'e gather the remains of those no longer here and carry them with great sadness an eight of arms across the dark seafloor to the gate where they will pass into the Dream and dwell forever in the embrace of the Great Father, P'lo, the Great Mother, M'lo, and all the He'e who have ever been and will ever be. All have lost fry in this attack and mourn them. They give into the Dream these young minds still so unformed they will have no separate existence in it. P'M'heen and P'M'aldil have lost fry of their own.

But P'aldil counsels against vengeance. "It is not us they care about, but the vast reservoir of hinu below us. It is to acquire the hinu that they attack. Hinu is not sacred to them, but valuable for its properties that bring and sustain life. If we left them to drain away all the hinu below us, they would not trouble us at all."

P'heen asks P'aldil, "How is it that you can know the intentions of these creatures?"

The Dream quiets as the elders await P'aldil's response.

"Because I have spoken to one of them in the Dream, to one who is called Gusman, and slightly to another, one who is called Harple."

There is a burst of voices among the elders in the Chamber accompanied by the flashing of many colors.

"How have you spoken to these creatures?" asks P'heen, channeling the collective thought of all the others. "They are not benthic worms that we can control through the Dream. Those that mutely follow our directives, but do not, in their lowly servile state, have the power of speech."

"I do not know," answers P'aldil. "It just began. A moment in the Dream that became many. But I do know this: the creatures like Gusman are thinkers — they have kino kinaka — like the He'e. They live in the Above, with many, many conurbations of their kind. In their Dream, they are like the He'e, dominant over all creatures — even those they fear will eat them."

"And do they fear the He'e?" asks P'heen.

"They do not. They view all creatures in the soul sea as lesser than them, such that may provide food to eat. They search everywhere for hinu and so they send their voracious radula into our conurbation. It is not that they desire to kill the He'e. It is that the He'e are in the path that leads to the hinu and must be scattered just as we scatter the clams and mussels when we build our dwelling places."

"But they kill us when we resist, break up our homes, destroy our fry that are our future. Are you saying that because they harm us only incidentally they have no blame for it?"

"Of course not," answers P'aldil. "We have to defend ourselves and our fry from them. But we will do it sadly because those from the Above are not our enemy by design."

"But they put our existence in peril, and that we must stop. Is that not so?"

"Yes," answers P'aldil, his arms flashing the pallor of sorrow.

It is M'toktai with P'toktai by her side who ask what they will do now, for few of the He'e in memory have ever acted purposefully to cause another sentient creature to die.

M'toktai says, "In the Dream, there is a thread of such an account of when the He'e came together in anger and battled each other in the same way that we drive off the muhe'e. Yet, all who were alive before the contest were also alive after. There is no precedent in the Dream for ending a life."

P'toktai says. "There is no precedent in the Dream for ending the life of one of the He'e. But we end lives of lesser creatures often to eat and sustain our lives, to guard our homes against marauders and mindless hunters. We have never taken the lives of others who think — like the blow holers — and by that thinking are as if they are also He'e."

And M'toktai, the murky brown of unsettlement darkening her arms, asks, "Doesn't it seem that if those inside the fish-thing — like those P'M'aldil encountered in their sally through the dark waters to the Above or the one P'aldil calls Gusman — are aware and knowing, they have the same desire we have to live and grow and abide in safety and happiness?"

"Are you saying let them be?" asks P'heen. "Are you saying let them take the hinu because of their need of it, though the taking puts us and our fry in jeopardy?"

"The seafloor is vast beyond any full knowing of it," says M'toktai. "Though there are many of the He'e upon it, we take up only a trifle of its space. Can't we give the ones of the Above a piece of it that they can drink the hinu, and therefore leave us in peace?"

Few have seen P'heen in a rage. Tranquility is a trait of the He'e, deeply engrained in the Dream. True anger is rare, and rage even rarer among them, so what P'heen says now stills all of the eight-eights of the Chamber of Decision gathered. "Those from the Above may be intelligent and facile, with minds as quick and able as any of the He'e. Still, even though their minds seem to be the kino kanaka of fully formed intelligence, there is a void in them that allows them to kill without remorse and destroy without caring. So, though their minds seem as kino kanaka as ours, much of their thought is no different from the mindless creatures around us. I have had my own Dream, and in it I have seen these beings from the Above. I have seen them living in multitudes, eights of eights beyond counting on the floor above the sea. If they would live only there, leaving us alone, it would be possible for the He'e to abide beside them. But they don't. They threaten us, our fry, and our future. So we have to threaten them as well. Show them that if they don't leave our waters, we will remove them with great force."

Every iota of P'heen's skin flushes with the bright scarlet of righteous anger. Most of the others in the Chamber flash scarlet, too.

"And do what?" asks P'aldil.

"Drive them from the waters above us."

"Drive them from the waters, P'heen? They are many and strong, and in my own Dream encounters with them, I have seen they wield instruments that kill — and kill great numbers at once. If we engage them, we may triumph, and we may not. Either way, the Dream makes it clear that many of the He'e will become no more in the doing of it."

"You saw what their hard-shelled fish did, P'aldil. I have no wish to see that again, not now, not in the Dream. You speak to them in the Dream. Tell them — make them understand that if they do not leave the waters of our Above, we will drive them away and in that driving many from both sides will die and become no more."

P'M'aldil confer, arms twining in agitation, flashing anger and concern and the bright green of true thought of Dream-reinforced reason.

"I'll speak to the one called Gusman — and the other one in whose dream I can barely enter, the one they call Harple — and tell them to say to the rest, 'leave now on your own or we will have to expel you.' I'll say it to him and hope he can make the rest understand."

"Good," say M'P'heen. "Tell them we will be preparing what we need to drive them away."

It is dark in the roiled waters above the damaged conurbation. Veils of the seafloor silt drift in it, dimming the He'es' view of their dwellings, dimming even their voiced clicks, which soften in the drifting silt and return to them soft-edged and uncertain. And so the He'e, hoping P'aldil can turn aside the anger of those from the Above, prepare for the first time for war.

Chapter 48

The Above: Platform Faith

Gusman lay on the cot staring up at the ceiling. He was bored, but too tired to read the spy novel Harple had brought him. Instead, he counted the holes in the acoustic tiles. He remembered doing this day after day in elementary school as he and his classmates waited impatiently for the final bell to ring. He smiled as he remembered that he never did make it to the final hole before the bell rang and they all bolted for the door and freedom. He noticed his breathing was completely even and timed to match the slight undulation in the hum of the lights and ventilation system. It was like he was listening to himself sleep. But he was awake. *Perhaps this is what deep meditation is like.*

"Gusman, what you feel is the pulse of the Dream. The whole of the Dreamtime, everything living and not living pulses to the same rhythm."

"P'aldil?"

"I am here."

"How do you know my thoughts?"

"I just know them. I do not know how I know them. Perhaps you know mine in the same way I know yours?"

"I have a question about the Dream, as you call it."

"Tell me your question."

"Do the He'e share their thoughts with other creatures, like you are sharing yours with me?"

"Yes, we see the thoughts of other creatures in the Dream. For the lesser creatures, who understand little the workings of the soul sea, the Dream gives us the ability to control them so they may serve the He'e, as it was intended by P'M'lo, the first Father and Mother. For the greater thinking creatures, we can sense their thoughts and cause them to be calm or confused or to know fear."

"And what of your conversation with me?" asked Gusman.

"It is not the same. What you and I share and what I share a little with the one called Chuck is different and new to me."

"You speak with Agent Harple… Chuck?"

"Yes, but it is not so clear. He listens but cannot speak back."

"What have you told him?"

"The same as I have told you. To go away."

"And what of the other humans here with us? Do you talk to them?"

"They are in the Dream, but it is confused and distant. We tell them to leave, but they do not seem to comprehend."

Gusman wondered whether the strange behavior aboard Platform Faith was linked to the apparent telepathic power of the He'e.

There was a silence between them. Gusman tried something new. He tried to concentrate on what he sensed P'aldil was feeling. There was nothing at first and then he felt it.

"P'aldil, are you there?"

"I am here."

"I sense that you're upset."

"It is true, Gusman. I am deeply troubled."

"Why?"

"The He'e have been attacked by your humans and many are no more."

"I don't know what you're talking about."

"How is it you do not know what occurs in your conurbation?"

"My what?"

"Conurbation, where creatures gather to live, build homes, make their lives together as a community."

Cities, Gusman thought. They have cities.

"Creatures like you attack us and kill us and you are ignorant?" P'aldil went on.

"I don't know anything about that. I am a prisoner."

"What is a 'prisoner?'"

"It means that I am isolated by my kind and cannot communicate with them. I cannot leave this place."

"Why, Gusman?"

"Because they believe I killed another human."

"Is that what your kind do? Kill without thinking? Kill when they do not need food? Kill for no reason at all?"

"Sometimes. But I did not do such a thing."

"So, you are different than the other humans?"

"No. I am the same as most other humans."

"So, you wish to kill the He'e for no reason other than to satisfy your desire to kill without remorse?"

"No, most humans only kill when they feel threatened."

"But the He'e pose no threat to the humans. The humans invaded our conurbation with their many-toothed radula and have sent metal fish-things to our smoker and laid egg sacks that explode and kill the He'e."

"The humans want the oil — the *hinu* as you call it — and they will do anything to the He'e or any other species to get it."

"But, Gusman, I have told the He'e that the humans are thinking creatures."

"We are very intelligent. But we will stop at nothing to get what we want."

"Then, Gusman, it must be that the humans believe they rule above all other creatures. But they are wrong. You must tell the humans to leave us alone. If they do not, we will refuse them the hinu they desire."

"My people will never believe me."

"Why?"

"They will not think it possible for me to talk with you and they will think I'm insane."

"What does this word, 'insane,' mean?"

"That my brain does not work and I see and hear things that are not there."

"Then humans are stupid creatures."

"Sometimes, P'aldil, we are very stupid creatures."

"Many of the He'e wish to kill the humans so they will not attack the He'e anymore."

"How can the He'e do that?"

"We will go to the place of the great, hot nothingness where the humans live, and we will kill them."

"But the humans have powerful weapons and they will use them."

"They already have."

There was a silence.

"P'aldil, are you there?" asked Gusman urgently.

"I am here, but I feel heaviness in the Dream. Many will soon be no more. I must go, Gusman."

"Why?"

"We must prepare to kill the humans. Gusman, you must hide, and I will try to find you and protect you from the wrath of the He'e."

"Wait, P'aldil. Let me try to talk to the humans."

"You told me they would not believe you. Did you tell me something you knew not to be true?"

"No. Perhaps they will not believe me, but I will try to convince them. Can you get the He'e to delay their attack?"

Another silence.

"P'aldil?"

"Yes?"

"Can you delay them?"

"Okay, I will try."

"Where did you learn the word 'okay?'"

"From you, Gusman. It means 'yes,' does it not?"

"Yes, it does."

"Gusman?"

"Yes?"

"What of the human, the one called Chuck?"

"Yes, he is the one who made me a prisoner here."

"I can pulse with him, but it is murky, like when sand is stirred in still water."

"Can you get him to listen to me?"

"I will try, Gusman."

"Good."

"Gusman?"

"What?"

"It will be okay."

Gusman laughed. "Why in the world do you think it will be okay?"

"Because to think otherwise is to dream of a world with no He'e."

Chapter 49

The Above: Platform Faith

What had started for Harple as the relatively straightforward task of writing a case status report had degenerated into a rambling and speculative narrative. Was Gusman guilty of murder — perhaps multiple murders — or was he not? There was significant circumstantial evidence pointing to him regarding the Drake homicide... assuming it was a homicide. As for Noguchi, the evidence was direct and raw. There was a video that seemed to show him pushing Noguchi over the side of Platform Faith or at least not restraining him. Harple's sentences ran on in stream-of-consciousness form. Inferences followed by suspicions followed by dead ends and plot twists.

What was he to make of Anna Campos? She was obviously Gusman's lover or, if not, there was clearly something between them. Did she have a part in this? And what of Morrissey and that ruthless Texan, Bobby Smith? They wanted to control him. They wanted him to focus everything on Gusman to the exclusion of other evidence. They were hiding something, but he didn't know what. And what was going on down below with these smart octopuses? Or were they octopi?

Harple realized he had not been writing for a while, that he had been lost in a daydream. He shook his head to clear out the cobwebs and then put his fingers back on the keyboard to resume his ramblings.

When he looked at the screen, the last sentence read, "You are all in danger. Go see Gusman."

Harple felt a wave of something visceral strike him in the gut, a feeling that was neither nausea nor the jitters, but something in between and worse than either.

Fear.

He must have written those words, but he had no memory of doing so. First the strange dreams and now this. *Was he losing his mind?*

Then he had an idea. He printed the last page of his report. Then he grabbed a thick black marker from his briefcase and crossed out all but the final two sentences on the page.

He stood and crossed the room to his suitcase, and for the first time since he arrived on Platform Faith, he unpacked his service weapon and holster. From another compartment in his suitcase, he retrieved the magazine. He pulled the Glock from its holster and inserted the magazine with a satisfying *click*. He put it back into the holster and clipped it onto his belt.

Before he left, he looked at the monitor. It was 2:00 a.m. Gusman was, of course, asleep.

When Harple turned the corner of the corridor leading to Gusman's makeshift prison cell, he almost collided with Anna Campos.

"What are you doing here, Dr. Campos?" He found himself embarrassed that his tone was so cop-like.

Harple expected a hostile response. Instead, with a confused shake of her head, Anna Campos quietly replied, "I don't know. I went to bed and here I am."

Harple's voice softened and he put his hand briefly on her shoulder. "Dr. Campos, it's okay. I understand. Maybe you were sleepwalking."

"Is Gusman all right? I need to know."

Harple paused. "Well, let's find out." Harple knocked on the door of Gusman's makeshift cell. "Gusman, it's Agent Harple and Dr. Campos."

From behind the door, Gusman barked groggily, "What?"

"Gusman, Dr. Campos and I are here to talk to you."

Harple unlocked the door and held it open for Dr. Campos to enter.

Gusman rose from his bed. He looked bleary eyed and tired, his four-day growth of beard accentuating the look of imprisonment.

Anna ran to Gusman, hugging him. Harple did nothing to stop her. He hung back while the two embraced, whispered to one another, and generally ignored Harple. He felt embarrassed for being an intruder, but he wasn't about to leave the two of them alone. Not now, not after all that had happened. Truth be told, he also felt a little envious of Gusman. Anna Campos was a brilliant and beautiful woman.

Harple cleared his throat to get their attention. "Sit down, both of you, please. Gusman, I have something I want to show you."

Harple pulled out a printout of the last page of his report from his jacket pocket, unfolded it, and handed it to Gusman.

"What do you make of this?"

Gusman looked at the paper. Anna Campos looked over and read it as well. She exhaled strongly, a whirr of air that meant "Wow."

Gusman handed the paper back to Harple.

"Why is everything blacked out but that one sentence?"

"Because you can't see the rest."

"'You are all in danger. Go see Gusman.' What do you think that means?" Harple asked.

"Who sent it to you?"

"No one. I believe I wrote it. It was working on a document on my computer, but I don't remember writing it."

"It is a warning, obviously, from…" Gusman paused, the barest hint of a smile forming. "A friend."

"P'aldil?"

"I don't know, maybe."

"Look, Gusman, I don't know why I am doing this, but I'm going to level with you. There is something strange going on here. Since I arrived, I've had these weird dreams."

"Me, too," said Anna.

"I wish they were only dreams," said Gusman with a droll grimace.

"Maybe I'm crazy," said Harple, "but is it possible that this P'aldil creature is somehow communicating with us through a means we don't understand?"

"By some extra-sensory telepathy. Isn't that what you're getting at?" asked Anna.

"Yes, something like that," Harple replied. "And you and I have experienced it to one degree or another, right?"

Gusman nodded. "In spades," Gusman murmured.

"So, Gusman, you need to tell me what they've said to you. Nothing will leave this room or wind up in any report." Harple nodded at the paper still in his hand.

Gusman said, "If I tell you what P'aldil has said to me in my dreams and you report it, they'll think I'm crazy."

"I'm no psychiatrist, but having intimate conversations with sea creatures is probably considered a strong indication of schizophrenia," said Anna brightly.

"Unless they're real," replied Harple.

"Well," said Anna, "group schizophrenia must be pretty rare. I mean if you are having a conversation with the same creature, that's got to suggest something quite interesting is happening. Since Gusman told me about his conversation with P'aldil, I've been wondering if all the strange behavior of the crew is related. Drake, Noguchi, the bizarre dreams that I have been having, all of it."

"You want to know what he said to me?" Gusman looked at Harple.

"Yes," said Harple.

"He said you should give me your gun and keys and then handcuff yourself to the bed."

Harple rolled his eyes.

"Come on, Gusman, be serious," pleaded Anna, slapping him on the leg.

"He told me the He'e, as the creatures call themselves, are really pissed because the company sent down a submersible that dropped explosives on their habitat and killed a bunch of them. They're planning to invade our little paradise and get even. P'aldil wants me to reason with the company and get them to go away so there won't be a bloodbath."

"How did you respond?"

"I told him the truth. That I was locked up in this fucking junior jail cell and that no one would believe me anyway."

Anna said, "I think you've got a good point."

"They'll not only think Gusman's crazy, they'll think I'm crazy too." Harple shook his head in defeat.

"So, you believe me?" asked Gusman.

"I don't know what to believe at this point," Harple replied.

Gusman laughed. "Well, if it's any consolation, I'm not sure I even believe me."

Harple lowered his voice and said slowly, "I'll say this much — if intuition matters, I've got a feeling that something really bad is about to happen."

"From my perspective," Gusman replied, "it couldn't get much worse."

Chapter 50

The Below

P'M'dnoki'alihikaua is a *stalwart pair whose voices command all when trouble threatens. "There is no precedent in the Dream for an action like this," P'dnoki'alihikaua warns the Chamber of Decision. "These are not muhe or mano that attack us mindlessly for food. They are a hoa paio enemy of proven strength. The eggs their metal fish dropped..." He searches for a word, struggling to describe the scene that replays in his mind. He searches the Dream for anything in their past to explain, but there is nothing. "Dropped eggs that erupt. If the one, this Gusman, who P'aldil has touched in the Dream is to be believed, then the others of his kind are many eights more numerous than all the counting of the He'e. If those eggs are the least of their..." P'dnoki'alihikaua again searches for a word for this evil, and finally grasps a term that seems closest, "their pa'ahana, tools of evil, then many of the He'e will be no longer if we join battle against them."*

P'M'heen rest among the others of the Chamber of Decision on the smooth swept sand of the sea bottom near a chimney of the smoker untouched by the bombs. The gush of the smoker eddies here and faint tongues of its heat play among them. A colony of glow fauna fixed on the side of the chimney cast a soft blue glimmering onto the sand. P'heen has listened to P'M'dnoki'alihikaua and has listened to P'M'aldil, who have warned of the same danger. P'heen and M'heen's intertwined arms play together seeking comfort from their fear.

Although P'heen has deep worries, he flushes with the blue of certainty as he says, "We know the ugliness Gusman's kind can bring. I hear and believe P'aldil when he brings us

Gusman's warning that his kind covet the hinu of the soul sea and will take it for themselves, no matter the cost. The hinu is plentiful in most of the places where the He'e dwell at the bottom of The Below and so the cost, the number of He'e who will be no more, will be countless if we do not defend our dwellings. I will tell the assemblage that we have no choice but to bring the kaua war to Gusman's kind."

Saffron rivers of agreement run up P'M'dnoki'alihikauas' arms and the others of the Chamber of Decision. None of the He'e wish for a fight, but with the need decided, the stalwarts are eager to prepare. P'dnoki, having heard P'aldil tell of how the gas-filled stones erupted at the top of the Above, asks if their frightening blast and power can be used to make war.

"Their dwelling is a massive metal construction," M'aldil says. "For all their force, the stones' bursting did it no damage. Perhaps a larger mass of the stone could wreck it. But if Gusman's kind are as numerous as we believe, we could scavenge the seafloor for all its bursting stone and still hardly touch their numbers."

This thought silences them all and they rest for eight-eights of beats, their arms almost still, their motion in thought diminished to the slow throb of the sea water through their gills.

After a time, M'aldil says, "We do not have to counter force with force. It wasn't force that stopped the mano as P'aldil and I rose to the Above. We stopped it as we would stop any wild thing we wish to make a meal of."

P'dnoki scoffs, "I don't wish to eat those from the Above. How would they taste anyway?"

The white light of mirth ripples on him and his mate joins in, saying, "If their taste is as evil as their deeds, a single bite would be as potent as k□kala, the bladder fish, venom. Even the least of our fry would avoid them."

"Venom!" says M'aldil.

"What?" says P'heen. "Our venom might destroy a few who come close enough to us. But there are multitudes of them. It is foolishness to think we could hurt them all."

P'aldil's arms are thrashing now, flashing and luminous in his excitement. "Of course," he says. "Not venom of death, *but venom of fear; the way we hunt the mano. Had M'aldil not used the venom of fear on the creature we encountered in the Above, he might have removed more than my arm with the eruption of his weapon. Even if the bursting rock won't have the force to do damage to those above, if we fill its spaces with the venom of fear, it and our pulsing will drive them away. None will be killed, yet we will prevail."*

"Maybe we'll eat a few of them after all," says P'dnoki, engulfed in more flashes of his own mirth.

— «» —

In the Dream, the waters fall away. The searing brightness is muted almost to the dimness of the seafloor on the structure Gusman calls a platform. Behind are lights in many colors — softer, not so bright, arrayed on the metal intricacies of the platform towering above like the self-lights of the benthic creatures that light P'aldil's undersea urb. Further, the Above is as black as the bleakest stretches beyond the urb of the He'e. Motes of light are scattered across it.

Gusman stands in a closed cave inside the metal urb, but his thoughts wander in the Dream to the platform's edge, where his small, strange eyes are fixed on those far away lights — those he calls 'stars.' The figure of a huge octopus seems to rest on the platform's fence, seven of its arms intertwined in the fence's rails, one arm a stump puckered at its end.

"The mâ, the others who are with you, have done us terrible harm, Gusman. Many of the He'e are no more because of that harm. There cannot be more of this dying. We will not allow it. We ask you to stop and to leave this platform," P'aldil says.

"I am sorry for those you have lost, P'aldil, for those who are no more. But I am not Superman. I cannot make everyone leave."

"What is this 'Superman?'" P'aldil asks.

"A human who is more powerful than all the other humans."

"I see. You are not Superman. You are ordinary man."

Gusman laughs. "True." He pauses to collect his thoughts. "Do you want revenge for the deaths of the He'e?" he asks.

"Revenge is 'ho'opa'i,' which is to slap as if to admonish a misbehaving fry. Are you just-hatched fry who misbehave

*or are you parents accountable for your misbehaving fry?"
P'aldil asks.*

*"Misbehaving fry, that's a good way to put it, P'aldil. No,
I'm afraid we are adults — parents, as you say — and very
much responsible for our actions."*

*"Gusman, if you were fry, we would admonish you like fry.
But you are worse; you are parents who behave like fry and so
slapping you is not enough. You must leave this platform now
or we will make you leave. You must leave this platform and
all of the Below because we can't trust you there."*

*Gusman still stares out at the stars. Like all the He'e,
whose sea bottom world changes slowly, P'aldil is patient. He
wishes to ask why there is the blackness now, why the searing
brightness of the Above has gone. He wishes to ask how
Gusman and the others manage to live in this place of such
heat and brightness. He wishes to ask how they can survive
without the sea that sustains life. He wishes to ask Gusman
many things, but now is not the time and he may never find
time to speak of it.*

*He realizes that Gusman is speaking, saying, "If it were
up to me, P'aldil, we would leave this platform now. We would
leave you alone. But I'm not the boss here."*

"Boss?"

"The one in charge. The one who runs things."

*"No single one runs things for the He'e. Those who know
take charge for each circumstance. 'alihikaua is our name
for one who leads when there is danger. Akolohe leads when
we enjoy mirth. Akauka leads when there is sickness. None
knows all things equally. Why would we want a 'boss' when
the He'e must have different talents for different..." P'aldil
searches the Dream for the right word, "...quandaries? I know
that is not your way to say that, Gusman. It is hard to find the
cognates. We do not think alike."*

*Gusman pauses and P'aldil understands that he has not
ended the conversation, but is also searching for the right
words. Finally, Gusman says, "I am a leader for the operation
of mechanical things. Things we use to build and create other
things, and for the crises that may come from the use of those
things — machines, we call them. But when there are conflicts*

among us, there are other leaders. We call such a leader the 'boss.'"

"One leader for most things? Ah, that is confusing." P'aldil drops his arms then shivers for an instant in his surprise. "So, Gusman, is there a boss who will decide if you will leave this platform?"

"There is," Gusman says, "and I'm afraid I know what his answer will be."

Chapter 51

The Below

They rise: twice *eight-eights of He'e in baskets beneath the buoyant stone. They joke about how human kanaka will taste as if this were a hunt for shrimp or bonefish.*

"They are evil and so their taste must be evil. Who would eat one?"

"Would they eat us? You are smart, P'maguzeh, so would their tongues be smart if they ate you?"

The light of mirth ripples on many nearby.

"P'aldil says their tongues are soft and that they have shells, but their shells are inside like the fishes. Because of this, their arms are not supple like ours, but bend only where the sections of their shells join inside. Seawater will not sustain them; they have no gills and cannot take the life essence from it. They are hollow inside, he says, and take their stuff of life from the void of the Above."

Another says, "The human kanaka sound hideous — shells inside, eyes as small as smoker vent marbles, beakless as unhatched fry, unable to take life from the waters."

The talk ripples among them, within the Dream and without. Their mirth rises as it always does when the sense of strangeness rises. As P'M'aldil had done on their own journey, these pū'ali soldiers carry their meals with them, but hunt with practiced skill among the rough-skinned, tough-fleshed niuhi and the more succulent māmaka. Their ascent seems more a traveling feast than an invading force.

P'aldil wonders whether their mirth guards them from thoughts of the death that will soon come.

— «» —

Their flotilla rises for nine hungers until, as P'M'aldil had discovered on their journey, the Above begins to glow with a light of its own. The mirth of the He'e turns to subdued voices and nervous flickers along arms and mantles. Something different happens now than what happened to P'M'aldil. This time the Above darkens as they rise. M'ku'ekepa, shaper of inanimate things, has created eye coverings for the soldiers to shield their vision from the searing light of the Above. M'ku'ekepa had been eager to show off these coverings, "On the inside of each are colonies of maka that will darken as the light brightens. So you will be able to see even in the brightest blaze of the Above."

"Why does the Above grow darker as we approach it?" P'dnoki'alihikaua asks P'M'aldil, who share a basket along with five other He'e, including P'dnoki's mate. "You said the Above is filled with light. This changes things."

"I don't know why it is dark now. It is dark sometimes when I speak to Gusman in the Dream. It changes things for the better, though," P'aldil says. "Still, the human kanaka make their own light, and even that manufactured light is far brighter than any the He'e have experienced."

"We will just have to see," M'dnoki'alihikaua says and ripples with the humor of her own wordplay.

They rise until the metal bulk of the platform is in touching distance. Masses of barnacles and mussels crust the surface of its pontoons. Schools of fat fish swarm the slow-moving shoals in the platform's shadow. Green growths the Dream calls 'ele'ele, a seaweed the He'e have never seen near their homes on the seafloor, tangle the deep blue water and shift gently in the currents eddying along the platform's massive metal bladders. Immense gatherings of fish dart away as they come near.

"We are less than a hunger from the end of the waters," P'aldil says, entranced again by the richness of life here at the top of the Above.

"We are ready," P'M'dnoki answer. There is no need to review the strategy. It is all in the Dream, and in the Dream, all speak with each other as if they were together in a single council space, seeing each other as clearly as if there were

no space between them at all. They will ride their craft up to the end of the waters. One He'e will stay with each of the craft, ready at P'M'dnoki's call to loose their terror ink. The rest will climb aboard, since P'aldil has seen that there are many holds and grabs along its sides that even in the absence of water the He'e soldiers can use to make their way up to the platform's living spaces.

"I think the darkness will be in our favor," says P'aldil. "I have learned from Gusman that most of the human kanaka seem to sleep when the light is dimmest."

P'aldil knows Gusman and his kind know fear — not just the timeless fear the He'e share within the present when the giant Muhe'e attack — but a strange, formless fear of things not yet; a fear somehow rooted in the unknown. In their timeless lives, the He'e have little sense of the unknown, little fear of it, and little way to discern its shape. Their spirits rove the soft shape of the Dream and chatter of their plans and prepare.

All the He'e soldiers wear caps fashioned of hu'akai sponge over their mantles. Wet, it keeps their gills moist, so they can absorb the stuff of life. "The kanaka are not so different from us that they can do without the stuff of life. It must be around them somehow as it is in the waters around us. Wear this over your gills; the water within the hu'akai will absorb the stuff of life from their strange space without water and will pass it to your gills and so you will live without water around you," M'kauka, the healer, had told P'M'aldil and the others of the raiding party as they had prepared for their journey.

"How long will it allow us to travel in the space without water?" M'aldil asks.

M'kauka flushes with the violet of uncertainty. "I believe as long as your gills stay wet, the stuff of life will reach them. You should be able to stay there for at least a hunger and perhaps more," she says. "If you return to the sea and fill them again with seawater, you should be able to return to that strange space as often as you need."

The He'e soldiers wear shells like those of the giant seafloor clams. These are thinner than a tubeworm's skin, yet very hard. They are fashioned from the stuff the burrowing smoker clams exude. P'alaku, the maker of such things, had tried to explain the process of their making to the Chamber of Decision.

"No need," P'heen says dismissively. "If you say the shells the clams make this way are tough and impenetrable, we have no need to know why. You say they are the same stuff as the kaimana we have used to shield our home from the digging jaws of the humans' worm device."

P'alaku says, "We know the humans have pa'ahana tools of evil that can travel swiftly across distances in water or in the attenuated substance they breathe. In the Chamber of the Strange, there are the bits of metal deposited like seeds in the carapace of the dead metallic creature that sank to us eight-eights of dreams ago. These seeds were deposited in patterns. Some say the humans possess pa'ahana that spray these metal seeds, like the thing that exploded when P'aldil came to the surface and severed his arm. These kaimana shells we will wear are strong, but we do not know how strong. They cannot be impervious, but they are very tough. I do not believe, nor find in the Dream, that any of the humans' pa'ahana are likely to do them damage, even the thing that sprays the metal seeds."

"We will find out," P'aldil replies mirthlessly.

"It is time," say P'M'dnoki.

"It is," P'aldil agrees.

They don their shells and snap them closed around themselves, their arms extended through eight holes in the shells. Slits near their gills allow water to enter and fill the hu'akai sponge. Transparent roundels of the shell cover their eyes. Rosy mirth plays upon their arms at the sight of the black shells.

"We look like fool clams," says a young He'e named P'tothanni. "We look like clams who have mated with eels. See, our arms wiggle like sharp-toothed kuna eels." He snaps an arm at an older He'e, who parries it with a gruff flash of gray on his own arms.

"Enough," says P'aldil. "Let's go to the platform."

— «» —

In a deep, small place in the Dream, P'aldil thinks of Gusman and wishes him to survive. But he does not see how this will happen; the humans will be destroyed. They must be destroyed. He is as anxious as when fry play too close to the smoker.

The He'e breach the surface, crossing the interface between the seawater and the strange place of the Above. It's good there is darkness, P'aldil thinks, because even for him and for M'aldil who have both experienced it before, the sensations of the transition are awful. The craft are arrayed in a crescent along a flank of the platform. Their buoyant stones bob in an unfamiliar current that rises and falls, lifting and dropping the stones along the interface between water and not water. Were they human, it would be chaos. Fear would overcome them. But they are He'e, and the Dream gives them strength and direction. Twice eight-eights of He'e warriors flow up the nets to the surface of the rocks and view for the first time the vast bulk of the platform.

P'M'dnoki give the order. Noiselessly, the He'e soldiers slip from the tops of the stones back into the familiar seawater and move quickly toward the platform. P'M'aldil are the first to reach it and they climb silently up onto its curved bladder and then onto the hard poles that hold it up. The bright, hot absence that is everywhere and nowhere stings at their eyes and dries their skin, but they are unharmed. They lead the arriving army of He'e climbing the stairs and ladders and holds to the first deck of the thing the humans call Platform Faith.

Chapter 52

The Above: Platform Faith

Gusman was awake. Not just dreaming that he was awake. It was real. He was certain of that. He paced his cell, crossing in two strides. He pinched his arm to make certain he was awake. He felt the pinch. And yet, P'aldil was talking in his head.

"Gusman," P'aldil said, "you must make yourself into a ball, like the *N'duja*, and hide." His voice sounded urgent, as if he were right behind him, speaking into his ear.

"How can I hide? I'm locked in a small room and there's nowhere to go."

P'aldil answered, "Is it like a cave with a large rock at the entrance?"

"Kind of."

"Gusman, it is important that there is a rock in front of the cave."

"Well, there's a door and it's locked, if that helps."

"A door is like the thin plate on the artificial fish that came to harm us?"

"Yeah, I think so."

"Gusman, make yourself into a tiny ball. Stay behind the door and perhaps you will not be eaten."

"Eaten? P'aldil, what in the hell is going on?"

"What is this thing you call 'hell?'"

Gusman was losing patience. "I don't know. A mythical place, deep and dark, where there is fire and stone."

"Ah, that sounds like the place where the He'e live. So, it is a good place, this hell?"

"Forget it. Just tell me why I might be eaten."

"It is war. I do not know this for myself, but it is said that your kind taste good. Those who attacked the metal beast that dropped the eggs that erupt — the ones we killed — were eaten. It is said they were quite succulent, like meat of the *moano ukali-ulua*, although some complained of a bitter aftertaste."

"War. What war? What are you taking about?"

"War between my kind and your kind."

"Am I dreaming this?"

"It is part of the Dream, Gusman. Everything is part of the Dream."

"P'aldil, I have been through a lot lately. I don't want to be eaten."

"Hide behind the door. Make yourself into a little ball and I will come for you."

"Come for me?"

— «» —

Smith and Morrissey stood over the computer monitor in the compartment Harple was using as his office.

Gusman was walking around his cell, talking to himself.

"What the fuck is he mumbling about?" asked Smith.

"Hard to say. It's like he's sleepwalking. But his eyes are open."

"The fucker's lost it."

Morrissey laughed. "From the looks of things, you're probably right."

"Maybe that's not such a bad result," Bobby Smith said, his words drawn out long, the drawl especially thick.

"Maybe. Could solve a lot of problems."

Smith locked eyes on Morrissey and said, "Too bad we can't put Harple and the Mexican gal in that room with Gusman. Would be mighty convenient if the two of them died at the hands of a madman who then took his own life."

Morrissey wasn't sure the Texan was kidding, so he didn't say anything. But he felt a hard chill run up his spine.

There was a click and a sudden gust of air from behind the two men as Harple swept in. He stopped, an expression of surprise rapidly turning into the flushed look of anger.

"What are you doing here?" he asked.

Smith smiled, but there was nothing friendly in it.

"Calm down there, son," he said.

"Excuse me? You have no right to be here. You need to get out right now."

"This is my ship, Mr. Harple, and I'll leave when I'm good and ready."

"No," said Harple. "You'll leave now or you'll find yourself in custody."

"Son, you're sounding real stupid right now," Bobby Smith said, spitting out the words.

Harple took a step back and squared his shoulders. He wasn't backing down.

Morrissey held up his hands. "Just calm down," he said evenly. "Nobody's going to do anything stupid here. We'll leave. Won't we, Mr. Smith?"

There was an uncomfortable silence. The ball was in Bobby Smith's court.

Smith let out a loud exhale, his lips pursed. It was the sound of resignation, perhaps only momentary, but the tension began to ebb.

"Excuse me, Special Agent," he said and started to walk past.

Then all hell broke loose.

Chapter 53

The Above: Platform Faith

Twice eight-eights of *He'e soldiers creep up the ladders to the top of the two enormous metal orbs, half submerged, from which the great legs holding up the platform rise. In the murky light they view for the first time the vast bulk of Platform Faith looming above them. The waterless miasma that forms the essence of this strange world above the Above is dark, but not completely without light. There is a large, bright disc shimmering far above them beyond the platform itself. And all over the miasma are tiny white lights, some steady, some twinkling, like the light emanating from the small fires of certain smokers. Platform Faith is as tall as one of the largest smoker chimneys, and as dark, but is covered with lights on its many corners and edges that are brighter than any on their dwellings in the urb. Lights hard and intense and steady, without the wash of seafloor currents to soften them.*

Without further orders, the He'e ascend the great orb, holding onto the crossed metal bars attached every three eights across its expanse. In the Dream, someone says, "Are these creatures so foolish that they provide us with the perfect grasping surface to climb?"

There is mirth, but it is momentary, because in the Dream there is apprehension of what is to come. P'M'aldil are the first to reach the top of the floating orb and they glide without noise up onto the flat expanse of the low space where these humans sometimes moor. They lead the arriving army of He'e flowing up the stairs and ladders far up into the miasma to the first deck of this conurbation the human enemies call "Platform Faith." Light flares. A harsh noise, human voices, ululates. From the water where the netted rocks bob, there is a cascade of booms, rock shattering, and a cloud rising darkly.

A humming, a pulse, the human voices screaming.

The He'e soldiers spread out in groups across the platform to explore its caves and smoker towers. Their collective rage pulsates at the human aggressors who attacked their urb and now must die.

P'M'aldil lead two eights of He'e into a doorway of the tower and into a long, metal-walled corridor. Boneless and able to slip into the tightest of spaces, even in their clam shells, the He'e have no fear of being trapped. Yet this place, so different from the endless open space of the ocean floor, arouses a distress in the He'e none have felt before. They move farther into this waterless void, sliding carefully on a floor weirdly flat and smooth and more solid than any but the hardest of benthic stone. Shuttered openings interrupt the walls at intervals. The sound through the medium the humans call air is dull, the noise of their motion attenuated as if from a great distance.

"There are chambers leading off from here," says a young He'e called M'wiwo'ole, as unafraid as her name implies. "But the openings have coverings and do not give." She pushes an arm hard against one.

"No," P'aldil says, "they are held closed with this." He curls the tip of an arm around a handle and pushes down. They hear a click and the door swings away to a sort of dwelling place. P'aldil has seen one similar through Gusman's eyes; but to the others, the strange constructions that are a bed, a desk, a chair, and a dresser are meaningless things. Not meaningless is the bellow of sound from the human in the room, backed into a corner. Its mouth, from where the sound comes, is wide, the noise itself a ragged gust. M'wiwo'ole advances into the chamber, her arms traveling before her, one approaching the human who backs farther away, the sound it makes growing louder. The room floods with light so bright that even the dimming shells cannot filter it entirely. Male or female? M'wiwo'ole cannot discern, though the sense emanating from P'aldil through the Dream is that this is a human male. It is larger than M'wiwo'ole is, though stumpy and compact in

build, its undersized arms awkwardly articulated, ending in a fingered, grasping appendage. With one of these, it has grabbed for something metallic and keen edged.

"I know this thing. In the Dream, it cut at and prodded my severed arm," P'aldil warns. "It is sharp, dangerous. Keep away from it."

Unbidden, in the reflex of defense, M'wiwo'ole's arms begin a marquee-like flashing, black against white. For the human, clearly already under the influence of the fear venom, the flashing is too much. Keening more loudly, it drops the knife, bolts past M'wiwo'ole's restless arms and out into the corridor, running directly into one of the He'e, who places his arm in front of the human's legs. The human flies through the miasma for a distance, still keening and expelling much gaseous eminence from the hole in its face. The creature, seemingly dazed, slowly rolls onto its back. P'hal'lea, who is close by, moves quickly to straddle the head and sinks its beak into the mouth hole, punching through the semi-hard osseous matter that makes up the roof of its mouth and into the soft and sweet-tasting meat beyond. The human stills and is no more.

P'hal'lea sups on the cavity meat. When he has his fill, he rises. Red blood from the human and bits of flesh and bone cover him, the stumpy human, and the floor.

"What does it taste like?" asks P'aldil.

"It tastes like the sweet ama shrimp!" he says with mirth.

The He'e explore further, wondering at the strangeness of the artificial light which seems to have no bioluminescent component and at the chambers large and small that are full of devices which P'aldil has had only fragments of explanation from Gusman. What a wonderful and terrifying life these humans must lead here above the Above.

Outside, on the open deck of the platform, a group of the He'e soldiers face three eights of humans who emerge from a bright opening in one tower. The humans rush forward, some of them brandishing tools of evil that flare with bright light at the end of long tubes. The tools flare and buck, and some of the He'e are struck with projectiles. Those struck in their arms are briefly full of pain until their venom-borne analgesics can deaden it. But those striking the He'es' shells simply stick without harm.

A voice from one of the humans, "They're wearin' fuckin' armor!"

Terrified sounds and outrage are somehow comprehensible and a sign of the humans' confusion.

Some of the humans retreat into the tower and emerge soon after with their own sort of shells on their faces with goggles protecting their eyes and grilled openings over their mouths. The cloud of the fear venom seems not to touch the humans breathing through the gills and they approach the He'e soldiers. They attack the He'es' shells with the butt ends of their pa'ahana — tools of evil. The shells hold, and one by one the He'e grasp the humans in their heavy arms and then draw them into the flaps that cover their beaks. A bite, the venom courses, and the humans are lifeless.

P'aldil and the others with him have emerged from the platform's interior in time to watch this struggle with the humans.

P'aldil, watching the humans die, thinks, "We should not kill as these fry-thinking humans do. But they leave us no choice."

There comes a booming voice, echoing from many places at the same time, "Get off, get off now!" At this, the few human attackers still living begin to retreat, their ineffectual tools of evil raised in a sort of futile defense.

"They are going," P'M'dnoki say. "We should not allow them to go. We should kill them all as a lesson to the humans."

P'M'heen would agree, but P'aldil objects loudly, his arms flaring the bright orange of warning, saying, "Look, we have killed many of the humans. They are no longer attacking us. We are not fry-minded wa'awa'a fools like them. They have our warning. Let them leave."

The crosshatched flicker of disagreement courses up P'heen's arms. He says to P'aldil, "They did not spare us; we will not spare them."

At the far end of the platform, they see a huge bright-skinned metal thing, big as the biggest smoker tower, begin to stir. A shaft spins, wide flat arms atop it whirl and the entire thing shudders. The remaining humans back away toward it, and more humans, maybe three eights of them, emerge from various openings in the platform and swarm toward the thing, pushing one another violently aside to enter it. Some of the humans crush their brethren underfoot in their panic.

"On board now. We're pulling out," comes the booming voice again.

P'aldil has been watching, but he doesn't see Gusman. Is the human still on the platform? He detects a faint echo of Gusman's life force in the Dream, but there are too many voices — human and He'e — cascading in cacophonous waves across the Dream.

The big thing begins to rock; its spinning arms whirl faster with a battering beat. Something within it howls a rising note and the arms begin to turn so fast they cannot be seen.

"Attack them," pulses P'heen, and the He'e race to the thing, swarming it, crawling inside, slaughtering the humans as they go. One of the He'e ascends to the top of the thing, reaches up and is cut into bits by the whirling blades.

The thing begins slowly to lift off, its door still open, the He'e still on it, inside of it, and all around it. It rises into the miasma, but then, no higher than two eights from its resting place, it shudders and tilts, its blades slamming into the rail, sending fiery sparks where metal meets metal, and it drops over the side of the platform.

There is a reverberating splash, then silence.

The He'e pulse slowly at the loss of their kind; so many are no more — the fry and old ones who died in the urb, and now the warriors who have died fighting the aggressors.

P'aldil enters the Dream and says, "Some humans have survived. I sense their life essence. One is Gusman."

"Where are they?" asks P'heen.

"Above in the heart of this place."

"Find them," P'heen orders.

Chapter 54

The Above: Platform Faith

Someone pulled the fire alarm and the interior hallways exploded in flashing lights and pulsing sounds. In a British accent, a woman's prerecorded voice came over the Public-Address system and repeated: "This is an emergency. Please make your way immediately to your designated emergency response station."

Morrissey and Smith, who had just started down the hallway, looked at each other and Bobby Smith said, "Goddamn it." He unclipped the two-way radio on his belt and pushed the button to raise the control room, which was manned 24-7.

"Control room, do you read me?"

There was no answer.

He tried again.

Again, there was no answer.

"What the fuck?"

"That's weird," said Morrissey.

"Shit, something must really be happening."

Both ran for the stairs at the end of the corridor.

Behind them, Harple came out into the corridor. He started running after them. "Hey!" he yelled, but they had already disappeared around the corner.

"Shit," he said under his breath.

When he reached the end of the corridor, he noticed the elevator propped open. A body lay slumped face down on the floor, his legs sticking back into the hallway, preventing the door from closing. There was blood everywhere. Harple fought the instinct to abandon the man and follow Smith and Morrissey up the stairs to the deck. But his training and conscience took control of his emotions.

He knelt beside the man and started to turn the body over.

What he saw made him rear up in horror.

What remained of the man's face was an empty, gelatinous hole, smeared with a black substance that smelled so foul he involuntarily recoiled. A wave of nausea came over him.

Then he heard a whooshing sound and a thump, and when he looked up, he saw that a giant octopus encased in some kind of shell and incongruously wearing sunglasses had dropped down from the elevator's ceiling. Harple jumped back, propelling himself farther into the hallway. The thing slithered toward him. Its color undulated from gray to pink to blotchy purple-blue.

He heard himself screaming.

The creature raised itself and sprayed him with some kind of fluid. It burned his eyes and skin and paralyzed him with fear. It was like he was watching himself from outside of his body, unable to will himself to move.

The thing latched onto his leg, its grip all-powerful, like a muscle made of a thousand smaller, undulating muscles, pinning his leg to the ground.

He wanted to reach for his gun, but couldn't move his arms and his heart was beating so hard he could barely breathe. He knew, without a doubt, he was going to die.

From somewhere beyond his own screaming, from beyond the sound of the recorded woman's voice telling him over and over that he should leave this place, he heard a woman's voice yell, *"Chinga te."*

A blast of thick, billowing gas hissed by his face and enveloped the octopus in a white powdery cloud. The creature immediately let go of Harple's leg and retreated into the elevator.

With the creature's grip loosened, Harple's willpower returned. Still seated, he pulled his gun from his holster and with the ingrained muscle memory from countless trips to the firing range, he leveled the weapon and fired off seven bullets of his fifteen-round clip into the body of the creature.

Most of the bullets bounced off the creature's armored shell but a few hit its arms.

Blue blood oozed from the wounds, but the creature seemed only momentarily stunned.

Anna Campos threw the empty fire extinguisher at the creature and lunged toward the elevator, punching the 'up' button. Somehow Harple had the presence of mind to pull the dead body toward him, clearing the elevator door. A few seconds later, a familiar ding issued and the elevator doors closed.

Harple dropped the weapon on the floor and brought his hands to his throbbing head.

Anna knelt down and yelled above the continued din, "Are you okay?"

"Yeah, I think so," said Harple. "My head hurts like a son of a bitch and my heart feels like it's going to come out of my chest."

Anna gently grabbed his wrist and took his pulse. It was racing.

"You smell disgusting," she said, averting her gaze. The odor made her sinuses burn.

"It sprayed me with something."

"Yeah, the ink of this species seems to have neurotoxic properties. Can you stand?"

"I've got to." Harple rolled onto his knees and pushed himself slowly to a standing position. He let Anna take hold of his arm and help him up.

Once standing, Harple swayed a little as he got his bearings.

"I think I'm okay. Just a little shaky."

Anna leaned down and picked up Harple's service weapon. She handed it to him.

"Thanks," he said, holstering the weapon.

"What's going on?" she asked. "I heard that alarm and thought there was a fire, but when I got here, I saw that thing crawling toward you."

"I don't know what's happening."

"What about Gusman? He's locked in that room. I've got to find him. Can you walk?"

"I think so."

Like an old man, Harple moved slowly. Anna offered him a hand, but he waved her off. "I'll be okay," he said.

"Come on. We need to find Gusman."

Harple motioned down the hall. "The stairs."

Anna was already moving.

Chapter 55

The Above: United States Naval Base, Guam, Western Pacific

The secure communications unit of the US Naval Computer and Telecommunications Command was tucked neatly behind some barracks dating back to the Vietnam era. It was a solid, no-frills piece of construction: windowless, with double thick tilt-up concrete walls and a steel door requiring biometric identification to enter. A gigantic air conditioning unit set among an array of antennas and satellite dishes sat on top of the flat roof.

Inside the dimly lit interior, a half-dozen communications specialists were at work, each seated in front of a computer panel. For more than a century, Guam had been the forward base of American sovereignty in the Pacific, its Rock of Gibraltar. Once a coal fueling station that allowed navy ships to traverse the Pacific without having to take on fuel at a foreign port, it was now more important as an air base and early warning station. Befitting the gravity of their mission, there was little casual conversation and even less joking among the naval personnel who manned this post.

And so they all turned around when one of them, a dusky young woman of indeterminate ethnicity, tripped as she rose from her chair.

"Skipper," she said excitedly to the duty officer, "I'm getting an unsecured radio transmission reporting some kind of an attack."

"Calm down, sailor," responded the lieutenant, who himself could not have been more than twenty-two. "Let's see what we've got."

He walked to her station and stood over her as she brought up the recording of the transmission.

The voice they heard was loud and male. There was fear in the voice, intensified by the crackle and snap of the radio transmission.

"Mayday. Mayday. We are under attack. They're everywhere. We can't stop them. Guns don't work. We're all going to die."

A hissing sound followed for a few more seconds and then the transmission ended.

"That's it, sir," said the young woman. "There was nothing after that."

"Do you have coordinates?"

"Um, yes," she responded and gave him the information.

"What's around there?"

She quickly entered a few keystrokes. "Um... It looks like there's an oil platform there, sir," she said, looking up at him.

"Oh, God," he said. "It may be a terrorist attack."

He spun around and barked an order at one of the other specialists. "Jones, try to contact that platform and see if we can establish a communications link."

He ran back to his desk and picked up the phone directly connected to the US Pacific Fleet's headquarters in Honolulu.

"Sir," he said, "this is NCTC Guam. We have a mayday transmission from a location aboard an oil platform approximately six hundred nautical miles west of Midway. They are reporting an attack."

There was a pause as the lieutenant listened to a question from the other side of the line.

"A single transmission, sir."

Another pause.

"Yes, the word 'attack.' No mention of terrorists. We are forwarding the transmission now."

— «» —

One hour later, after the President of the United States was briefed and had given his consent, orders were relayed to the *USS Bonhomme Richard*, the command ship of Navy Expeditionary Strike Group Seven, headquartered in Sasebo,

Japan, to proceed without delay and at full speed to Platform Faith. Upon reaching the objective, it was to take control of Platform Faith, kill or capture any hostile forces, and rescue any surviving members of the crew. United States Satellite Command had already redirected its spy satellites to the Platform and reconnaissance aircraft were on the way from Guam.

Chapter 56

The Above: Platform Faith

Harple and Anna stood at the top of the stairwell just behind a fire door. On it, large black-stenciled letters read 'B Deck,' the deck where Gusman was being held.

A few hours earlier, they would have thought nothing of simply walking through the door. Now they hesitated. Harple pulled out his gun and, with an audible exhale, cracked open the door and peered through.

"Can you see anything?" Anna whispered.

"Not much."

Harple pushed it open another few inches and looked down the corridor. B Deck was lit only by red emergency lights and was quite dim, so he waited for his eyes to adjust. The recording of the woman's voice telling them to evacuate to the main deck kept repeating.

There was nothing there. He crouched down and pushed the door open far enough so he could step through.

He entered the hallway and stood, signaling to Anna to wait. He looked both ways. There were no open doors or papers scattered in haste. No dead bodies or lurking creatures. Just an empty corridor.

"Clear," he whispered.

They headed down the corridor toward the cabin where Gusman was being held. Both stepped lightly as if that would somehow make them inconspicuous. When they reached Gusman's improvised jail cell, Anna leapt in front of Harple and rapped loudly on the door.

"Gusman!" she yelled. "Are you okay?"

There was rustling inside, but Gusman did not respond.

"Gusman?" asked Harple, feeling in his pocket for the key.

"Yeah, yeah, I'm here," Gusman croaked. "Get me out of here."

As if to dramatize the point, the muffled sound of an explosion came from the main deck above.

"Jesus," Harple said.

"What was that?" asked Anna.

"I don't know. But we have a bigger problem. I don't have the key."

"Where is it?"

"I must have left it in my cabin."

From the inside, Gusman yelled, "We have to get out of here! Let me out."

"Gusman, this is Harple. We don't have the key. I need to go back for it."

"We don't have time for that," replied Gusman. "This place is under attack. We need to get off this platform. Try kicking the door in."

"Okay."

Harple holstered his gun and tried — unsuccessfully — to kick in the door. Then he used his shoulder. It didn't budge. The steel door was manufactured to withstand much more force than a human foot or shoulder could bring to bear.

"Is this what you're looking for?"

Anna and Harple turned around.

Smith and Morrissey stood behind them. Smith tossed the set of keys to Harple.

He started to say "Thanks," but stopped speaking when he saw the gun in Smith's hand. Morrissey looked puzzled.

"Put that gun down," Harple ordered. "We need to get Gusman out of there and we all need to get off this Platform. It is under some kind of attack.

"I don't think that works for me, young man," said Smith.

"What?" Morrissey said, looking surprised. "We have to get everybody out of here. What are you doing, Smith?" Morrissey backed away a step.

"Sorry, Morrissey," said Smith, and calmly pointed the gun at the older man's head and pulled the trigger.

Morrissey hit the ground and ceased to move, blood oozing from a wound above his left eye.

It was so quick and unexpected that Anna didn't even react. She just stood there, slack jawed.

But Harple did. He had two choices: lunge at Smith or try to shoot him. He chose the latter, which caused him a crucial half-second delay while he fumbled with the keys — as Smith had undoubtedly intended when he threw them to Harple — before he could reach his gun.

It was the wrong choice, or maybe there was no good choice because Smith shot the FBI agent once in the chest.

The force of the bullet threw Harple, still trying to reach for his gun, off his feet and against the corridor wall. He slowly slid down the wall. As he tried to speak, only a gurgling sound and a trickle of blood emerged. His head fell to his chest.

Anna screamed. From behind the door, Gusman was yelling.

"Why?" asked Anna.

"Loose ends, missy," he said with a nonchalant shrug of his shoulders. "Now close your eyes," he said almost gently. "It will be easier that way."

She did as he ordered and knew, as surely as she knew that the sun rose in the east and set in the west, she was about to die.

Chapter 57

The Above: Platform Faith

Anna heard movement in front of her and opened her eyes. Smith was looking over his shoulder, the gun still in his hand. What she saw was almost incomprehensible. An army of giant octopuses, many wearing the same sunglasses and armor as the one she and Harple had encountered in the elevator, slithered in total silence down the hallway toward them. Their bodies pulsed in colors that ranged from angry purple to deadly black.

Smith completed his turn, raised his gun, and fired a half-dozen times in quick succession down the crowded corridor, the bullets missing or simply bouncing off the creatures' armor.

"Jesus," he said under his breath as he turned and ran down the hallway.

The creatures did not pursue Smith. Instead, they circled around Anna, the wounded Harple, and the corpse of Morrissey. They filled the corridor, silent and undulating gently to the same slow rhythm.

Then one of the creatures slithered over to Morrissey's body and gently crawled onto his belly.

The octopus turned blood red. It moved slightly, then plunged its sharp beak into Morrissey's soft abdomen.

The creature spent what seemed like an eternity feeding off Morrissey's corpse. Anna stood completely still, barely breathing, as if perhaps they might not notice her if she were quiet enough. Gusman had gone silent again behind the steel door.

Finally, the octopus moved off Morrissey's body, revealing a completely empty abdominal cavity. As the thing moved back to its original spot, it left a trail of blood mixed with bits of human tissue and fabric on the floor.

Anna's mouth felt bone dry and she could taste vomit at the back of her throat. She used all her concentration to stay still, hoping somehow the creatures would let her live. She wanted to call out to Gusman, but didn't dare. She wondered why the creatures had not fed off Harple.

Then the creature that ate Morrissey moved toward Anna.

She took a large gulp of air and tried to move backward, but the corridor wall halted her movement.

The creature continued toward her, its gray skin pulsing yellow and pink starbursts. In the far off reaches of Anna's mind, the scientist in her wondered whether these changes in color conveyed mood. The weight of scientific evidence had always been that the changes in color of cephalopods were solely for the purpose of camouflage or mating. Was something much more sophisticated happening here?

It stopped in front of her. She held her breath, her fear so overwhelming it seemed like time had stopped. She stared into the creature's eyes, which seemed to be staring back into hers. Then it lifted one arm. Anna closed her eyes, expecting, for the second time in less than ten minutes, that she was about to die.

She waited. Then she felt a slight sensation on the left side of her face. It was not unpleasant. It was dry and smooth and very gentle.

She opened her eyes.

The creature's arm stroked the side of her face so softly she could scarcely feel it.

From somewhere far off, she heard Gusman's voice.

"It's okay," he said. "It's okay. He won't hurt you."

Chapter 58

The Above: Platform Faith

P'aldil touches the *face the face of the female with the sensitive end of his makauna arm. Her skin is soft, like the skin of the fry when it first emerges from the egg sac, but covered in tiny, downy, translucent hairs. He looks into her eyes. They are intelligent like the eyes of the great blowholer called Kohol☐, which has lungs to hold gases but no gills and lives in the warm waters far above the He'e. Perhaps he only imagines this intelligence because she is the one named Anna, the semi-mate of Gusman, and he wishes her to be so out of his respect for Gusman. Her respirations are rapid. Gusman keeps telling him in the Dream not to harm the woman Anna.*

"You worry too much, Gusman. Why would I eat Anna Campos?"

"Because you just ate Morrissey."

"Morrissey was not the semi-mate of Gusman and he was near death."

"He was still alive?"

"Only a little."

"Just get me out of here, P'aldil. Push open the door."

P'aldil moves away from the female named Anna toward the horizontal slab of metal that Gusman calls a door.

He lifts one of his arms to push open the door. It doesn't move. "Gusman, the door is fixed."

"Push harder."

P'aldil tries two arms, then three. The closest of the He'e, a strong creature named P'nakua, adds two of his arms to P'aldil's three, but the door will not move.

Gusman says, "I thought you guys were strong."

P'aldil is without mirth because his exertions have made him irritable, He says, "We are not Super-He'e."

The others think it mirthful, though, and flash with momentary joy.

Then Anna Campos speaks. While the gathered He'e cannot understand her human words, her voice is loud and firm, causing a ripple of agitation.

"They need the key," she says. She points at the human with the yellow hairs on the top of his head who lies slumped against the wall. "Harple had the key before he was shot."

"What is this key?" asked P'aldil.

"It is a small piece of metal you insert in the handle of the door. It releases the lock and lets the door open."

The human named Anna puts her hand appendage to her mouth. She understands that P'aldil has spoken to her noiselessly in the Dream and she seems surprised. She tries to make herself small again.

P'aldil, too, is surprised that he can speak so easily to the one called Anna. It must be a matter of proximity, but the other He'e cannot enter this part of the Dream. It is a special gift of P'aldil. He translates the words of the humans and the others flash fiery yellow in amazement.

P'aldil moves to Harple and starts to search all around him with his arms. Then he notices something and stops. "This one is alive. I feel the rhythms of his body and the beat of a heart, but it is very weak."

The semi-mate of Gusman suddenly abandons her torpid state and moves quickly to the body of Harple.

"Please," she says to P'aldil, who understands that she wishes him to help the near-dead human called Harple.

The He'e ripple in anticipation. They are entertained.

The human female lowers her body down to the floor. Tenderly, she wraps her arms around the body and maneuvers it to a prone position, resting the downy pink head on her legs. She strokes the face of the almost-dead human while making low, rhythmic sounds. The He'e pulse in wonderment — these creatures are capable of caring in the rare periods when they are not killing. Then she opens the thin, pliable carapace covering the front of his body. There is a small puncture hole in his torso. It looks like the anus of the m'yona, but larger. Red human blood gurgles in and out of the wound as the dying human weakly respires.

P'aldil calls to M'aldil, who has the power of healing. She comes over. They have all witnessed how the human was wounded by the explosive seed-firing tube and she understands what she must do without the need to exchange thoughts. It is her gift, freely given to the wounded. But to another creature like the humans?

P'aldil pulses the urgency of the task.

In preparation, M'aldil turns dark gray as she withdraws from the Dream to concentrate all her power on the healing task. The human named Anna, who still cradles the head of the dying Harple, stares at M'aldil. M'aldil senses intelligence and the intensity of her caring, like the caring she has for P'aldil and her fry. This surprises M'aldil, as she has doubted P'aldil's claim that the humans are not simply cruel predators like the Muhe'e. M'aldil wishes she could share the Dream with Anna so she could explain to her what she is doing, but she cannot. In any case, she can feel that Anna is calming — her breath slowing, her heart beating more quietly then before. Do these humans know how to trust, she wonders?

Then, M'aldil's concentration is broken when, from inside the room, there is a pounding on the metal barrier and Gusman makes a loud sound with his interior gas box. "What is happening?"

The He'e feel the intensity of Gusman's vibrato expiration. Only P'aldil understands the words.

P'aldil turns angry pink and fires back at Gusman in the Dream. "Stop making noise Gusman. We are trying to save the one called Harple from death."

"Okay, fine," responds Gusman, again in words. He ceases his vibrations.

M'aldil summons her concentration again. She stretches her ho'omao arm straight out in front of her until it thins to a point. It is now a half an arm longer than her other seven. Then she passes it over the wound in the torso of Harple, circling it several times before touching it, probing along its wet edges. Her eyes turn gray like her body and she no longer sees images. Instead, she sees with the end of her ho'omao arm as it probes inside the wound, first in the shallows and then deeper within the human's body. She floods the wound with the fear venom, which paralyzes the flesh inside the wound and slows everything down, deadening the nerves and making them less angry. What paralyzes and panics the brain of a creature when sprayed on its eyes and mouth is beneficial when placed inside a wound.

As she probes deeper, she finds fragments of bone and sinew, which she gently extracts, depositing them on the abdomen of the human. Finally, she feels something hard and foreign. It has traveled past through bone and muscle and lodged near the irregularly beating heart.

"There is metal inside," says M'aldil. She realizes that she means to say this to the human named Anna.

"It is a bullet. Remove it or he will die," replies Anna Campos.

The He'e hear this exchange in the Dream. They are shocked and there is agitated clamor. They have never heard an alien voice. Even Gusman does not speak in the Dream except directly to P'aldil.

"She speaks to M'aldil, but I do not know how," P'aldil explains.

M'aldil understands Anna's words and probes around the metal fragment, which, through her touch, she can see as clearly as if she were examining it with her eyes. It is thick and heavy for such a small thing. She knows this metal. It is called kepau and it is found in abundance near one of the cone smokers. It is softer than other rocks and is affected neither by salt nor sulfur, yet it turns molten in the presence of great heat, but then returns to a solid state when the heat is removed. In the great recesses of the Dream, they know of the ancient one named P'rant'i, who lived in the first generations that followed the death of P'lo and M'lo, the Great Father and the Great Mother. P'rant'i was a great combiner of things. He discovered that kepau, if heated and rolled, could be formed into tools to probe and to strike. But with that good, there was bad, as P'rant'i died a slow and agonizing death from touching the softened kepau. And from the death of P'rant'i, the He'e forevermore refrained from changing the essence of kepau from one thing to another.

Gently M'aldil extracts the metal through the hole in the human's chest, all the while flooding the wound with the sticky healing secretion that all female He'e possess when they are mature enough to mate. It is used to coat the wounds of the growing fry. She does not know whether it will heal human flesh, but she uses it anyway. It is how these things are done.

She places the fragment of kepau on the almost dead one's abdomen with the other detritus she has extracted. It is so small that the He'e wonder how such a small thing can harm these humans.

"They are fragile creatures," says P'heen, "which is good."

"It is strange," M'aldil says to P'aldil, "but this wound would be minor were it sustained by a He'e, unless it was lodged behind the eyes. But on these creatures, it can kill them."

The human named Anna speaks more noises from her mouth.

"Thank you."

The human removes her own soft carapace and places it under the head of the Harple, who is still near death but perhaps a little further away than before.

Then, as the He'e watch, she puts the feelers at the end of one of her arms under Harple and pulls out a bit of metal: "The key," she says. 'I thought he'd fallen on it."

She stands and walks to the door. P'aldil lets her pass.

"Gusman, I've got the key," she utters and slides it into a hole in the metal barrier. She turns it with the appendage at the end of her arm and the door swings to reveal the lighted cave-like space beyond.

Out steps a human male, who immediately entangles his arms in hers and then they touch their mouth orifices together.

The Dream erupts in questions.

Chapter 59

The Above: Platform Faith

Her body clings to his. Gusman kisses Anna, who says in a whisper, "Thank God."

A second later, everything surrounding him floods Gusman's consciousness: the blood spattered on Anna's face and clothes, her wild look and the tears running down her face, the overpowering smell he can't place, the eviscerated body of Morrissey, the chest of the wounded FBI agent rising and falling, and the giant octopuses, silent and staring, filling up the corridor. Most of them seem to be wearing coke bottle-thick sunglasses and are encased in shells that look like opaque, greenish-blue glass.

"What the...?" he stammers, but his words are interrupted by a familiar voice in his head.

"Greetings, Gusman. It is I, P'aldil."

There, a few feet from him sits a large octopus whose skin flashes gray and pink with streaks of blue. He reaches out and gently touches Gusman's head with one of his arms.

"P'aldil?" he asks, and without thinking, he starts to offer his hand in greeting. He quickly pulls it back when realizes the absurdity of his gesture. He wipes his hand on his pants leg to cover up the gaffe, which seems even more ridiculous. Behind him, Anna suppresses a giggle, which seems completely out of place. He is not sure if he is speaking or talking in his head. He's not even sure he can tell the difference anymore. She steps away to check Harple's pulse. Gusman heard the shots; he can guess what has happened.

P'aldil moves a little closer, still keeping one of his arms pointing at Gusman's head.

"Is this a dream?" Gusman asks, perhaps to himself.

"Of course, Gusman. This is the Dream."

"I can't believe this."

"What is this word 'believe,' Gusman?"

"To decide if this is really happening."

P'aldil cocks his head slightly to the side. Many of the other octopuses also cock their heads to one side.

"Gusman, I do not understand."

"What don't you understand?"

"What you mean when you say, 'really happening?'"

"That I am not imagining what I see — dreaming it."

"I am confused, Gusman. There is only the Dream. Everything flows through the Dream. Every creature, every rock, the water, the strange miasma, this place; it all exists in the Dream."

"Forget it," responds Gusman, waving his hand in front of him, as if to push something away. "We can talk about this some other time. The question is what do we do now?"

"The invaders are dead. It is over. We shall leave."

"The people will come back with stronger weapons, P'aldil."

"But, Gusman, this is over now. There is no need for more humans or He'e to die. There has been enough death."

"I agree. But it is not that simple. Humans are both vengeful and curious. It is a dangerous combination. They will not stop until they find out what has happened here. You are a new species to the humans. They will want to learn everything about the He'e. They want your oil and they will stop at nothing to get it."

"They eat the dead. That will not be understood." It was Anna speaking in the Dream. She walked up beside Gusman and took his hand.

P'aldil responds, "It is true. But the *uhane* of the humans — what you told me you call the 'soul' — is no longer here. It now flows in the Dream. Their bodies are just meat for the benthic creatures and the scavengers to eat. Perhaps it is different for you. For us, this is as it is meant to be."

Gusman says, "We eat octopus. I guess now they are returning the favor."

P'aldil sees no signs of mirth on Anna's arms.

"Whatever the truth may be," Gusman says, surveying the eviscerated body of Morrissey. "You have eaten the bodies of the humans you have killed. Our people will consider that barbaric."

"What is 'barbaric?'" P'aldil asks.

"I guess evil. Do you understand the word evil?"

"Yes, we understand evil." P'aldil finally moves his arm from where it has been resting on his head all this time and sweeps it in a circle in front of him before resting it on the floor. He seems to rise, to grow taller and larger. It is menacing, though perhaps not meant to be. Anna moves her body closer to Gusman's. "Evil is what has been done to us by your kind. It is killing not for food, nor for defense, but to kill without reason or because other life gets in the way."

"They will not understand," says Gusman, shaking his too-small head.

"But M'aldil saved the one called Harple. He is not dying so quickly now. He may live. Does that not show that we are not evil?"

Gusman shakes his head again. "They will come with weapons more powerful than the He'e possess. They will kill you without mercy when they find out what has happened here."

"We will return to the urb," says P'aldil. "You will tell your kind that we mean no harm. That we regret the death of the humans, but that they attacked and killed us first."

"They will not understand."

"Then I will stay to explain it to them."

Chapter 60

The Above: Platform Faith

The Dream erupts.

What P'aldil proposes is beyond comprehension and the He'e fear for him. M'aldil says that if P'aldil stays, she will stay with him.

P'heen forbids it and the other elders pulse in angry agreement.

Surely P'M'aldil will perish if they stay behind in this miasma. Already some of the He'e have begun to feel strange pain in their eyes and a burning sensation around their beaks. They want to return to the urb, to the familiar world, that place of soothing water and darkness, punctuated by the hazy illumination of the lighted fishes and the filtered light where molten lava flows up through the vents. The Above is a place of fear and danger and a frightening new enemy, but, most of all, it is a place utterly devoid of moisture, and they feel this alien and unnatural sense of desiccation in every cell of their being, a sensation for which the He'e have no word because, in the entire history of the Dreamtime, the He'e have never experienced it before.

P'aldil begins to address the He'e.

"The humans are like no creatures we have ever encountered. From the beginning of the Dream, we have known these to be truths: that among all the creatures, only the He'e possess knowledge of good and of evil; only the He'e remember the past and plan for the future; and only the He'e know that all creatures exist to serve a purpose, even if they cannot know what it is. Yet, with every mysterious object and dead creature that floated down from the seas above, which

we now know were humans or their creations, we feared that we were not the only sentient creatures — that there was at least another. And now they are among us. They are thinking creatures and, although their bodies are weak and vulnerable, they have powerful weapons so dangerous they can deliver death to the He'e from a great distance in a way that we cannot deliver to them. Yet, I have learned from the human Gusman that they also know the difference between good and evil, but it is not our good nor our evil. And I have learned from Gusman that they want the hinu."

"To salve the wounds of their fry?" asked one of the He'e.

"No, to make their world work. They make it combust and make objects move and lights grow intense. And they will not stop until they have it all."

"But to have it all, they must destroy the urb."

"That is true."

"And you say they know good from evil?"

"In a fashion," responds P'aldil. "And it is for that part of them that knows good that I will stay here and communicate to them."

"You will die."

"We all die."

There is silence for a moment in the Dream.

Then P'heen speaks. "We will return to the urb as speedily as we can. Discard all you have brought that will slow your descent. When we return, we will fashion the kaimana into a shield to cover the entire urb and we will be safe from the humans forever."

The He'e warmly pulse the azure of resolution and of relief.

P'aldil joins with them, but it is not the truth for he knows that, kaimana shield or not, they will never be safe again.

Chapter 61

The Above: Platform Faith

Under the cover of darkness, four SEAL teams approach Platform Faith from the sea, the motors of their rubber boats silenced. Their orders are to scale the giant legs of the platform and secure the deck. If necessary, helicopters from the *Bonhomme Richard*, which had just completed a grueling sixty-hour journey at full speed from its home base in Sasebo, Japan — and was now at anchor two miles from Platform Faith — would then ferry a platoon-sized force of Marines to complete the assault.

They really didn't know what to expect. Their intelligence was fragmentary and contradictory. Clearly there had been an armed attack by a force of indeterminate size and intent. Yet there was no evidence of ships or planes in the vicinity. In the ocean surrounding Platform Faith, the only unusual things were the satellite images showing dozens of small, spherical, shadowy objects of varying size on the ocean surface. The analysts were stymied. Were they man-made or a natural phenomenon? Distress signals had been sent out during the initial stages of the assault. Then, for fourteen hours, there was no further communication. Every effort to contact Platform Faith was met with silence. No demands had been received. The NSA detected no unusual electronic chatter from terrorist sources.

As the assault teams were being assembled, the New York office of Clearsea Energy received a phone call from a cellular phone located on Platform Faith from an employee named Gusman. He claimed that the entire crew was dead except himself, a Doctor Campos, and an FBI agent named

Harple, who was seriously wounded and in need of immediate medical attention. When asked about the assault, he said the platform was now safe now and that 'it was complicated.' Then communication was lost.

As the four rubber boats neared the platform, they encountered the objects in the water that had been detected in the satellite images. They were unusually large floating volcanic rocks enmeshed with seaweed webbing. While they didn't seem to pose any hazard, the team leaders on each of the four boats requested instructions. After consulting with the Pentagon, their commander aboard the *Bonhomme Richard* ordered them to continue the assault, but to move forward with extreme caution.

Nearly in unison, the SEAL teams reached the enormous pontoons that held up the platform. Silently, they began their assent up the ladders attached to each of the four steel legs. Some natural light from the stars and the sliver of a moon illuminated the clear night sky, but they would not have been able to see without their night vision equipment. They didn't linger. Staying still made them targets, and they had no idea what to expect when they got to the top of Platform Faith. All they knew was that at least a few people were purportedly alive and friendly, but from their vantage point, they saw nothing. No noise, no lights, no activity whatsoever.

They climbed silently up the wet, metal ladders. The ascent seemed to take forever. The men tried not to look down. Within minutes, they were hundreds of feet above the surface of the water. Above them loomed the solid blackness of the platform. They stopped just underneath the hatches that opened to the deck. They waited for all the teams to get into position. Finally, the last of the units reached the top. All that stood between them and the platform were four locked steel hatches. They paused to check in with one another and their command aboard the *Bonhomme Richard*.

It was a go.

Acetylene torches quickly cut through the hinges and the SEALs began to push through, climbing the last flight of metal stairs that opened onto the four corners of the platform. As they ran up the stairs with a fluidity of motion gained through constant practice, they unclipped their short Heckler and Koch submachine guns, silenced and scoped, bursting onto the surface of the platform in groups three, fanning out in all directions.

The top of the platform was littered with bits of glass and clothing but was otherwise completely deserted. It smelled like rotten seaweed, and in places the surface was slippery with what appeared to be blood.

Within three minutes, they had achieved their initial objective of securing the exterior of the platform. There had been no injuries, no casualties, and no contact — friendly or otherwise — with any human beings, alive or dead. Having encountered no resistance, and ahead of schedule, they were ordered to proceed to the next stage of the assault: securing the interior of the platform without waiting for the arrival of the marines.

Since setting sail from Japan, the SEAL teams had been practicing for the assault and were prepared for what came next. The forty-odd SEALs huddled in teams outside each of six doors to the interior. As expected, all were locked. Clearsea Energy had supplied them with the codes for opening the doors, but, fearful that they might be wired by explosives, they decided to blow them instead. Charges were affixed to the locks and the SEAL teams temporarily retreated to cover.

A few moments later, through their ear buds, they heard the demo guys yell "fire in the hole," followed by the flash and bang of explosives. The four teams moved slowly into the interior, which was eerily lit by dim red emergency lights. They checked for trip wires and booby traps. There was nothing. Now they went faster, with movements that were almost dance-like in their precision. They had studied the blueprints of Platform Faith and knew where they were going.

There were no bodies, but the smell was more intense: fishy; the fetid stink of static, tropical air; ammonia; and something that those among them who had witnessed death close up recognized — the faint odor of blood and decaying flesh.

Chapter 62

The Above: Platform Faith

Gusman declared, "this place is a 'pig sty,'" but, try as he might, he was unable to explain the concept to P'aldil. The floor was slick with water. There were empty tuna, salmon, and sardine cans strewn about. P'aldil complained that the canned fish tasted oily and dead and the bones were missing. Somehow, though, P'M'aldil managed to eat them. The place reeked, but that was a bigger problem for the humans who, unlike the cephalopods, seemed to distinguish between good and bad smells. P'aldil and M'aldil simply catalogued each new smell. The humans had a distinct odor, something like a blowholer, but with the overlay of the frightening predator smell of the *muhe'e*. P'aldil had not told Gusman this because he did not wish to offend him.

When P'M'aldil started to feel sick, the He'e explained that they needed to be kept wet. So Gusman and Anna spent day and night pouring water over their skin and into their gills. This contributed to the generally disgusting — at least from the human's perspective — state of the place.

P'aldil was incredulous when Gusman explained that Dr. Campos was an expert in sea creatures, especially cephalopods — creatures like the He'e. How was it that humans knew about the He'e and the He'e knew virtually nothing about humans? Or that a human could, upon achieving maturity, spend most of its life engaged in such study.

P'aldil felt comfort when Dr. Campos sprayed water on him. She would stroke his arms gently as she sprayed the water and P'aldil could sense that she felt no fear. His colors undulated slowly and M'aldil had said that perhaps he would like to stay here permanently with the human female. P'aldil scoffed.

It was different when Gusman did it. He sprayed the water, but never touched P'aldil. P'aldil asked questions to initiate conversation, which Gusman would answer, but it seemed as though he lacked curiosity and preferred to remain quiet.

P'aldil wished he could enter the Dream more easily with Anna Campos. There were fragments of words that passed between them, and sometimes they understood each other. But it was not like Gusman who was fully in the Dream.

When they weren't dousing P'M'aldil, the humans were tending to Harple, who was still unconscious, but had stabilized. His breathing was slow, but steady. They had raided the infirmary and found an IV, which Anna knew how to start. She had, it turned out, served as an army medic to put herself through college and grad school. They had him laid out on the same steel table that they had examined P'aldil's severed arm.

Suddenly, P'aldil raised up on his arms. "I smell humans."

"Where?"

"Below us, entering the human urb," he said, pointing one of his legs at the door to the dining hall.

"Quickly," he said, "you must get our protective shields of *kaimana* for us."

Gusman understood and explained to Anna. They hurried to the storeroom and retrieved the translucent shields and helmets. Although they were large and awkward to grasp, the material was thin and light. They managed it in two quick trips.

P'M'aldil donned their equipment with amazing speed. M'aldil flashed the fear colors and P'aldil tried to reassure her that it was just a precaution, that the humans would not hurt them.

"Your words are slippery, like the eel," she said. "They do not comfort me."

Chapter 63

The Above: Platform Faith

The SEAL team split into two groups, one huddling to the left and the other to the right of the doors to the mess hall. They moved quickly and silently into position, their eyes fixed on the hand signals of their commander. They had fully adjusted to the dim red glow of the emergency lighting and removed their night vision equipment.

They waited in silence for their orders to breach the door. Without air conditioning, it was hot in the corridor and the air was still and stagnant. The full body armor they wore felt leaden and constricting and they were sweating profusely. The linoleum floor under their feet was sticky.

From the room beyond, they heard the hum of the emergency lights and an odd squishing sound.

Somebody or something was in there.

Chapter 64

The Above: Platform Faith

There was an explosion and a momentary flash of light as the charge blew the doors open. They waited for a few seconds to see if there was any resistance, then a half-dozen black-clad Navy SEALs entered the room, their assault rifles held at shoulder height. The red dots of their laser sights rested on the chests of Gusman and Anna, who were dazed and temporarily blinded by the sudden explosion and bright flash of light. Both had instinctively covered their heads with their arms.

The SEALs did not see the two octopuses, who had slid next to the now-blown entry doors and made themselves flat and still. They had turned themselves red to match the exact hue of the emergency lights. They were nearly invisible.

Uncovering their faces and taking in the sight of the armed, crouched figures through the dim hazy red glow of the emergency lights, Anna raised her hands in surrender. Gusman did the same.

It took the SEALs perhaps a full second to stop their forward movement and freeze as they began to comprehend the scene in front of them.

Two people. No weapons. A lot of water. The place reeked, like an aquarium in need of cleaning.

Nobody moved.

Except P'aldil, who was straining so hard to be still that when he stiffened one of his arms he hit a table behind him, causing one of the metal buckets they were using to keep the octopuses hydrated to come crashing onto the floor.

One of the SEALs turned in the direction of the sound and, overreacting, fired twice in the direction of the sound. The trajectory of the bullets took them far above P'aldil, imbedding them in the far wall.

Instinctively, P'M'aldil acted as one, rearing up and spraying the SEALS with fear venom.

The SEALs became confused and were unable to react. Several dropped their weapons, and others shook their heads as if they had just been sucker punched.

The two octopuses moved forward, pushing the SEALs out of their way with their strong arms, and disappeared into the corridor.

Gusman must have been sprayed, too. He found himself on all fours, trying — without success — to stand up. Anna was a few feet away, lying face down on the floor. He crawled over to her, leaning in close to her.

He could see she was breathing. Was she conscious?

"Anna," he whispered, brushing the hair from her face. "Anna," he whispered again, this time his tone more urgent. "Can you hear me?"

She groaned, then let out a croupy-sounding, barking cough. Her eyes fluttered open and, for a second, seemed unfocused and disoriented. Then she fixed on Gusman's face and he saw recognition flow back into her eyes. She smiled weakly and brought her hand to touch Gusman's, which was stroking her cheek softly.

"I'm okay," she said.

They stared into each other's eyes as if there were no one else in the world.

Rough hands yanked Gusman up to his feet by his arms and shoulders. Before he had time to register what was happening, his wrists were bound, and a hood was being shoved over his head.

"Take him topside," a voice growled.

Afterward, in their debriefing, the SEAL team flatly contradicted the stories of Gusman and Anna, and insisted they saw no alien creatures and that they must have been momentarily overcome by the noxious atmosphere and slippery surface.

Chapter 65

The Above: Platform Faith

One of the other SEAL teams found Bobby Smith hiding in a locked utility closet on another part of the platform. When they kicked in the door, they found Smith seated cross-legged with his hands on his head, smiling up at them, a look of tremendous relief on his face.

"Am I glad to see you boys," he said in his deepest Texas drawl as the red laser dots danced on his torso. "I was scared shitless those terrorists would find me."

They were taking no chances and handled him roughly, cuffing him and putting a hood over his head. But he expected that and took it in stride. They found his weapon on the floor of the closet. One of the SEALs picked it up and bagged it.

The SEAL team leader only asked him one question. "Are you injured?"

"Nah, I'm just fine. Damned happy you're here."

He was brought to a young naval officer, who did a quick field interrogation. It didn't take them long to confirm his identity as the Chief of Corporate Security for Clearsea Energy.

"Sir, you check out — but for now, I apologize, I have to leave on the handcuffs. You understand. Standard Operating Procedure."

"Of course."

"Tell us what happened here."

Smith regurgitated his carefully concocted story.

"We were attacked by an armed terrorist group. I can't tell you much. I was in my quarters and heard on the monitor the distress signal go out from the communications room, saying we were under attack. Then the emergency lights went on. I grabbed my weapon and ran into the hallway. I saw a member of the crew. He yelled that terrorists were attacking us and that they were slaughtering the crew. I proceeded down the stairs to B Deck, I ran into two mutilated bodies. Then I saw something moving on the other end of the corridor and fired my weapon."

"Did they fire back?"

"No. But it was clear that I would only get myself killed if I went forward, so I decided to find a safe hiding place and wait it out until help arrived. I found the utility closet and didn't come out until you found me. Did anyone survive?"

"Yes, sir. Three people. Two men and a woman." He looked at his clipboard. "Gusman, no first name, and... Campos, first name Anna. The third man is severely wounded and unconscious. We have not identified him yet."

"That's all?"

"Yes, sir. Unless there's somebody else hidden here that we haven't found yet."

"Did they shoot people? Take them hostage?"

"There are no bodies. We don't know how or even if they died. So, I can't say, sir."

"Jesus Christ," said Smith. "They took the bodies? Bastards. Son, I was a Texas Ranger for many years and I saw a lot of terrible things, but nothing like this."

"Yes, sir."

"Strange thing," Smith said, shaking his head slowly, "that Gusman and Dr. Campos survived."

"Why do you say that, sir?"

"Well, there was a murder investigation going on before the attack. An FBI agent was sent here to investigate and had placed Gusman under arrest. At the time of the attack, he was confined to a locked room. There was a personal relationship between Gusman and Dr. Campos. It's a helluva coincidence that those two survived."

"Yes, sir. I'll pass that along."

Chapter 66

The Above: Platform Faith

Gusman could not see anything, but he could feel, and he could listen. Two men held him, one at each arm. Their grip was firm, but not painful. They shuffled him down several corridors and outside onto the platform. He felt the change of pressure and the warmth of sunlight on his face. It must be well past dawn now. From there, they crossed the deck. He heard male voices in the distance. They were calm and businesslike — men doing their jobs.

They stopped.

One of the men guiding him said, "Five stairs. Be careful."

He stepped forward hesitantly onto the first stair and then he started up. As his foot reached the final step, the men let go. Other strong, competent hands took over, grabbing him by the arms and shoulders and pulling him up.

"Watch your head," one of them said and a hand cradled his skull and pushed it down under a low threshold.

"Okay, we're going to sit you down and buckle you in." It was the same voice — low-pitched, vaguely southern, young.

It suddenly smelled different. Metallic and oily. It was hotter, too, and more humid. He started to sweat.

Someone cut the plastic strap holding his hands and brought his arms around to the front of his body and cinched a new plastic tie around his wrists.

He was lowered, and shoulder straps were placed over his head and across his chest. He heard the tight click of the seatbelt as it latched. He tested it with his body. He was buckled in tight.

Then he heard the sounds to his right. Metal sliding along a greased channel.

"Okay, Skipper," someone said.

There were two or three clicks in rapid succession and the rotors started. They were in a helicopter.

"Where are you taking me?"

No one answered.

He could feel the helicopter rise and then take off.

"Hey," one of them said, "you got another piece?"

"Yeah, sure," responded another.

The windows must have been open because as they flew, he sensed wind on his face through the hood and the air got cooler and fresher.

"Can't you guys take this thing off?" Gusman asked.

"Nope," one of them grunted. It was a nonchalant, disinterested grunt, like he just didn't feel like making much of an effort, the very lightness of tone conveying scorn in a way that a firm and harsh 'no' could not. To these men, Gusman was not worth shit.

They were in the air for only a few minutes. Then they slowed and landed. Firm hands pulled him up and then transferred him to another set of hands that guided him down the stairs and onto the deck of a ship.

He could feel the sway of the deck in the current and the suddenness of it, combined with his inability to see, caused him a momentary wave of nausea.

"I feel like I'm going to throw up."

"Okay. Just stand him still for a minute," a female voice said.

"Sir," she said, "you just need to catch your breath. You're on board a ship and you need to get accustomed to it."

"Yeah," Gusman croaked. After a few seconds, the nausea passed. "It's okay."

They started moving again, entering a corridor, turning several corners, taking an elevator down, and crossing more corridors. Occasionally, he heard voices. Sometimes they stopped abruptly as he passed. Were they shocked to see a prisoner with a hood over his head and his hands manacled in front of him?

Finally, they came to a stop. He heard a key enter a lock and a metal door slide open. He was led in and seated.

His arms were lifted, and the ties cut off. He rubbed his wrists, which were chaffed and sore.

After his hood was removed, it was easier to breathe and Gusman took a couple of deep gulps of air. The air was fresher now that he was no longer inhaling the foulness of his own expired breath.

A female naval officer in a camouflage uniform stood in front of him. Behind her were two male soldiers. One of them held the plastic handcuffs that had been removed. Both looked impassive.

She was about thirty years old with her blond hair pulled back into a tight ponytail. Her high cheekbones gave her a slightly Slavic look. She wore no makeup or jewelry. On her uniform, where her name tag would normally be, there was just a strip of fabric. She did not introduce herself.

"Mr. Gusman, you have been transferred to a United States Navy vessel for interrogation. You are being confined to the brig. You have a sink, a toilet, and a bed. Someone will be back in a little while. Do you have any questions?"

"Can I see a lawyer?" he asked.

"No. Not at this time. Any other questions?"

"No," he said.

"Are you injured or sick?" she asked

"No. I think I'm okay."

"All right then. As I said, someone will be back to talk to you shortly. Please change into the clothes that are on the bed. Put your own clothes, shoes, and personal effects in the bag." She gestured to a clear plastic garbage bag sitting on the bed.

They turned around and left the cell. There was a loud click as the lock was engaged from the outside.

Gusman took stock of his new home. It contained a steel cot with a thin mattress, one pillow, white sheets, and a gray blanket. On the bed was a small, white towel. Next to that was the plastic bag containing the change of clothes. Across the room were a stainless-steel sink and a toilet. The toilet did not have a toilet seat. *Nice.* Above the sink was a shelf and mirror, also made of stainless steel. On it was a plastic water cup, a toothbrush still in its packaging, a small tube of toothpaste, and a tiny bar of soap like the ones the hotels give out, but in a plain wrapper with no writing on it.

The only place to sit was the bed, so there Gusman sat. The tiny cubicle was immaculate. It smelled strongly of disinfectant, which seemed to grow in intensity the longer he was in the room. Maybe it was the odor, but whatever the reason, his head ached again. He massaged his temples. The pressure gave him momentary relief, but as soon as he took his fingers away, the pain returned more intensely than before. His mouth tasted of bile and so he decided to brush his teeth. Grabbing the towel, he walked the two steps to the sink. It had one of those pressure activated faucets. He pressed down on it and the water ran anemically for a few seconds before it shut off. He did it again, this time filling the cup with water. It was cool, but not cold, and tasted vaguely of metal and chlorine. He stared at his distorted image in the polished, stainless steel mirror. Great, he thought, you can't break steel into shards. Suicide proof. *How depressing.*

The mint flavor of the toothpaste was soothing, and it felt good to brush his teeth again. Finally, relieved to feel even slightly refreshed, he turned back to the bed and emptied the contents of the plastic bag onto it. There was a yellow jumpsuit, a white T-shirt, a pair of white cotton briefs, a pair of white socks, and a pair of slip-on, one-size-fits-all black plastic sandals. He stripped. The T-shirt and the underwear were a little big. The jumpsuit was way too big for him. He unfolded it. A large black letter 'P' — for prisoner, he presumed — was ironed on the back. He had to roll up the sleeves and the pant legs to get it to fit halfway decently.

He stuffed his clothes and shoes into the bag. His only personal effects were his wallet and his watch — a cheap Timex digital he had bought recently to replace the last cheap watch he had lost.

Gusman sat down on the edge of the bed to wait. For what, he wasn't sure.

— «» —

It had long since ceased being a shock when P'aldil's voice appeared in Gusman's head, although he wasn't expecting to see his gray-pink octopus face staring back at him in the mirror. Actually, truth be told, Gusman was happy to hear from P'aldil — although it was depressing to contemplate that he had reached the point that a giant octopus was rapidly becoming his best friend.

"Gusman, are you there?"

"Yeah, I'm here."

"Where are you?"

"In jail, for a change."

"I recognize your laughless mirth tone. You seem to spend a lot of time in that jail place."

"Ever since I met you, good buddy."

"Are you in pain?"

"No, I'm fine. And you? How are you?"

"I am healthy. But there is great fear. You are right: the humans are powerful and must be deterred from attacking the He'e. Tell me, what do they need most from the waters?"

"Fish and oil — *hinu*."

"There are too many fish to deny them that. But oil. I wonder, Gusman, if their *hinu* was cut off, would they be deterred from attacking us?"

"They would be very pissed off, and maybe slowed in their response, but in the end, it would be the same, I'm afraid. With one exception."

"And what is that, Gusman?"

"If you could cut off their supply of offshore oil all over the world. They need the oil, the *hinu* in the sea. The hinu in the land away from the seas will not last forever. You must make it clear to them that you control the *hinu* in the sea and they will get none of it without your cooperation."

"Then we must enlist the help of the faraway He'e who live in the outer reaches of the Dream."

This will not end well, thought Gusman.

"Tell them, Gusman. Tell them the *hinu* in the sea is ours. We won't surrender it to humans."

"Yeah. No problem. I can tell them. Except for the minor problem that they will think I'm completely insane."

Chapter 67

The Above: Aboard the
USS *Bonhomme Richard*

Against his better judgment, Gusman decided he would waive legal representation and just tell them everything. His story was so crazy he couldn't conceive of them believing it. And honestly, he had another motive: to help P'aldil save the He'e from further blundering attacks.

He had reached a new low: altruism.

Gusman's interrogator seemed neither surprised nor incredulous when he began to discuss his interactions with the He'e. The young man — he said his name was John, which Gusman didn't believe — just kept asking more questions, drilling down to the tiniest details of Gusman's story. His expression was blank; his voice monotone and nonjudgmental.

"Sir, how do you spell P'aldil?" the man asked, without the slightest change of expression.

Time seemed to be moving slowly in the windowless room. The young officer's relentless questions made Gusman sleepy. They kept shoving coffee and food in front of him. He wondered whether they were drugging him. He didn't care one way or another. Perhaps his lack of concern, his odd sense of inner calm, was just the effect of the drugs.

He asked if they were drugging him and the officer laughed a little derisively and said, "We don't do that kind of thing."

"So, you draw the line at waterboarding?" he asked, immediately regretting it.

"Sir, please, shall we proceed?" the young man asked calmly.

Gusman was unconvinced, but he didn't care enough to make a big point of it. In any case, it felt good to unburden himself. He had done nothing wrong — except to be in wrong place at the wrong time.

Repeatedly.

After a while, they gave him a break, walking him back to his 'quarters' as they called his cell. They had him in leg chains, which made it hard to walk. In addition to extreme fatigue, he had no idea what time it was, which contributed to a strong feeling of disorientation. He collapsed on the bunk and slept a dead, dreamless sleep. The best he'd had in ages.

The next thing he knew, a woman's voice was waking him.

"Mr. Gusman, time to get up." She pressed a finger gently, but insistently, into his shoulder. His brain stumbled into consciousness.

"Where am I?" he groggily asked the blurry face above him.

"Aboard ship, Mr. Gusman," she replied. And then he recognized her, the young female officer from before. The memories flooded back.

"Is it time for more questions?"

"Yes, sir," she said.

She touched his shoulder to help him to his feet. It was a sympathetic gesture. Why, he wondered?

The next session focused on what the young interrogator, John, called "the terrorist attack."

"I didn't see any terrorists," Gusman said flatly.

"Well, then, what did you see?"

"Well, I was in a cell for most of the time of the attack. By the time Anna and P'aldil let me out of there, all I saw were He'e…"

"Now remind me again, who are the He'e?"

Gusman grew impatient because his interrogator knew quite well who the He'e were. He had explained it to him a dozen times already. But then he realized the kid was just doing his job, just trying to trip him up.

"Okay, as I've told you about a thousand times, the He'e are a deep-sea octopus species — and P'aldil is one of them."

"Go on."

"So, what I saw was the He'e. They were everywhere up and down the corridor. Morrissey's body was on the ground. Harple was still alive, but in bad shape. And Anna."

"What about Mr. Smith?"

"He wasn't there. Anna told me that after he shot Morrissey and Harple, he fired at the He'e and ran. I never saw him."

"When was the last time you saw Smith?"

"I don't know. A few days before, when they locked me in that room."

A little later, as John walked him through the chain of events yet another time, he suddenly paused and, staring straight into his eyes, asked, "Mr. Gusman, would you be willing to take a polygraph test?"

"Sure. What have I got to lose?"

The young man-made no effort to answer the question. "Now tell me, Mr. Gusman: what do you think that these creatures you've described want?"

"They want to stop us from invading their habitat."

"And how do you suppose they intend to do that?"

"By attacking off-shore oil facilities like they did here."

"And how do you know that?"

"P'aldil told me."

"When?"

"Yesterday."

"You must be making a mistake, Mr. Gusman. You were here yesterday."

"No, I'm not making a mistake."

"Are you telling me that P'aldil spoke to you while you were confined here on this ship?"

Gusman sat back in his chair. His ankle chain rattled. "That's exactly what I'm telling you."

"He was here on this ship?"

"No, I don't think so."

"But he talked to you."

"Yes, he appears in my dreams sometimes."

John slapped down his pen on the table. Anger flashed in his eyes. "Come on, Mr. Gusman. That's impossible."

"Hey, suit yourself. If you don't want to believe me, you don't have to."

Chapter 68

The Below: Platform Andrew, the North Sea

Deep in the Paleocene rock beneath the cold water of the North Sea, there was a bit of unusual movement at the well-head of Platform Andrew. Named for the Patron saint of Scotland, Platform Andrew had brought good luck to the shareholders of British Petroleum for nearly thirty years. No one witnessed the movement and perhaps there was no relationship between the shadowy presence and the disaster that followed. But the pressure in the well began to drop steadily. Samples of the oil revealed an unknown, gummy substance and small, clear, and very hard rocks mixed in the oil. Eighteen hours later, the flow of oil stopped completely.

The next day, a submersible reached the sea bottom to inspect the wellhead. Everything looked normal except a few meters from the shaft were a group of large stones arranged in a circle with lines of smaller stones radiating from the bottom half of the circle. Later, when photographs of the rock formation were examined, something became immediately obvious: the large circle of stones was made up of eight stones as were the eight lines of smaller stones emanating from circle. Stranger still, the stones were not of local origin. Of course, the bigger problem was that, when the inspection covers were removed from the wellhead pipes, it was discovered that the pipes were completely filled some kind of hardened, concrete-like aggregate material, rendering the well completely inoperable. As this had never before been encountered, no estimate could be immediately given as to how long it would take to bring the well back online.

There was an obvious suspicion of sabotage. Photographs taken at the wellhead site were sent to Scotland Yard and MI-5 for analysis. Neither could match the strange rock formation with the symbol of any known terrorist group. Inquiries were sent to Interpol and the foreign intelligence services of France, Germany, and the United States to see if they had any information.

Meanwhile, BP routinely reported the shutdown to the UK's Department of Energy and Climate Change, which, in turn, included it in its daily output report for North Sea wells under British authority. The shutdown caught the attention of a stringer for the *Oil and Gas Journal*. When he made a call to the media relations office of BP-Scotland in Aberdeen, he was told that the company had no information to release on the 'incident,' and that if he wanted more information, he needed to take the matter up with headquarters in London. Sensing something unusual happening, he called a woman named Glenda he had met a few weeks earlier at a club who had given him her number. She was a secretary in BP's media relations office. He had been pretty drunk the night they'd met, and he didn't remember much, except that she was a stout girl with ample cleavage and an open, friendly face.

But Glenda remembered him and was very friendly. He flirted for a bit and then asked her if she knew anything about the shutdown at Platform Andrew.

"I thought you called to talk to me," she said coyly. He could practically see her furrowed brow and the petulant turn of her lip over the phone.

"Come on, love. I called to ask you out, but sometimes I just can't help myself," he said coyly, making his accent sound a whole lot more working class than it normally was.

"I'll ring you back," she said.

Glenda was good for her word.

"They're all hush-hush about this one. I think Scotland Yard is involved. Something happened down there that completely stopped production. It will be months before it comes back online."

"Is that all you know?"

She lowered her voice to a whisper. "Nobody will talk to me. Someone said something about the Official Secrets Act."

"Seriously?"

— «» —

Six hours later, *Oil and Gas Journal* posted the following online story on its homepage:

14:26 GMT. Aberdeen, UK. British Petroleum's North Sea Platform 'Andrew' ceased production yesterday. A spokesman for BP refused to comment on the reason for the shut down and would only say that the matter "was under investigation." Production will be restored in the "near future," according to the company. Britain's Department of Energy and Climate Change, which regulates oil production in the North Sea, is also refusing comment until its own investigation is completed.

Chapter 69

The Above: Asmari Oil Reserve, Bandar Abbas, Iran

Their orders were clear. The Supreme Leader had decreed that the Iran National Oil Company should double its investment in drilling new oil wells, even in the oldest off-shore fields, like the Asmari field in the Persian Gulf. The truth was — and everybody knew it — that Iran's oil production was gradually and inexorably declining. What Iran's oil men kept telling the country's leaders was that investment was needed in new extraction techniques — gas injection, fracking — that could boost production at the fields. But they would hear none of it.

The platform was a kilometer off the coast, at the edge of the Asmari field, just east of the main seaway through the Straits of Hormuz. From the drilling platform, two US destroyers could be seen in the distance maneuvering to get a closer look. A small patrol craft from the naval branch of the Iranian Revolutionary Guards was executing slow, lazy circles around the rig.

It was hot and dirty work. They were pushing the drilling equipment hard — perhaps too hard — to try to get through the layer of Paleolithic rock that lay just beneath the sand and shale at the bottom of the Persian Gulf. But they were under strict deadlines, and the crew was promised bonuses if they struck oil. Then they hit something that was hard. The crew boss told them to increase the drill speed to try to break through. He ordered them to inject more drill mud into the borehole to accommodate the increased speed of the case-hardened steel bit.

The men closest to the drill shaft felt it first. A heavy vibration in the steel casing that surrounded the drill shaft, followed by a whining sound that seemed like it was coming from deep below them, from the depths of the sea. The vibration became a noticeable wobble in the shaft. The wobble increased until it felt as though the entire platform was torqueing. The crew members looked at each other with fear and let go of the shaft, running for the edges of the platform.

There was a deep roar that sounded like it was traveling from the center of the earth right through the metal of the now wildly bucking drill shaft.

Then nothing.

The shaft continued to spin — much faster than before — but the bucking stopped. It was obvious to everyone what had occurred: the drill bit had sheared off in the wellhead.

The crew leader immediately reported what had occurred to management. He was ordered to stop anyone from leaving the platform pending the arrival of a detachment of Revolutionary Guards, who would launch an investigation. All cell phones were to be confiscated.

The US destroyers moved in even closer. A drone that had been aloft for hours continued to snap high-resolution photos.

By early evening, the platform was crowded with investigators. The crew was thoroughly interrogated, then sent home with strict instructions not to discuss the incident.

The head of the investigation — a Major Ishfahani — was convinced from the outset that the accident was likely the result of sabotage, although his interrogations yielded no evidence that any of the crew were involved. It was probably the CIA or the Mossad sending Iran a message. The movement of the American destroyers was very suspicious. A month earlier, the army had released a video of a simulated Iranian rocket attack on the new Israeli Leviathan offshore gas well in the Mediterranean. The Jews had a nasty habit of responding to such propaganda by doing the real thing. So perhaps it was their handiwork.

On the second day of the investigation, Major Ishfahani sent a team of deep-sea divers down to the wellhead to inspect the damage and photograph the site. Upon reaching the scene, they radioed an assessment of the damage back to the platform. There were fragments of metal and opaque crystalline rock radiating from the wellhead, indicating an explosion. They took samples. But the strangest thing, which they caught on a video feed, was a rock formation obviously left as a calling card by whomever was responsible for what was, Major Ishfahani believed, almost certainly a terrorist attack: a circle of eight rocks with a trail of eight lines of rocks descending from the bottom, each line made up of eight rocks.

The Americans, who had buried sensitive sound detection equipment throughout the area to detect electronic signals sent by Iranian submarines, picked up large parts of the transmission, which was relayed back to the Pentagon for analysis.

Major Ishfahani sent everything back to Tehran. Photographs of the strange terrorist calling card were distributed throughout the intelligence services of the Islamic Republic. No one could identify it. An ethnic Azeri file clerk, who was on the payroll of the foreign intelligence service of the neighboring Republic of Azerbaijan, copied a photograph of the stone calling card and smuggled it out of the country. The Azeris, loyal allies of the United States and Israel, duly sent it along to the CIA and the Mossad.

Chapter 70

The Above: Gulf of Mexico

It was in the shallow waters off the Gulf of Mexico that offshore oil drilling first began in the 1930s. The water was warm and the crude sweet, light, and remarkably close to the surface. The near-shore oil fields — the earliest — are now mostly exhausted. After the end of their useful economic life, oil wells are sealed at the ocean bottom and a large concrete plug put in place. Then the oil rigs are either totally removed or sometimes the rigs — already encrusted by sea life — are tipped over to create an artificial reef. For the next six hundred or so years, the metal gently disintegrates, eventually returning the rig, like all things, to its elemental state. Occasionally, the plug comes loose and there is slight leakage of oil. While there is too little oil to cause major environmental damage, the oil companies immediately send divers down to reseal the plug.

It is routine.

A passing shrimp trawler was the first to radio in the news that he had spotted a small oil slick in the gulf approximately two miles south-southwest of the city of Galveston, Texas. A Coast Guard cutter was dispatched along with an oil spill prevention and response team from the United States Environmental Protection Agency. They deployed a boom to isolate the spill and the team began to vacuum it up. It was quickly ascertained that the oil was not from a leaking tanker or other vessel but was rising from the ocean floor. Measured by the hour, the volume of oil — while small — was increasing.

Within thirty minutes, a public information officer from the EPA regional office in Galveston issued a press release indicating that an oil slick had been discovered, its location, and that it was likely "either naturally occurring or the result of a ruptured wellhead seal from an abandoned offshore oil platform."

The EPA informed ConocoPhillips, which had once operated the offshore well prior to its decommissioning that there was a possible leak at the site of the wellhead cap. Under federal law, ConocoPhillips was liable in perpetuity for any oil that leaked from the site.

The company immediately dispatched its own cleanup team to the site, including divers.

Over the course of the next twelve hours, the amount of oil leaking from the site steadily increased, although the total volume was still small.

A local television station in Galveston sent a helicopter over the site to get footage of the leak. The station broadcast a short news segment that afternoon. The reporter interviewed a spokesperson for the EPA, who said that the situation was "fully under control" and that a cleanup was underway. The probable cause of the leak was a failure of a cap in a former offshore wellhead, which she characterized as an "extremely rare event." ConocoPhillips did not comment on air but issued a press statement taking "full responsibility" for the leak and pledging to clean up any leak and reseal the well.

It was a local story. So far.

The dive team was sent down to the site of the wellhead. The divers confirmed that oil was leaking from the cap.

They made two surprising discoveries. First, the cap was not cracked, and the seal was not broken. Rather, oil was leaking through several two-inch holes bored cleanly through the cap. There were no concrete fragments in the area. Such a hole could only have been drilled with a tool.

Second, near the wellhead was a clearly man-made formation of rocks: a circle of eight stones from which eight arms of eight stones each, descended.

"Looks like sabotage to me," said one of the divers excitedly into his mic. "Shit, I think we got eco-terrorists on our hands."

Chapter 71

The Above: Aboard the
USS *Bonhomme Richard*

Anna was angry, but there wasn't much, it appeared, that she could do about it. In the twenty-four hours since they were removed from Platform Faith, she had been interrogated nearly continuously by a polite, but very insistent naval intelligence officer who identified himself as Lieutenant Commander Hawkins. He had a receding chin and thin, bony cheekbones — a combination of features that made him seem condescending and arrogant. She did not like him. They let her sleep, but only a few hours at a stretch. She had no idea whether it was day or night.

At first, Anna's interrogator seemed focused on the assault and appeared convinced that Platform Faith had been the subject of a terrorist attack.

She vigorously corrected his misimpression. "I know it sounds crazy, but that's not what happened."

"What did happen?"

"The platform was overrun by a previously unknown species of cephalopod. They killed many of the crew."

"Really, ma'am?" he said with obvious disbelief.

"Yes, really. You can ask Special Agent Harple, who will confirm what I say."

"Special agent Harple has not regained consciousness. He is in critical condition and has lost a lot of blood. If he regains consciousness, we will certainly interview him."

"If he lives, it's because one of those octopuses removed a bullet fragment from near his heart."

"Is that so?"

"Yes."

The man frowned slightly. "You are certain there were no terrorists?"

"Absolutely certain."

"Not according to Mr. Smith."

"That murdering asshole," she blurted. Fists clenched, she flushed and looked away.

The officer cocked his head slightly and leveled his glance at her. One eyebrow was raised. It was obvious he did not believe her. "Who did he murder?"

"He killed Mr. Morrissey, then he shot Agent Harple, and he was about to shoot me."

"And you witnessed that?"

"I sure did."

"As you can imagine, Mr. Smith tells quite a different story."

"Then Mr. Smith is a liar as well as a murderer," Anna shot right back. "He knows quite well what happened on Platform Faith. The only reason he didn't shoot me is that an army of those octopuses were coming down the corridor and he ran. If you don't believe me, go look in the galley refrigerator. There's a leg of one of those creatures in there. A few weeks ago, there was an incident where a few of the creatures surfaced near some crew members and there was a confrontation of sorts between them. The creatures escaped, but one of the crew shot off its leg. It's a new species. Any decent marine biologist will be able to verify what I am telling you. There are detailed notes of my examination of the leg in my quarters."

"We'll be sure to check that out," he said calmly. "But that doesn't prove that Mr. Smith is a murderer."

Did he just think she was crazy? Anna couldn't tell.

"Dr. Campos, tell me about your relationship with Mr. Gusman."

"What do you want to know?"

"Everything."

Chapter 72

The Above: Austin, Texas

For the first time since she was a child, Annie was worried about her brother. It was like he had fallen off the end of the Earth. She sent him numerous texts and emails. She left messages on his cell phone. She even called the human resources department of Clearsea Energy in New York. They told her he was on Platform Faith.

When she questioned further, the woman from HR said, "Perhaps, ma'am, your brother does not want to talk to you."

It wasn't like Gusman to be completely unresponsive. Sure, her brother wasn't exactly big on detail. He would send mostly monosyllabic texts back in response to her chatty emails. Occasionally, he would write something longer or they would have a real conversation. But he was always prompt. He never simply ignored her like he was doing now.

A few hours later, she happened to turn on the local television news, something she rarely did anymore. She was half paying attention when a story came on about an oil leak at the site of a former offshore platform near Galveston. It piqued her curiosity, and she decided to make some calls. In any case, it would divert her attention away from wondering why her brother had gone silent.

Her first call was to a guy she knew at the EPA. He was a dedicated environmental regulator, and out of frustration some years earlier, he had begun to slip her information that the government was trying to keep under wraps. She had never burned him, and they had developed a relationship of trust.

When he answered her call, the first thing he said was, "What took you so long?"

This time his information was juicy. He described the event in the Gulf as "way, way out of the ordinary."

"Wait," he whispered, "I need to go into another room." When he came back on, his words were rushed, like he was out of breath. "So that was no ordinary leak from a wellhead seal cracking or something."

"What do you mean?"

"We're not sure, but the video shows that concrete in the wellhead was riddled with holes, as if someone had drilled into it."

Annie was skeptical. "Come on. Who would do that... and how?"

"Well, it's like nothing we've ever seen. And all the photos were classified. The security people from DC swept in here and took everything. They said they were taking over the investigation."

"I assume that's pretty unusual."

"I've never seen anything like it. But it gets even weirder."

"How so?"

"You know how it's all just sandy bottom down there, right?"

"Yeah, the rocky substrate starts further down the continental shelf."

"Right. Well, catch this: next to the wellhead was a formation of stones that had to have been placed there by somebody."

"Are you telling me it was like a calling card? A terrorist thing?"

"If it wasn't that, what could it be?"

"What did the formation look like?"

"Well it was a circle of stones — eight of them, actually — with eight arms, each made of eight stones, radiating from the circle."

"Bizarre."

"Very."

"Does that match the symbol of any known terrorist organization?"

"Not according to the FBI."

"Can we get together and talk about this?"

"No way. I've told you too much already." He hesitated and then said, "There's something else. Your brother's on that Clearsea platform in the Pacific, right?"

"Yeah. Why?"

"I overheard one of the security guys who flew out from DC tell another one of them that a team of them was headed to out to Platform Faith for an investigation and that it was very confidential."

"What?"

"Annie, I need to go."

The line went dead.

Chapter 73

The Above: Aboard the
USS *Bonhomme Richard*

Exhaustion took Gusman down hard. They were letting him sleep only a few hours at a time and then waking him up to resume his interrogation. One minute he would sit down heavily on the bunk in his cell, and the next he was drifting away, too tired to bother taking off his clothes.

"I feel mirth," said P'aldil, "for the first time in eight-eights of a smoker's life."

"Huh?" responded Gusman, who was just waking from a deep sleep — his wakefulness, he knew from experience, was probably a dream. "What are you talking about?"

"We have sent the humans a message. Do you want to know what it is?"

"I can hardly wait," responded Gusman, rubbing his chin and feeling stubble there. His temples throbbed, and his mouth was dry.

"The faraway He'e stopped the *hinu* from flowing in three places."

"Oh, God. Where?"

"Two places where the waters are warm and one where the waters are cold."

"Well that doesn't tell me much."

"I am very excited about this, Gusman, because it was I who sent this thought into the Dream. And there is another thing. I asked the faraway He'e to leave behind something to remind the humans that it was we who had visited this calamity upon them."

"What are you talking about?" Gusman asked, his irritation plain. P'aldil, of course, was oblivious.

"It is a circle of eight stones with eight arms sticking out from it."

"Clever."

"Tell them."

"You know they'll probably think I'm crazy."

"What is 'crazy?'"

"When you see things that are not there and hear things where there is no noise."

"You cannot see me, and you cannot hear me. But we are in the Dream. So, we are both crazy."

"Jesus, forget it. It's not worth explaining."

"What is this 'Jesus?'"

— «» —

Gusman looked up at the ceiling of the cell. Nothing had changed except his latest conversation with P'aldil, which may have been real or not real; a dream or not a dream — perhaps both. It did not matter.

They would come to interrogate him, and he would tell them about the oil and the stone calling card the He'e had left behind. And they would believe him, or they would not.

Chapter 74

The Above: Sacramento, California

Noah Reiner's ring tone was the theme song from the movie *Jaws*. When he heard the first of its relentless beats, he looked down at the screen and saw that it was Annie Gusman. A jolt of nervous excitement passed through him and he sat upright in his booth at the Pine Top Grill. He looked around at the other patrons, but no one seemed to notice. He let it ring two more times before he answered, not wanting to look overeager.

Their last email exchange had resulted in Noah's blog achieving an unprecedented level of public attention and he attributed his newfound notoriety to his breaking the story about Clearsea Energy. He was hungry for more.

And more he would get.

"Noah, that event in the Gulf…"

"You mean the leak near Galveston?" he interrupted.

"Yes. I have reason to believe that more was happening out there than just a routine oil leak."

Noah was aware of the oil spill in the Gulf, but it was small and contained. He had already blogged about it, but he blogged about a lot of things and he didn't think it was particularly noteworthy.

"What do you mean?" he asked

"It may have been sabotage."

Noah felt his nerves go taught and his heart start to race.

"What evidence do you have of that?"

"I have a source inside the government. What he says is that the leak in Galveston was caused by somebody boring holes into the concrete cap on the wellhead."

"How did they get equipment down there without being detected?"

"They have no idea."

"Wow!" he exclaimed, immediately regretting his boyish response.

"But he told me that whoever did it left a formation of rocks at the bottom, like a kind of calling card or a message."

"Did he say what it looked like?"

"Yes, he did. He said it was a circle of eight stones with eight 'arms' coming out of the bottom of the circle, each made up of eight stones."

Noah drew the design on a napkin. "You know what this looks like?"

"I have a theory. Tell me yours?"

"It looks like an octopus."

"That's what I thought," Annie replied.

"The Earth Liberation Front, EMETIC, Thermcon, Oceanic Avengers. None of them have an octopus as a symbol. Is this a new group?"

"I don't know. I've never heard of anyone using that symbol."

"What about Islamic State... those type of guys?"

"That seems far-fetched. They kill people. Anyway, they pump oil themselves and could care less about the environment."

Noah was silent for a few seconds and then said, "Well, whoever it is obviously has resources. You can't drill holes in a two-foot thick reinforced concrete slab without some very heavy underwater drilling gear. I can't see how they could have done it without a large boat and heavy generating equipment."

"I agree. That's why I called you. Dig into it, Noah. Tell me what you find."

The call ended. Noah was excited and deeply flattered.

He set to work.

First, he scoured the Internet for some references to the octopus in political discussion or if any radical groups used octopus imagery. All he found was an obscure pre-Second World War ultra-right nationalist group in the Balkans that seems to have disappeared by 1937. And, of course, there was the early twentieth century muckraking novel *The Octopus* by Frank Norris. There were plenty of octopus references around, but they had no association with radical politics. His favorite? A small chain of Australian hamburger joints called "Octoburger," whose logo was a smiling octopus tightly clenching hamburgers in its tentacles.

As the morning wore on, he switched topics. He read everything related to the Galveston oil leak. He started looking for other recent incidents. After a while, he found a little article in the *Oil and Gas Journal* from two days earlier, which recorded an unusual temporary shutdown at a BP platform in the North Sea. The article had no byline, so he emailed the *Journal* to ask who wrote the piece. While he waited for a response, he moved on.

It was like looking for a needle in a haystack or, more accurately, a small oil slick in an endless ocean of news.

After he had lunch — a greasy gardenburger that he was certain no self-respecting patron of the Pine Top would ever order — he decided to take a break and visit a class of website that sometimes yielded a different kind of environmental news. These were defense and intelligence sites that followed the endless wars of the Middle East and Africa, where human conflict and environmental degradation went hand-in-hand. One of his favorites was called Debka.com, an Israeli site that boasted of its supposed inside ties to the Jewish State's intelligence services. Often Debka's information was highly speculative — and right more often than not.

It was on Debka that he found an interesting little piece that had just been posted the previous day entitled, "Is the US or Israel Hitting Iranian Oil?"

Reliable intelligence sources say a covert attack destroyed an Iranian National Oil Company off-shore oil rig that was drilling for new deposits in the Persian Gulf near the port city of Bandar Abbas. As two United States Navy destroyers patrolled nearby, the giant drill started to wobble and then apparently exploded at the site of the borehole. Within hours, a unit of the Revolutionary Guards had landed on the platform and evacuated the crew. DEBKA has learned the Iranians believe their platform was sabotaged. Internal signal traffic intercepted by Western intelligence agencies indicated the IRG believed the attack was carried out by a previously unknown group calling itself Hasht Paw, the Farsi word for "Octopus." The terrorists, according to intelligence sources, left behind a collection of stones resembling the eight-legged sea creatures on the ocean floor. However, they also suspected that this may be a 'false flag,' a diversion used by the CIA or the Mossad to try to obscure their own responsibility for the attack.

Could it be that the Iranians had it all wrong? That the attack wasn't carried by some intelligence agency hostile to the Iranian government, but was something much more breathtaking: one of three nearly simultaneous attacks on three separate continents? Did these attacks represent the emergence of a new and audacious eco-terrorist group able to plan and simultaneously carry out complex undersea sabotage operations? Noah started to write down on a legal pad the resources that would be necessary to perform these operations: crews, divers, heavy drilling equipment, and ships of sufficient size to traverse the world's oceans. How was a ship able to enter the Persian Gulf — one of the worlds most heavily monitored shipping lanes — undetected? And why leave their calling card on the ocean floor? What was the point of carrying out these attacks without claiming responsibility or making demands? Every question seemed to spawn ten more questions.

None of it really made sense.

He needed to talk to Annie. He called, but she didn't answer. He left a message on her voicemail.

He decided not to wait. He would put it out on his blog and let the chips fall where they may. Three hours later he posted his story. It was entitled "Coordinated Undersea Attacks on Big Oil?"

Three hours and one minute later, his webpage crashed.

He went to his Facebook page. His account was closed.

Chapter 75

The Above: The White House, Washington DC

In the basement beneath the West Wing of the White House is the Situation Room. Built early in the Kennedy Administration and modernized forty years later, it is cramped and claustrophobic, hardly commensurate with its status as the nerve center of the free world. To make it less so, the White House staff had placed a large flower arrangement in the middle of the conference table. If it helped, the positive effect was marginal.

The president looked tired. As if the endless crises in the Middle East, the weakening economy, and his endless fights with Congress were not enough, now there was this.

"Come again, Admiral?" he said, tilting his head as if he had he had not heard it right the first time. The other members of the President's National Security team were looking down at their hands.

"Mr. President, sir, what I said is that we have had to revise our earlier determination that the attack on the Clearsea Energy platform was carried out by terrorists. It now appears that the deaths were the result of an attack by predatory and..." He paused and cleared his throat. "Intelligent sea creatures."

"What kind of sea creatures?" the president asked, his tone simultaneously acidic and patronizing — like he was talking to a crazy neighbor. Before the admiral could answer, he held up his hand and turned to his National Security Advisor. "Bob, is he pulling my leg?"

"I'm afraid not, Mr. President. We don't pull legs down here. But look on the positive side: at least we're not dealing with some new affiliate of Al Qaeda or a rogue nation with an ocean-going navy."

The president was not the least bit amused. He looked angry and confused.

"Okay, Admiral, proceed. But first answer my question."

"Um, Mr. President, we think it could be a species of cephalopod. Octopuses, sir."

The president took off his reading glasses and rubbed his temples. Then he looked up and smiled. "All things considered, I think I would prefer terrorists. All right, Admiral, lay out your evidence for this."

The admiral, the Commander of Naval Intelligence, slowly and systematically went through the case for a predatory sea creature attack. As he spoke, everyone around the table thumbed through the thick written report that had been passed out to each of them. No one wanted to meet the stare of anyone else in the room.

"Mr. President, there were no satellite images, no radar readings, heat signatures, or any other objective evidence of ships or planes being anywhere near Platform Faith on the day of the attack, either before or after. There have been no claims of responsibility, no Internet chatter. Complete silence. There was human and animal blood and tissue found at the scene, but no bodies. Three of the four survivors told consistent stories about a sea creature attack. One of those witnesses was an FBI agent sent to Platform Faith a week before the attack to investigate a possible homicide. Yesterday, he woke up from a coma resulting from injuries sustained in the attack. Although he could not remember how he sustained his injuries, as he is apparently suffering some trauma-induced amnesia, he confirmed the general narrative told by the crew member named Gusman and a Dr. Campos, a scientist who was employed by Clearsea Energy — and who, according to the company, was sent to the facility to examine some fish specimens for environmental compliance. The fourth survivor, Clearsea Director of Corporate Security, a man named Robert Smith, contradicted the stories of the other three, claiming it was a terrorist attack. However, Mr. Smith seems to have been hiding during the attack and never saw either terrorists or sea creatures. Incidentally, Gusman and Campos claim it was Mr. Smith who shot Special Agent Harple and another man named Morrissey. Smith denies that allegation and suggests that Gusman and Campos, who were in an intimate relationship, were responsible. This is plausible because Mr. Gusman was the prime suspect in two earlier suspected homicides aboard the platform."

"Sounds messy. Well, what do you think?" asked the president.

"Sir, Special Agent Harple had a chest wound. There was no exit wound, so we cannot confirm the wound was caused by a bullet, although the surgeon thought the wound was consistent with a bullet entrance wound. Without bullet fragments, this cannot be confirmed." He hesitated for a moment.

"Go on," said the president, irritation obvious in his voice.

"Well, sir, according to Gusman and Campos, one of the creatures removed the bullet fragment."

There were guffaws all around the large conference table.

"You're telling me these creatures not only attacked an oil platform, made almost the entire crew disappear into thin air, and also performed surgery on a wounded FBI agent?"

"Affirmative, Mr. President."

"Oh, for Christ's sake," the president said. "This is insane."

A wry smile crossed the admiral's face. "Yes, sir, that was my reaction. But there is confirmatory evidence. Dr. Campos claimed that a few days before the attack, two of the creatures surfaced and were confronted by some crew members of Platform Faith. In the altercation, an arm of one of the creatures was severed and recovered by the crew. We found that arm on the platform and a preliminary examination by scientists we have brought in appears to confirm that this is a new, very large species of octopus. And although the crew members are missing, as I said, there were human blood stains and tissue found throughout the platform, indicating that there was some kind of violent struggle. Some of that blood and tissue was not human in origin."

"What about surveillance cameras on the vessel?"

"The attack apparently occurred at night and, shortly after the attack commenced, the electricity was cut, and the cameras lost power. There are no usable images."

"Is that it?" the president asked.

"Oh, no, Mr. President. There is more. Considerably more." He reached down into his briefcase and retrieved a clear plastic bag marked Top Secret across it.

"Please pass this to the President," he said, handing it to one of the President's aides.

"The bag contains what looks like small, translucent rocks that were retrieved from the deck and interior spaces of Platform Faith after the attack. However, these are no ordinary stones. Our analysis has identified them as a material known as the 'buckyball stone' and this is the hardest substance known to exist. This molecule has only been synthesized in a laboratory. If these creatures had possession of naturally-occurring buckyball, it would be a game changer in the defense world."

"What does Clearsea Energy have to say about this?"

"They deny everything, but my understanding is that when the FBI interviewed employees at Clearsea as part of the terrorist investigation, there were inconsistencies in the company's account of events. Most importantly, a lot of records are missing regarding recent activities at Platform Faith in the period immediately before the attack. In any case, we do not believe that Clearsea is being forthright with us. Other information from the NSA regarding Clearsea's communications through its satellite network is in the process of being analyzed. We will know more in the next twenty-four to forty-eight hours."

"We need to get on that. I always felt there was a 'trust deficit' with that son-of-a-bitch Enrique Gonzales," said the president, smiling. "He's such a phony."

There were nods of agreement around the room. Gonzales had once accused the President, when he was the Attorney General of Texas and the President was starting his run for the highest office, of having a 'trust deficit with the American people.'

"What else?" asked the president.

"Well, sir, there have been three other attacks on offshore oil facilities that have occurred since the attack on Platform faith. None, however, have involved fatalities."

He looked up to make sure the president was following him.

"Keep going," said the president, gesturing with his hand.

The admiral systematically detailed the incidents in the Gulf of Mexico, the North Sea, and the Persian Gulf, culminating with the signature stone 'calling card' left by the perpetrators at each location.

"If you turn to page one sixty-three of the briefing book, you will see photographs of the three stone formations."

They opened their briefing books to the page and stared at the circles of eight stones with the projections of stones radiating from them.

"What does it mean?"

"Well, this is pure speculation, but according to the witnesses Gusman and Campos…"

"Who sound crazy to me," interjected the President.

The Admiral continued. "They are symbols representing cephalopods — octopuses, sir. The octopus has eight arms and a circular body. According to Gusman, who claims to communicate with one of the creatures through mental telepathy—"

"Now stop right there, Admiral," the president said, slamming down his hand. "This is insane."

"Mr. President, I know it sounds inherently incredible, but please, sir, hear me out."

"Okay, Admiral, but this is becoming increasingly impossible to believe, much less react to."

"Yes, sir, I understand. May I continue?

"Why the hell not?"

"Thank you, sir. According to Gusman, the attackers deliberately left behind these symbols to let us know that it was they, not some humans, who were responsible."

"Well, couldn't divers have left those?" asked the vice president.

"Yes, sir, that is possible. But something else has occurred."

"There's more? Good God!" said the president, sighing in exasperation.

"Yes. Three hours ago, a buoyant volcanic rock surrounded by netting composed of seaweed surfaced next to Platform Faith. Attached to it was a fish bladder containing the wallets, jewelry, and other personal effects of the disappeared crew members. The Navy has cordoned off the area. No vessels have been detected in the area."

"Including submarines?"

"Yes, Mr. President, including submarines."

"Does anyone outside of this room know about this? Foreign governments? The press?"

"Let me answer that," interjected the National Security Advisor. "So far, no one has connected the dots. What happened on Platform Faith has not been made public yet, but we're going to have to do something within a very short window. It's been five days since the attack and we have to inform the families of the dead crew members on Platform Faith what happened. There have been fragmentary news stories about the three other incidents, but no one has made public the 'calling card' left behind. Something is up with the Brits, though, because they have invoked the Official Secrets Act with regard to the North Sea incident. The Iranians think the Israelis did it. The Israelis think we did it. We limited the information release in Galveston and, although it made the local news, because there was so little oil that leaked, it was a minor story. Finally, there is a kid out in California…"

He adjusted his reading glasses and looked at his notes.

"Name of Reiner. Has an environmental blog with a decent following. He posted an article in which he actually got it right. You have the story in front of you. We were watching for it and shut it down."

The president winced but said nothing.

"Obviously that bought us a day or so, but it is evident, Mr. President, that this whole thing cannot be suppressed much longer. We need to make a decision."

"Agreed," responded the president. Then the president said something that surprised everybody in the room. "I think I have the nucleus of an idea."

Chapter 76

The Above: New York City

Enrique Gonzales had come a long way from the hard-scrabble East Texas farmworker shack where he was born to 211 Central Park West, where he now resided at the fabled Beresford Apartments. Built in 1929, the Beresford was an art-deco masterpiece with lavish lobbies, massive vaulted ceilings, and prices to match. He had purchased his three-bedroom apartment — with its spectacular view of Central Park — for $7.5 million at the height of the last recession. Now, a few years later, it was worth much more. Yet every time the liveried doorman opened the polished brass doors for him, there was a small voice inside of him that accused him of being a fraud. Lately, his nagging doubts were amplified by the on-going disaster taking place on Platform Faith.

Fortunately, it looked like he had turned the corner on his problems.

It was the end of a very long day. Bobby Smith had finally arrived the night before and they had spent the entire day planning for the public relations roll out to explain the terrorist attack on Platform Faith. For the last thirty-six hours, Clearsea's public relations team had been in nearly continuous meetings with representatives of the FBI, the Department of Justice, and the President's Deputy National Security advisor to go over the narrative and coordinate their public comments regarding the incident.

The President of the United States was scheduled to hold a press conference the next morning. His message would be clear and unequivocal. With twenty-three Americans missing and presumed dead and just four survivors, this was the worst terrorist attack on an American target since 9/11. The terrorists responsible would be hunted down and brought to justice. Although no group had taken responsibility, early indications pointed to Islamist extremists. Most importantly, the President would reiterate that Americans would never bow to terrorism and that Platform Faith would be back up and running very soon. Finally, he would ask Congress for a supplemental appropriation to enhance protection of America's vital offshore oil infrastructure.

For his part, Gonzales would hold a press conference in New York after the President's to announce, with grave sadness, the terrible loss of life resulting from the terrorist attack—but he would pledge that exploration and production would resume as soon as possible. He planned to read the names of each of the dead and to say something personal about them. In addition to the proceeds of the generous company-provided life insurance policies their families would receive, Gonzales would announce that a trust fund was being established to pay for the full cost of college for the children of those who had so tragically lost their lives.

These thoughts occupied his mind as he got out of his limo in front of the Beresford. He hadn't taken more than three steps when a man in a dark suit approached him and flashed a badge. Two other men came up to his sides, moving quite close to him.

He smiled briefly. "Mr. Gonzales, I'm Special Agent Telfer of the FBI. If you wouldn't mind, the Attorney General wishes to speak with you."

"Now?" asked Gonzales, too surprised to be angry.

"Yes, sir," he said, pointing to a black SUV directly behind them. "It should only take a few minutes of your time."

One of the agents touched him very slightly on the elbow. "This way, sir," he said quietly.

Gonzales hadn't noticed the Escalade with the distinctive blue-on-white US government license plates when he pulled up. *Had they been waiting for him?*

One of the FBI agents opened the door for him. "Sir," he said, motioning for him to get inside.

"Hello, Enrique, come on in," said the Attorney General jovially, thrusting out his hand.

"Tom, it's good to see you," responded Gonzales, shaking the AG's hand and sliding into the cool, black interior. The dome light shone a dim yellow, casting long shadows across the attorney general's handsome — if aging — face.

It was not lost on either man that had the election results been different ten years earlier, Gonzales might be sitting where Thomas Bishop now sat. The two men had known each other when Gonzales was the Texas Attorney General and Bishop was the Attorney General of neighboring New Mexico.

"That was a terrible thing happened out there on your oil platform."

"Dreadful. A nightmare for our company."

"For the entire country."

"Do you have any further information on which terrorist groups were responsible?" asked Gonzales.

"No, Enrique, we don't. Because, frankly, we have some doubt whether a terrorist attack occurred."

"What are you talking about?"

The Attorney General laughed. "Are you shocked?"

"Of course. Who wouldn't be?"

"That's a good point. But in this case, there are some folks who might not find that a revelation," he paused for effect. "I don't know exactly how to put it. There are some unusual elements to the story."

"Well, what do you mean?" Gonzales felt the pit in his stomach shift.

"You know, Enrique, it's amazing what information we have at our disposal these days. Those guys at the NSA really pay attention to satellite communications. And there are just reams of information that were relayed between your office and Platform Faith in the last several months. A lot of it is quite… revealing."

"What are you driving at?"

"Well, where should I start? Let's see. There was the back and forth about the refrigerated leg of a previously unknown sea creature — an octopus — that you never told us about and that we found in the galley. There were threats to harm certain Clearsea personnel — maybe even federal law enforcement agents — the withholding of information from regulators, doctoring records... You know, little things like that. That Chief of Security of yours, Mr. Marlboro Man, is a real piece of work. And that's just the minor stuff. There are the serious issues. Like your withholding of information regarding this stuff I didn't know even existed until yesterday. 'Buckyball,' it's called. Very strategic and on the list of materials that cannot be exported or traded. Until yesterday, we thought the damn stuff could only be synthesized in a lab. And then we found it on the deck of your oil platform... which we now know you knew all about and withheld from us. Did it not occur to you that the NSA would be listening into the chatter from your private satellite? Oh yeah, and then there are the submersibles you hired from Ironstone, one of which sank, killing two of their personnel. Did you think we wouldn't learn about that? For Christ's sake, Enrique, those guys are CIA contractors. Suffice it to say that Clearsea has withheld a lot of information which, if it were made public, would be deeply troubling to the public, your investors, and my criminal division."

"What do you want?" Gonzales responded quietly, resignation rapidly replacing indignation in his voice.

"Oh, nothing very complicated really." The pleasure the attorney general was taking in the humiliation of an old adversary was palpable.

"Just give it to me straight," Gonzales said.

"We can do this with your lawyers present, if you like," the attorney general said.

"That won't be necessary," Gonzales replied quietly.

"First, we want Clearsea to stick to the terrorism story, even though we both know that is crock of shit. That shouldn't be so hard, since it's in your interest. Secondly, your company will make no claim to the buckyball material, which will be the sole property of the United States government. You will surrender all your records, research — everything you've got on that stuff to us. Information regarding that material will be classified. Mr. Gusman and

Dr. Campos will be separated from your employment with a generous one-year severance package. They will then go to work for the Department of Defense. And don't get any Texas-sized ideas about silencing them. We will insure their silence."

"All right."

"There's one more loose end. Bobby Smith. I'd like to try him for the murder of your employee Morrissey and the attempted murder of that FBI special agent we sent out to your oil platform. But there isn't enough evidence and trying him would be… complicated. But he needs to be terminated from your company and you are to have no further contact with him."

Gonzales nodded and asked quietly, "What about the oil?"

"It depends. If — and that is a huge if — the oil can be safely extracted, we will let you proceed and you can pump to your heart's content. Unless, of course, the environmentalists eat your heart out first. But that's your problem, not ours. Oh, yeah. We will need you to agree to stop cease production if it's necessary for us to get access to that buckyball stuff, you will have to stop."

"And what if I refuse?"

"You won't."

"What makes you so sure?"

The Attorney General reached into his suit pocket and pulled out a piece of paper and handed it to Gonzales.

He opened it and began to read.

"It's a sealed national security warrant. You remember those. Ironic, eh? You campaigned in favor of the Patriot Act extension and I expressed doubts. Now, if you don't do what I want, I will take you and your company down with one of them. As we both know, one little whiff that your company is somehow associated with terrorism and its good night, Clearsea Energy."

Gonzales looked up from the paper and met the eyes of the Attorney General. He handed the warrant back but said nothing.

"That's yours, Enrique. You can keep it as a souvenir."

There was a long moment of silence between the men. Then Gonzales said, "Is that it?"

"You forgot to ask me something," the attorney general said.

"What's that?" asked Gonzales.

"What happens to you."

"Okay, Tom, what happens to me?"

"Nothing, Enrique, you lucky dog, as long as you keep playing ball."

Chapter 77

The Above: Aboard the
USS *Bonhomme Richard*

Gusman's two marine guards led him down a different set of hallways than the day before. Eventually, after a few twists and turns and a ride up an elevator, they brought him to a recreation room. It was a big, windowless room lit brightly by banks of fluorescent lights. There were a half dozen pool tables and a bank of arcade-style video games. The place was furnished with round tables and chairs, all made of heavy plastic. There was a stainless-steel counter that ran the entire length on one end of the room equipped with an array of coffee and soft drink machines. It looked like a fast food restaurant, except the art on the walls consisted not of advertisements for the latest cholesterol-laced super-sized special, but photos of various naval ships and aircraft, equally spaced from one another and screwed solidly into the walls so they would never be askew or fall should the ship encounter turbulent weather or conditions of warfare.

They sat Gusman down at one of the tables and stood next to him. One of them asked him if he wanted something to drink.

"Water, please."

The marine nodded and walked over to the bank of machines and filled a paper cup from a water dispenser built into the counter.

The two guards placed themselves behind Gusman, one by each shoulder.

A few silent and uncomfortable minutes later, the door to

the room opened and in came Anna Campos escorted by two guards of her own.

"Anna," he said, his voice cracking, overcome by surprise and emotion.

Gusman tried to stand, but one of his guards firmly restrained him with a hand to his shoulder.

"Gusman," she said, starting toward him.

Her guards gently, but firmly, stopped her.

"Ma'am, you can't do that. I'm sorry."

"Fine," she said, shaking off their grip.

They led her to the table and sat her across from Gusman. They did not — at first — stop them from reaching across to grasp each other's hands. Anna's eyes were moist and her smile warm and tender.

"Are you okay?" he asked.

"Not bad for being a prisoner, I guess," she said. Her voice broke a little, belying the strain.

One of the marines, young and blond, said, "Ma'am, sir, you need to let go of your hands. I'm sorry, but you're not allowed to do that."

Gusman complied, laughing. "Good point. I just slipped her a file."

"I know you wouldn't do that, sir," he responded, not without a little wryness in his tone.

"Because you'd have to shoot us, right?" said Anna.

"Yes, ma'am," he responded, with just the slightest trace of a smile.

Just then, the doors opened, and the four marines shot to attention.

A naval officer and a civilian entered the room.

The officer, dressed in a khaki uniform, walked with precision. He was older, maybe in his late fifties, gray at the temples, and movie-star handsome.

"At ease, marines," he said, removing his cap.

The four guards took a step back in unison and placed their hands at their backs.

"Mr. Gusman, Dr. Campos, I am Rear Admiral Franklin, and this is Mr. Lowell. He is here to speak with you."

The other man was a bit younger than the Admiral —

closer to Gusman's age — but rounder and shorter. He wore a rumpled blue suit that seemed like it had seen better days. His white shirt was a little gray from too many washings and his striped tie was loosely knotted and slightly askew. He had dark, alert, intelligent eyes, hooded by drooping eyelids and heavy brows. As he talked, he absentmindedly rubbed his bald head.

"Admiral, you and your men can leave us now," he said, looking up and blinking his eyes.

"Mr. Lowell, I think the guards should remain," responded the rear admiral.

"No, it will be fine. They can wait outside the door. I feel quite safe with these two."

"All right," the rear admiral responded stiffly. He nodded at the marines and ordered them outside. It was obvious that he did not approve of this breach of protocol.

"Thank you, Admiral," the man named Lowell said, smiling pleasantly.

When the door closed, Lowell said, "I don't know about you, but those guys make me nervous. They're all so stiff."

Neither Gusman nor Anna responded, though they exchanged glances with one another.

Lowell moved a chair to the end of the table and sat down heavily. He folded his hands in front of him and, with a pleasant smile, looked up at the two prisoners.

"Well," he said, "I suppose you are wondering why a landlubber like me would fly halfway around the world to talk to the two of you."

They said nothing, although Gusman smiled at the little man's self-deprecating humor.

"You see, I work for the government and, therefore, as the saying goes, 'I'm here to help.' Or at least offer you a way out of your present predicament."

Gusman finally spoke, "We're all ears, Mr. Lowell."

"Call me John," he said jovially. "Anyway, as I'm sure you can guess, some pretty smart people have been thinking about what to do with the two of you. And they have a plan for your futures. May I go on?"

Anna responded, "Do we have any choice?"

"None whatsoever, Dr. Campos," responded Lowell, pausing. "Now, I'm one of the few people at the White House who believes your story about these intelligent sea creatures attacking Platform Faith. The majority view is that you are crazy — or that you are perfectly sane but have concocted a crazy story and that it was terrorists who attacked the platform and you were working with them. Some of my more aggressive colleagues think because the attack occurred outside the territory of the United States, we can treat you as enemy combatants and toss the two of you in a dark hole in Guantanamo. The constitutional sticklers think we should just arrest you, charge you with conspiracy and murder, and hold you at a Supermax Prison until the government is good and ready to prosecute you. There is a lot of credible evidence against you from surveillance footage, Mr. Gusman, which appears to show you throwing a crew member over the side of the platform to the eyewitness testimony of the Chief of Security for Clearsea Energy that a terrorist attack occurred, during which you attempted to kill an FBI agent in furtherance of that terrorist attack and then tried to cover up the crime."

"That's total bullshit," Gusman said.

"Well, Mr. Gusman, you're in luck because I believe you and, more importantly, so does my boss, the President of the United States. And that is why I'm here to offer you a way out."

"What do we have to do?"

"It will really be quite painless. All you have to do is agree, in any public statement that you make, that Platform Faith was attacked by terrorists... of the ordinary *homo sapien* sort, probably of the middle eastern, variety. We'll give you the script and make sure that you are protected by layers of national security from having to tell the truth of what went on here."

"That's it?" asked Anna.

"Oh, no, it gets better. We are going to offer you jobs. Those jobs will have high-level security clearances that are conditional on your signing standard confidentiality agreements. Those agreements subject you to arrest and prosecution if you divulge your activities. The fact of the matter is that, if you ever breach the agreement, the matters which you would disclose are so inherently unbelievable that you'd probably wind up in a psychiatric lock-up for the rest of your lives."

"And what if we don't want to accept those jobs?" asked Gusman.

"It's pretty simple. You go to jail," Lowell answered brightly.

"So, we really have no choice?" asked Anna.

"Not much of one."

Gusman crossed his arms. "All right, suppose for the sake of argument we decide to go along with this. What are we supposed to do in these jobs?"

"Well, Mr. Gusman, you will do pretty much what you have been doing already: communicating with your eight-legged friend Mr. P'aldil. We need to understand the intentions of his kind, assess their capabilities, and determine a future course of action. As for you, Dr. Campos, you will be the Chief Science Officer for the project, with a hefty research budget and a state-of-the-art laboratory."

"And no way to publish the results of my findings, I take it?" she asked.

"Probably not for the foreseeable future. Perhaps someday."

"And if we agree with this, when do we start?" asked Gusman.

"Immediately."

"How long do we have to decide?" asked Anna.

Lowell looked at his watch. "How does fifteen minutes sound?"

Chapter 78

The Below

In the Chamber *of Decision, we wait, the Dream so still that nothing ripples. Our gills moving the life-giving water in and out in the same rhythm — four counts in, four counts out, eight times in total — is the only motion. Even the black smoker slows. The fish are gone into the darkness beyond the chamber and the benthic worms lie still. The He'e turn gray, then blue, then black, then pink, then gray, then blue, then black, then pink again… and again and again, each color the length of one undulation of our gills. It is all in perfect harmony. As it is across the entire urb, from conurbation of He'e to conurbation of He'e, each in the same rhythm, waiting and silent.*

P'aldil speaks. "We have done as Gusman asked; we 'sent a message' to the humans that 'we mean business.' I did not understand these words 'message' and 'business,' but after many attempts to grasp this strange human idea, I asked Gusman if 'sending a message of business' was like this: in the not-so-distant Dream, a mano had attacked our fry. Instead of sucking its delicious guts out until it was dead, we ate only enough guts that it was nearly dead and injected the fear venom in its mouth and eyes and gills and brought it to the conurbation of mano to show what would happen if they attacked our fry again.

"Gusman said 'yes' in that noisy way he speaks when he is correct. He said, 'I bet that showed those dumb sharks that you meant business.'

"And I said to Gusman, 'I am confused. The other mano simply ate the wounded mano like it was one of our fry. And

then they attacked us again and again. It is in their nature. So, this 'meaning business' does not work.'

"Gusman said, 'Have faith, P'aldil. We are much smarter than a bunch of mindless predators.'

"I did not wish to argue, so I stayed silent."

Suddenly, there is a ripple in the Dream. A voice, small at first, then louder — and the others sense it through P'aldil. It is Gusman, and the Dream erupts.

Gusman says that the humans wish to meet.

"Where?" asks P'aldil.

"On the platform."

P'aldil speaks for the He'e, "There is agreement in the Dream. This is not safe. They must meet us near the water, at the place where the humans took my leg that has now regrown, where there is escape from attack. It must be at the time of darkness of the gases, the time you call 'night.'"

Then Gusman says, "It is important that you bring some kaimana," and then he is gone from the Dream as quickly as he entered it.

There is great excitement and even greater fear in the Dream. They await the decision of P'heen.

Finally, P'heen pulses, "We must make our preparations,"

The others pulse in fear and anxiety. But P'aldil pulses the red flashes of excitement.

Chapter 79

The Above: Platform Faith

It was dusk, and the sun was red and low and hot over a dead calm sea. Gusman stood at the rail in the exact spot where Andy Noguchi had gone over the side. It had happened only a month before, but it seemed like an eternity.

Anna put her hand lightly on the small of his back.

"Do you think they'll come?" she asked quietly.

He did not turn around but kept staring out toward the setting sun.

"Ever heard of the 'green flash?'" he asked.

"No. What's that?"

"It's a Hawaiian thing. They say that sometimes if you watch the setting sun that at the precise moment it goes down, there is a sudden green flash of light. It lasts only a second."

"Have you ever seen it?" she asked.

"No, but I don't stare at the sun going down very often. It's probably tourist bullshit."

"Were you deliberately ignoring my question?"

"Yes. But the answer is, I don't know."

They watched in silence as the sun drew rapidly lower.

"Watch carefully."

"Okay," she whispered.

The sun dropped to a thin orange sliver on the horizon, hung for a second like it was reluctant to go, and then disappeared.

Gusman yelled, "Did you see that?"

"See what?"

"I saw it. For a split second. It was blue, though, not green. A blue flash. You didn't see it?"

"No, I didn't. Maybe I blinked. So, you really saw something?"

"Definitely. A blue flash."

"Like the color of octopus blood," she said flatly.

From behind them, they heard footsteps and turned around. It was Lowell.

"Okay, lovebirds. It's show time."

"How do you know?" asked Gusman.

"Sonar. They're about a half hour away."

"All right."

The three of them started back toward the opposite corner of the platform, where they would descend to the ocean to meet the He'e. Gusman was nervous and excited. This was the stuff of a thousand science fiction movies: aliens meet the government. Except it was for real. He could tell Anna was excited as well.

It was getting dark now. This time of year, the sun seemed to set faster or maybe time was bending a bit. *Why not?* thought Gusman. He had experienced reality bending. Was time immune?

"Who else is coming?" asked Anna.

"It will just be the three of us plus a couple of navy SEALS in case something goes wrong. Don't worry. The entire area is plastered with cameras. A lot of people will be watching. And if it goes south, there's an armada nearby."

"That's what I was afraid of," said Gusman under his breath.

"It's going to be dark, right? I mean that's what they asked for," said Anna.

"Yes. It will be dark. We have cameras that see in the dark."

They walked the rest of the way in silence. The metal stairs down to the surface seemed to go on forever. The light was fading, and as they neared the bottom, the stairs became wet and slippery from the ocean spray, which slowed their descent. At the bottom of the giant pontoon that held up the platform, a black rubber boat was securely tethered. The two SEALs in dark uniforms and watch caps waited for them. One stood at the bow and the other at the stern, his hand on the outboard engine that powered the craft.

The SEALS helped the three civilians into the boat. The ocean was still dead calm, like the surface of a lake.

The dusk turned to dark and it was night.

Little was said as they waited, and what conversation they had was short and direct.

Gusman realized he was holding his breath. He had to tell himself to breathe regularly. At one point, Anna reached over and stroked his hand. When he looked at her face, it was so dark he could barely make out the whites of her eyes. He thought maybe she was smiling at him.

Time seemed to stop.

Then he heard the voice of P'aldil.

"Gusman, we are near."

His body must have must have moved in response to P'aldil's words because he sensed the other four humans in the boat reacting, turning toward him.

"What is it?" Anna whispered.

"They are around here somewhere. P'aldil just spoke to me."

"What did he say?" asked Lowell.

"That they are close."

Although their eyes had fully adjusted to the night, it was almost impossible to see anything. The surface of the water was barely distinguishable from the sky above it, although the moon and the first rising stars provided faint illumination. The superstructure of the platform loomed above them, the massive forms of metal jutting in every direction, darker than the sky or water.

They heard it before they saw it. In the silence that surrounded them, it sounded louder than it really was: the whooshing of a buoyant object breaching the surface and settling back. It sent a series of gentle waves radiating away and caused the rubber boat to sway.

The thing they saw looked very much like the contraption that had brought P'M'aldil to the surface the first time: buoyant volcanic stones surrounding a seaweed net to form a basket. This time there were also other small objects attached around the outer perimeter of floating rocks, which were bioluminescent, glowing faintly with greenish-yellow light. In the darkness, it illuminated the scene in a soft and indistinct way.

There were three octopuses sitting on the top of the rock. In the twilight, color was hard to discern except for occasional flashing streaks of colored light up and down their long, undulating arms.

The humans shifted nervously, causing their boat to rock once more. Gusman felt tense and scared and fought the urge to escape. Suddenly, he became aware of the craziness of it all. He let out a small laugh, which was the first noise any of them had made since the He'e had surfaced. It sounded loud after the silence and a little deranged, like the utterance of some street person to total strangers passing by.

"Sorry," he whispered.

"No need to be sorry," said P'aldil. "It makes me mirthful to see you again."

"Are they talking to you?" asked Lowell in a voice that sounded both perplexed and aggressive. Gusman wondered how he knew.

"Yes," he replied. "That is P'aldil."

He pointed to the octopus to their left.

"P'aldil, can you lift an arm to show them who you are?" asked Gusman. He was speaking out loud, so the other humans could hear, but, of course, P'aldil could only speak in his head so there was no response. He wondered what Lowell and the two SEALs — not to mention the people all around the world viewing it through hidden cameras and satellite uplinks — were making of this strange encounter.

P'aldil raised an arm and shook it. "Greetings, members of Gusman's urb," he said.

Gusman translated. "P'aldil says hello to everyone." To Gusman's ear, it sounded hopelessly inadequate and entirely too banal for such an auspicious moment of cross-species communication.

"Hello," said Lowell loudly and slowly as if the creatures were hard of hearing and it was necessary to speak up to make them to understand.

In his head, Gusman heard a sort of buzzing sound — *The three He'e talking in the Dream,* he thought.

Now, the creature in the middle raised an arm and shook it.

P'aldil spoke again. "This is M'aldil. Together she and I are P'M'aldil."

"The one in the middle is named M'aldil. She's married to P'aldil," Gusman said.

"Married?" said Lowell.

"Yeah, happily, as I understand it. You got something against marriage?" Gusman asked with a laugh.

Finally, the last octopus raised an arm.

P'aldil spoke. "This is P'heen. He is the wise one and commands the Chamber of Decision."

"The one on the right is their leader. He is named P'heen," translated Gusman.

"And who are the other humans besides you and your mate?" P'aldil asked.

"They want the three of you to introduce yourselves," Gusman said to Lowell.

"Okay," Lowell responded. He raised his arm and said, "I am John Lowell, I work for our leader, the President of the United States."

Gusman said, in his head, "The one without hair on his head is named Lowell. He works for our leader."

P'aldil said, "Please tell Lowell that he is soft and round like the He'e, and he is pleasing to look at for a human."

Gusman said to Lowell, "They like you because you're pudgy."

"Seriously? He said that?" Lowell shook his head slowly.

"Yes, he did. Now, navy guys, you need to raise your hands and introduce yourselves."

Slowly, as if he feared they were somehow being mocked, the sailor at the front of the boat raised his hand and said "Morgan, E-5, SEAL Team Two."

The second one at the rear of the boat identified himself as Lieutenant Commander Espinosa.

A strange silence followed. The humans stared at the He'e and the He'e stared right back.

Gusman turned to Lowell and said, "I think you should tell them something."

Lowell cleared his throat. He started to speak, then stopped himself, reformulating his words. He started again and stopped once more. Gusman had not imagined Lowell as a man who would ever be at a loss for words.

"Why did you attack our platform and kill the crew?" he finally asked.

Gusman repeated the words.

Flashing red with vehemence, P'aldil responded, "The humans attacked us first, sending the radula mouth into the urb, killing our fry, and then attacked us again with the gas-filled, hardened fish that dropped the explosive egg sacks. We attacked the humans because they meant us harm and would not leave us alone. Since the beginning of the Dream, there have been predators that have attacked us, but none, even the evil *muhe'e*, kills with such force and so often as you humans."

"Is he saying something?" asked Lowell.

"Yes," Gusman replied. "He says that we attacked first by drilling into their habitat, then by dropping depth charges. We killed with abandon. They acted in self-defense."

"Jesus Christ, did those oil idiots you worked for actually use explosives on them?"

"I don't know. At one point, P'aldil told me there had been a devastating attack on them, but I was locked up, so I didn't witness anything firsthand."

Anna spoke for the first time. "I might know what he's talking about. Clearsea had a contractor here called Ironstone that was deploying submersibles right before the attack, but I assumed that it was related to repairing the drilling equipment."

"We knew about Ironstone being here, but nothing about their using explosives on these creatures."

Lowell paused, choosing his words carefully. "Tell him that the President apologizes for attacking his habitat."

"Gusman," P'aldil said, "you do not need to repeat his words. When you hear his words, they enter the Dream and I hear them through you."

Hearing this, Gusman wondered if this was evidence that octopuses experienced impatience.

"Tell the one called Lowell that P'heen says that we know that the humans value *hinu* above all else. Tell him that the faraway He'e can destroy the humans' *hinu* anytime as we have done three times in the distant seas and here."

Gusman repeated the words of P'heen to Lowell.

Lowell laughed, which seemed incongruous to Gusman and must have for the others as well, since the two SEALs turned around and looked at him.

"Well, I guess negotiation tactics cross the species barrier," he said. "First, there are the mutual threats, then the small opening, and finally the deal — if there is one to be made."

In his head, Gusman heard M'aldil ask P'aldil what a 'deal' was.

"Tell them that we have weapons that could destroy the He'e altogether."

P'aldil took in the ominous threat. But he flashed the calming blue to M'aldil and P'heen. He said to Gusman, "Has the time come to do as you ordered?"

Gusman did not speak out loud, but closed his eyes and spoke into the Dream, "Yes, now is the time."

From somewhere in the inner recesses of their floating rock, P'aldil slowly picked up an object in one of his arms.

The two SEALs stiffened, and their hands wandered down, nearer their weapons, which were concealed at their feet.

"He wants to hand you something," said Gusman to Lowell.

"What is it?" asked Lowell, but the question sounded perfunctory, as if he knew already.

"It is something the He'e call 'kaimana,'" said Gusman.

"Yes, we discussed that. Okay, let's get closer so he can hand it over."

"Yes, sir," the SEAL at the back replied.

The boat inched closer to the He'e.

When they were close enough, P'aldil held his arm straight out so he could hand over the object to the crew member in the front of the boat. The SEAL turned to Lowell and asked, "Should I take it, sir?" His facial expression seemed a combination of concealed fear and open disgust.

"Yes, go ahead," replied Lowell.

"He won't bite," said Anna.

The sailor took the object from P'aldil with two hands but handed it back to Lowell with one. Clearly, it was much lighter than expected. The thing was about a foot square and a half-inch-thick and translucent, like a thick piece of amber glass.

"It's light," said Lowell.

P'aldil said, as he had rehearsed with Gusman, "We believe that you would like to have this *kaimana*. It is hard and impervious both to heat and the hardest blows. If you do harm to us, you will never know how this is made and where it is found. Only the He'e have this knowledge. You say you can destroy us, but there are many multiple eight-eights of the He'e and you cannot destroy us all as you do not know where we reside — except for us, in this urb. Your *hinu* is not safe in any sea."

Gusman translated.

"And what do you propose?" asked Lowell.

"That you remain in your gaseous place and we remain in the sea. That if you wish the *kaimana* or the *hinu*, that you give us what we desire."

Lowell waited for the translation.

"And what is that?" asked Lowell.

"Your Dreams."

Lowell and the two SEALs perceived it as an all-encompassing white light. It was intense, but it did not frighten them, as it was also warm and comforting, and they felt at peace. The He'e, they understood, from the soothing light, as surely as the sun rose and fell each day, were their friends.

"They are so simple, like benthic worms with arms," P'aldil said into the Dream and he felt great mirth.

"Perhaps P'lo and M'lo have given them and their gaseous Above as a gift to us," said P'heen.

Gusman's jaw dropped and he said, "What?" but the others did not hear.

Chapter 80

The Below

There are fish *from the Above to eat, luscious and sweet as any meat in the sea. The humans have sent them as a gift. If it is all the He'e gain from this strange new contact with the humans, it may be enough. So, says P'heen, who ripples with mirth. He knows there is much more to come from the humans, much more to learn. Yes, the humans are more dangerous than the fiercest of the muhe'e, craftier, more filled with guile. No, they are not always trustworthy, sometimes they seem as simple as the youngest fry; sometimes they seem very wise.*

P'aldil says that trustworthy individuals exist among the humans. Gusman is one. The female named Anna is another. The numbers of the humans are beyond counting; more trustworthy ones must surely reside among them.

"And more we cannot trust for now," says M'aldil. "In time, we will learn which are which." She says 'time' and has also begun to understand what it means to the humans.

Yes, the fish called salmon taste wonderful. Just one attraction of the Above. There is much more above, though, P'M'aldil think, but nothing so rare and fine as the riches of this sea bottom. What in the Above can be as wonderful?

Appendix

In the Beginning

This is the *essence of the Dream of Dreams, from which all lesser dreams follow:*

* **In the First Dream,** *there is only P'lo, the Eight-Armed father, who dreams the waters of the world into being and they are cold.*

* **In the Second Dream,** *P'lo dreams M'lo into being. She is the mate of P'lo and the First Mother and she dreams all the creatures of the seafloor into life. P'lo and M'lo are the first He'e.*

* **In the Third Dream,** *P'lo and M'lo have a contest. Who can whisper into being the greatest gift to the He'e. P'lo, whose spirit is in the seafloor and the waters above it and the rocks below, says, "I wish the rocks below are hot and that their heat will heat the waters so they absorb all the essences of life from the rocks and gush up like a great hot current out of the seafloor through vents and into the waters."*

* "See?" P'lo the Eight-Armed says. "The heated waters rush into the seafloor's cold waters and lose their essence, which cools and combines into the many towers and chimneys and castles. In them, the He'e can live and raise their fry. That is the greatest gift I can wish for all the He'e."*

* M'lo is awed at the vast array of chimneys P'lo wishes into being and these places are the first of the He'e's dwellings. She is duly impressed and rests for a time among the chimneys, from which comes black smoke out of the vents, and considers what she can make real to rival P'lo's creation. She finds the dwellings agreeable but thinks the He'e cannot eat the hot*

waters or the chimneys or the smoke from the vents. The He'e are living things and must eat other living things or they will die. So, she says to P'lo, "I will dream food into being, so we and our fry can eat and stay strong to live long lives." But the first food she dreams into existence is the tiny creature too small to see with the eye or feel with clicks of echoes from it.

P'lo mocks M'lo, saying, "First Mother, the tiny creatures can eat the hot broth of the mineral essence. But the He'e cannot eat the tiny creatures. If the He'e have only this to eat they will starve and die and not be any longer."

M'lo flushes; her arms turn bright with frustration. "Then I will wish tubeworms, the fan wavers who share their lives with the tiny creatures, into being and the He'e can eat them and live long lives."

P'lo eats the tubeworm and scoffs. "Have you tasted the tubeworms? The He'e would rather starve than eat them."

And so M'lo dreams the benthic worms and the sea stars and the anemones into life. P'lo says, "That is better. At least the He'e can eat these things and not starve. But who wants to spend his life eating sea stars and worms?"

In a flash of anger, M'lo dreams the savory clams and mussels and shrimp of the seafloor into being and wishes the succulent crab into life. And she says, "That's enough! It is all the He'e need to eat and live."

And now P'lo says nothing. He is making a meal of a fat, meaty crab.

And each creature, those that crawl and swim through the seas, and those that do not move, has a life pulse and P'lo and M'lo can sense the pulse of every creature, each one different from the other.

In the Fourth Dream, *P'lo gives a gift to M'lo, for all the female fry in every generation and M'lo gives a gift to P'lo, for all the male fry in every generation.*

P'lo's gift to M'lo is the black liquid called hinu, which seeps from the rocks and has many strange and wonderful properties: it thins when it warms, turns solid when it is cold, and even combusts brightly in a pure stream of the stuff of life when it nears fierce heat. But it is as a healing agent for wounds that it is the lasting gift to the females of the He'e because it is they who shall be the healers. Still, P'lo warns M'lo that hinu must never be ingested, for it will kill the creature that swallows it.

M'lo's gift to P'lo is the kaimana, the transparent and flattened rock. It is harder than the hardest rock or clamshell. No dead thing or living creature can penetrate it, no heat can melt it, no cold can make it brittle enough to break, and no water can erode it. It is the lasting gift to the males of the He'e because it is they who are the defenders.

In the Fifth and Final Dream, *P'lo and M'lo gather their fry and give them this, which shall always be a Dream for the He'e:*

He'e are the mother and father of all living things, which shall serve the He'e, just as P'lo and M'lo are the mother and father of their fry.

The He'e have the power of the Dream and the clicks and the eye that sees much, but no other living thing shall have such power.

The He'e shall eat only living things and not dead things, as the dead things are food fit only for the creatures that serve the He'e.

The He'e shall never eat other He'e, as this will extinguish the Dream.

The Above, which is water beyond water, is the place of many creatures, large and small, some of which can eat the He'e.

Of all the creatures that are large and can eat the He'e, there is only one, the Muhe'e of eight arms and two tentacles and a powerful jaw, that kills the He'e with abandon. And because the Muhe'e is a creature that sometimes kills for the sake of killing and not for food, it is an evil creature for the He'e and for those that are and those that will be as long as the Dream exists.

P'lo and M'lo, the Father and the Mother of the He'e, have fry and their fry have fry and they spread across all the places where heat meets cold.

And when P'lo and M'lo are no longer here, the Great Dreamtime is no more and the He'e have only small Dreams.

If you enjoyed this read

Please leave a review on Amazon, Facebook, Good Reads or Instagram.

It takes less than five minutes and it really does make a difference.

If you're not sure how to leave a review on Amazon:

1. *Go to amazon.com.*

2. *Type in Dark Sea Rising by Barry Broad and Drew Mendelson and when you see it, click on it.*

3. *Scroll down to Customer Reviews. Nearby you'll see a box labeled Write a Review. Click it.*

4. *Now, if you've never written a review before on Amazon, they might ask you to create a name for yourself.*

5. *Reviews can be as simple as, "Loved the book! Can't wait for the Next!" (Please don't give the story away.)*

And that's it!

Brian Hades, publisher

About the Authors

Barry Broad was born in Los Angeles in 1957. He is a lawyer by training and has spent his professional career as a lobbyist, representing a variety of union clients from the Screen Actors Guild and the Teamsters to the Longshoremen and Jockeys' Guild. His work has brought him in contact with people from all walks of life and he has used those people and their stories to dive deep into the lives of the characters that animate his fiction. He earned his law degree from the University of California, Davis and attended King's College, Cambridge University, in England and U.C. Davis as an undergraduate. Barry Broad is the author of two espionage thrillers, *Eve of Destruction* and its sequel, *Requiem for the Damned*.

Drew Mendelson is a novelist and short story writer born in 1945 in Kansas City. He has worked as a labor journalist and photographer and as a political speech and op-ed writer for California's governor, state senators and state treasurers. Drew is a Vietnam War combat veteran. He and his wife, Susan, now live in Sacramento, California. He holds a master's degree in creative writing and is a longtime member of the Science Fiction and Fantasy Writers of America. His other longer published works include two science fiction novels, *Pilgrimage* and *Marin 2120 CE*, and a Vietnam War novel, *Song Ba To*.